Germania

Roman Empire 9 CE

Germania

Roman Empire 9 CE

John Wilson

Library and Archives Canada Cataloguing in Publication

Wilson, John (John Alexander), 1951 - Germania: Roman Empire 9 CE/John Wilson

ISBN (paperback) 978-1-990483-24-0

Cover design and photography by John Wilson

Interior map by Malcolm Cullen

Originally published in 2008 by Key Porter Books

For Sadie.

A note on dates and numbers.

The Romans either numbered their years from the date of an emperor's accession or named them for the consul that year. They couldn't know that future generations would number years from the birth of a local mystic in Judea.

The thirty-sixth year of Augustus's reign is what we would call 9 A.D. or 9 Common Era. Lucius wrote his document under the shadow of Vesuvius in the first year of Emperor Titus's reign or 79 CE

Roman numbers can appear cumbersome: I is 1, V is 5 and X is 10. Numbers to the left are subtracted, numbers to the right added, thus 4 is IV and 6 is VI. To add to the complexity, the Romans sometimes wrote 8 as VIII and sometimes as IIX. Rather than load up the story with Xs, Vs and Is, I have varied the numbering of the military units.

A Roman Legion was divided into ten cohorts, which were themselves divided into six centuria. I have written out the numbers for centuria, given Roman numerals for the cohorts and used actual numbers for the Legions: thus Lucius is part of the First centuria of the IXth cohort of the 19th Legion.

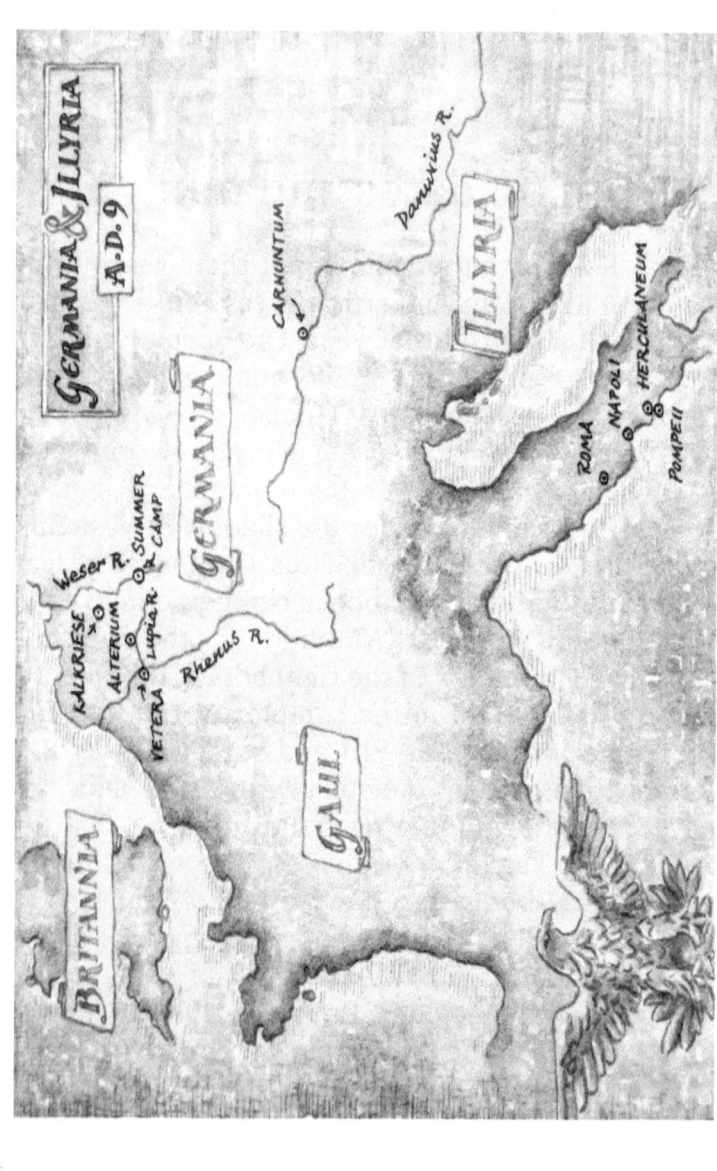

GERMANIA & ILLYRIA

A.D. 9

Danuvius R.

ILLYRIA

CARNUNTUM

GERMANIA

Weser R.

SUMMER
CAMP

KALKRIESE

ALTERUM

Lupia R.

VETERA

Rhenus R.

ROMA

NAPOLI

HERCULANEUM

POMPEII

GAUL

BRITANNIA

Herculaneum

The reign of Titus Caesar: Year 1
24th August, 4:00 p.m.

The advantage of living a span of near a century is that one becomes an historian, whether one likes it or not. Even if I had not chosen a life of examining the past, I would still be doing just that, simply because I have seen and heard so much. Over the course of my many years, I have met countless people—good and bad, noble and slave. I have seen wars, heard the screams of men dying in battle, and caused not a few of those screams myself. I have seen ten Caesars rise to power, although I admit fully three of them rose and fell within the span of a single year. I am a living, breathing archive.

This is not to say that I am dry and dusty like a room full of ancient scrolls. True, my skin is as wrinkled as one of Hannibal's elephants, my joints ache and my remaining hair is as white as the snow on Mount Olympus. But my mind is still sharp and I take continued joy and pleasure in the bright sun outside and the cooling breeze from the bay through the shutters. I also watch and listen with interest to the unusual activities of our previously friendly neighbouring mountain.

But I must not digress if I am to fulfill my task. I have spent much of my life in emulation of the great Greek historian, Herodotus, travelling, listening and discovering so that I may write a history of my age. My work is almost complete and, as you may know, the volumes already published have met with some praise. However, the story is not yet finished; I have one volume still to write.

It is a simple task to recount the doings of great men and Julius Caesar, Augustus and Tiberius stride lightly across the pages of my books. They come and go with such ease because I did not know them. Some I admired and some I did not, but they are what the Gods made them and I accept that. It is an entirely different matter when I write of myself and those I knew. That is why I have delayed this final volume. It is a part of my own life that I must write now, and its remembrance is painful to me. But I must delay no longer. If my work is to be complete, I must include this tale as well.

So, dear reader in the unknown future, I will tell you a story of when I was young. It is a tale of dark, evil forests—frightful places filled with the victorious howls of barbarians and the screams of dying soldiers—and of a time that scarcely seems imaginable now. But it is also the place and time that made me what I am; a place and time that contains the ghosts of some of the finest people I have ever known.

But I get ahead of myself (it is a habit of age). Whoever you are, you will wish to know something of who is talking to you.

My name is Lucius Quinctillius Claudianus and I sit—in truth I lie propped up by pillows—in the *cubiculum* that Pius Gallus, grandson of my beloved sister Livia, and his wife Calpurnia have so generously made available for me. Pius's villa lies in a beautiful situation, just by the northwestern gate of the town of Herculaneum on the scenic coast of the bay of Neapolis.

I do not leave my room much now as it pains my joints greatly, but I used to enjoy short walks through the surrounding olive groves or down to the shore where I could look over the bay to the island of Capri, where Tiberius Caesar forgot his responsibilities and lived out his days in vile debauchery. I still occasionally have my personal slave, Pallas, help me to the roof, where I can sit on a warm day and contemplate the sea before or the mountain behind.

I have just returned from the roof and it is what I saw there that has prompted me to begin this tale. Although the sun still shines above and the sky to the west is as blue as a robin's egg, the picture is altogether different to the east. There a cloud hangs, turning the landscape below it as dark as midnight. It is no ordinary cloud, such as presages a thunder storm, but an unnatural one that blossoms up in a vast column from the unknown depths of the mountain. Zeus himself must inhabit that cloud as it is dressed in an ever changing pattern of great branches and sheets of lightning that compete with the sun in illumination.

The cloud rises far above the height of a soaring eagle and extends, like the windblown crown of a clifftop pine, far along the coast over our unfortunate neighbours in Pompeii. I fear that they must be having a most uncomfortable time in the city as dust and ash appear to be falling steadily upon them from the cloud.

We are lucky in Herculaneum that Vesuvius's fury is aimed at others, but still the road from the town is busy with refugees. Within the past hour, Pius and his family have joined them, leaving Pallas and myself to fend for ourselves, although the frailty that prevented me accompanying Pius necessitates Pallas undertaking the fending. The good man has brought me my papyrus, ink and quill, and keeps me both informed of events and supplied with fresh olives and wine.

I do not share Pius's fear of what Vesuvius has in store for us. The Gods may plan our destruction this day or not, it is not my place to presume. Whatever they have in mind, I am long past running about like a headless chicken at the first sign of danger. But it is an imprudent man who does not take note of what the Gods do. Even if Vesuvius falls back into peaceful slumber, I cannot expect my tenure here to last forever. If I am to finish my final volume, I must first begin and I thank the mountain for reminding me of that. I have no excuse. The events of a lifetime ago are as vivid still in my mind as if it were yesterday, so I shall take what time I have left and inscribe the small piece of history that I was both blessed and cursed to be a part of. No one else can do this. I am the last of Varus's lost legions.

~~~~

I was born at my family villa on the plain near Pisanus when Augustus had ruled, and the Republic had been dead, for only sixteen years. My family was not of the highest rank, no Patricians in the Senate, but we were respectable and could boast an honourable, if distant, descent from the great military hero and eventual vanquisher of Hannibal, Scipio Africanus. I think it was Scipio who started the vein of soldiering in our blood and many of my ancestors spent their lives with the Eagle, the symbol of the conquering Roman Legions, in the farthest corners of the world.

In fact, it was soldiering that had brought us to where we were. My grandfather fought with Julius Caesar in Gaul with the 25th Legion, Antiqua. He rose to the much respected rank of *aquilifer*, standard-bearer, and was commended by Caesar himself. Upon his retirement from the Legion, he was awarded the land on which I was born.

My father sought to join the 25th, but it was disbanded during the chaotic years of the Civil War and he served instead with the 19th in Sicilia and Gaul. At the first opportunity, he retired to work the land where I grew up, complaining that, with Caesar long dead, there would never be another general of his like and nothing left in the world worth fighting for.

Still, my father revelled in the memories of his life as a soldier, and I spent many an evening at his knee, listening to tales of long ago battles and almost forgotten wars. My favourite was of how the 19th was awarded its name, Scorpio.

During the revolt in Sicilia the 19th, being the newest Legion, was always given the rearward position on the march. In the heat of the summers in that land, this was a particularly unpleasant duty as my father and his companions were continually breathing the dust and stumbling in the ruts of the Legions who had passed before. In addition, it was their responsibility to protect and hurry along the large baggage train that followed the Legions everywhere.

On one occasion, the 19th was the last of four Legions passing through some rugged country. The army was negotiating a narrow pass and the first three Legions had successfully crossed to the plain beyond when the rebels ambushed the last Legion and the baggage train. They blocked the pass to prevent help arriving and swarmed the 19th in vast numbers.

My father was convinced that his last hours had come and, at this point in the tale and with a suitably dramatic flourish, he would uncover his thigh and show me the long, white scar caused by a Sicilian spear. But he was destined to live and fight another day.

Through superior discipline and bravery, the Legion fought back the attackers and even reopened the pass and brought the baggage train safely through. As a consequence they were awarded the name Scorpio—in honour of the creature who has such a sting in its tail—and ever after, insisted proudly on bringing up the rear on any march.

As a child, my head was filled with these stories of forgotten battles and long-dead men. It created in me a fierce and lifelong love of the past, but at that early age, my prime desire was to emulate the heroes of the stories rather than record their activities. Much of my childhood was spent practicing with wooden sword and blunt javelin and, when the weather did not cooperate, sitting in the atrium of our villa reading Caesar's account of his conquest of Gaul and the works of Herodotus.

Through hard work and frugality, my father prospered and eventually came to acquire a modest fleet of merchant vessels with which he traded grain from Egypt, oil and wine from Hispania and slaves from Africa. My mother, an intelligent and practical woman, ran the household and maintained the farm when my father was away. My three sisters, Livia, Drusilla and Poppaea, were destined to marry well, and my older brother, Marcus, was groomed to take over the business. I was happy to allow the world to unfold this way as I had determined that I would follow in my father's footsteps with the Scorpions.

On the morning of my thirteenth birthday, my father announced that, through his contacts, he had secured for me the position of apprentice *signifer* in a centuria of the 19th Legion. From that humble beginning, I could rise to full *signifer* and carry the standard for the centuria. In time, I might even emulate my grandfather, become an *aquilifer* and carry the Eagle Standard for the entire Legion.

I was ecstatic. A year earlier than I had expected, I was beginning the journey of my young dreams.

Accompanied by my father and leaving behind a tearful mother, chattering sisters and a well-wishing brother, I set off one summer morning in the twenty-ninth year of Augustus's reign to take the oath and join a baggage train of raw recruits and returning wounded, heading out to meet the famed Scorpions in distant Germania. My adventure was beginning.

Vetera

The reign of Augustus Caesar: Year 29
25th October

B ack on his father's cleared and groomed farm, Lucius never imagined that there were so many trees in the entire world. The small group had been walking through dense forests for days now and there was still no end in sight. Massive oak, beech and pine trees, bedecked in damp hanging moss, threatened to overwhelm the narrow dirt road and disappeared within a few feet into shadowy darkness. On the rare occasions they did retreat to provide a wider view, it was an almost equally sombre vista of treacherous swamps or deep black lakes.

The journey was gloomy, but safe. The small party was travelling on the west bank of the Rhenus River and the really dangerous wilderness was on the east side. On this side, the tribes had been defeated many years before by Caesar and most were now content to live under Roman rule, inhabiting settled communities and earning a living supplying the Legions with everything they needed from grain and fresh meat to Auxiliary soldiers.

Perhaps the place wouldn't seem so miserable if the sun ever came out, but it rarely did. Most often, a heavy, wetting mist clung all around and moisture soaked out of the saturated air to dampen everything. Lucius's uniform was only three months old and yet he had to work continually to keep his armour polished and stop the rust from getting a hold. It was October and he thought fondly of golden fields of wheat ripe for harvest and fat olives darkening on twisted trees. He longed to feel the warm sun on his skin.

"By all the Gods I hate this place." Lucius turned to look at the man trudging along beside him. Titus was the same age as Lucius's father, and as gnarled as an old olive tree. More than three decades of soldiering in Gaul, Africa and Asia had toughened his body to a sinewy fitness and weathered his skin to old leather. "The only fruit that grows in this forsaken place is the mould on my equipment."

"But the meat's good," Lucius responded. "What about that deer we ate in camp last night?"

"True, but meat alone is not enough. You're young yet. Wait until you've tasted apricots from Carthage and peaches from Persia," Titus said wistfully. "I once ate an odd fruit in Egypt. It was the colour of the sun, covered in a thick skin and the inside divided into many segments like a lemon, but sweet like you couldn't imagine. All the way from the Indies it was, but the food of the Gods." Titus snorted derisively. "In this land I even crave simple Roman pears, simmered in wine and seasoned with pepper."

Lucius smiled. It continually surprised him how Titus, a grizzled veteran of countless battles and capable of swearing strongly enough to shock

Jupiter, could wax on so eloquently about the daintiest gastronomic delight.

"That's the curse of a life spent feasting on dormice, oysters and lark's tongues."

"You might mock, lad, but a man must look after his stomach. An unsettled stomach and neither a philosopher nor a soldier are any good to anyone."

Lucius was glad he had been apprenticed to Titus. The old soldier was stern but kind. He never beat Lucius, restricting himself to a sharp clip on the ear if he felt that his pupil wasn't paying attention. Other recruits were not so fortunate.

Titus was the *signifer* for the First centuria of the IXth cohort of the 19th Legion, Scorpio. The first thing Lucius had been taught on the long journey from Rome was the Legion structure and his place very near the bottom of it. He couldn't take that place yet, as the Legion was at Vetera in Germania, several days march away, but he had to know it inside out.

As soon as he arrived at Vetera, Lucius's life would be the 19th Legion. He would be assigned to a *contuberium*, a tent group of eight men who ate, slept and fought together. Ten of these groups formed Lucius's centuria. Titus was the *signifer* for the centuria and his job, the one Lucius was being trained for, was to oversee the unit's finances. He organized the men's pay and savings, buying extra supplies as needed and planning and obtaining food for celebratory or religious feasts. On the march and in battle, he also carried the *signum*, a spear shaft decorated with the medallions the centuria had earned and topped with a carved open hand to symbolize loyalty. Nailed below the hand, the First centuria's *signum* also carried a carved, black-painted scorpion to let everyone know which Legion it was a part of.

Lucius's centuria was the first of six in the IXth cohort. Each cohort was made up of 480 men—except for the elite Ist, which was double the size of the others—and there were ten cohorts in a Legion. Each cohort also had a *signifer* to carry its standard, but there was only one *aquilifer* to carry the gold eagle for the entire legion. That was the role Lucius wanted eventually. But for the moment he was at the bottom of the legionary pile—a Legion was ten cohorts, a cohort was six centuria, a centuria was ten *contuberia*, and Lucius was one raw recruit out of eight men in a single *contuberia*.

With cavalry cooks, baggage handlers and mule tenders, a full-strength Legion was close to six thousand men, and that didn't include the officer's slaves, camp followers and general riff-raff that trailed after an army wherever it went.

The 19th was a formidable fighting force and Lucius was proud to be a part of it, but he was also nervous. Travelling in a loose group like this was simple and fast. Lucius and the other twelve soldiers had to do what Titus told them and Titus had to obey the centurion, Gaius Maximus, but it was fairly easygoing and everyone helped organize the slaves who brought along the supplies and pitched camp every night.

Soon Lucius would arrive at Vetera and join his *contuberium*. Then life would become much more structured and he would be subject to a host of rules he could only guess at but whose transgression could lead to severe punishment. Lucius knew he would be in Titus's *contuberium*, but what would the other six men be like? Lucius shook his head. Time would tell what Vetera had in store.

"Titus, tell me about my father when you knew him during the Sicilian Rebellion. He told many stories..."

"Hush." Titus raised his hand to cut Lucius off. The old soldier tilted his head and stared intently into the impenetrable trees to his right. Lucius stared too, but he could see nothing unusual. He looked at the rest of the party, but no one appeared concerned.

Gaius Maximus, centurion of the First and the only one of the group on a horse, rode to the front in full armour, his red cape and helmet plume the only colour in this green and brown world. The fourteen other soldiers walked in pairs behind Gaius. They were less colourful, dressed in plain round helmets, thigh-length armour made of dozens of small bronze plates sewn onto a long fabric shirt, woollen trousers and sturdy leather sandals. Each man was wrapped in a heavy brown cloak in an attempt to keep out the damp and cold, and each carried a *gladius*, a short stabbing sword and a *pugio*, a wide-bladed dagger. Spears, tents, cooking utensils, personal possessions and supplies for the legion were carried on three heavy ox-drawn wagons that lumbered along behind Lucius. At the very rear, half a dozen slaves tended to a small herd of a dozen horses for the Legion cavalry.

"I thought I heard something, but you can't make anything out in this damnable place. The air's so wet it absorbs all sound and the trees are so thick you can't see the length of a stadium. Could be an entire barbarian army within a slingshot of us and we'd never know."

"But this part of the country's pacified." Lucius looked around nervously. "Isn't it?"

"Supposed to be. West of the Rhenus is part of the Empire, but you can never trust a barbarian. They don't think the same as us. Always raiding and stealing. Still, we'll sort them out soon enough."

"What do you mean?"

"That's why the 17th, 18th and 19th Legions are up at Vetera. Germanicus is in charge of us all and he plans to sort these troublemakers out once and for all. Instead of sitting back and letting the barbarians across the river raid us, he plans to go on the offensive, take the battle to the enemy. If we beat them a few times on their own territory and then set up some forts to the east, that should do it. It'll be hard work and garrisoning those outlying forts won't be a picnic, but it should take the pressure off this side of the river. We might even see a few villas going up, although I can't imagine why anyone would want to come here. You can't grow grapes, olives, or anything worthwhile.

"Sometimes I think your dad had the right idea, taking a nice piece of land at home and settling down instead of marching and fighting the rest of his life. He's done well, with his ships and all." Titus stopped talking and looked ahead thoughtfully. Then he grunted. "Ah. That's not the life for me. I wouldn't know one end of a stalk of wheat from the other. All I know's soldiering, so that's all I do."

"You know food."

Titus laughed. "I do that. Maybe I could open a little food shop down by Neapolis or Ostia. 'Titus's Place. Delicacies from the farthest corners of the Empire.'"

"I could use some delicacies here," the man in front of Lucius said over his shoulder. "It's all very well to march and fight, and Germanicus is the best general in the Empire, but I prefer to do my fighting in a place where there are luxuries to enjoy at the end of a hard day."

The man's name was Pullo. He was a ten-year veteran returning to the Legion after recovering from a sword wound. He had not been expected to survive and took tremendous pleasure in scaring the new recruits by exhibiting the ragged, still red scar above his left hip.

"The women in Egypt, now there were some beauties. Best-looking women in the world, if you ask me. When I retire, I'm going there to find me a wife. You've been there, Titus! You can tell this young boy how beautiful the women are along the Nile."

Titus smiled broadly. "They are beautiful indeed, Pullo."

Pullo nodded, content to have his opinion validated. "Dark eyes you could drown in," he went on wistfully. "I remember one in Alexandria—"

If there was one thing Lucius had learned about soldiers, it was that they spent a disproportionate amount of time reminiscing about all the places they had been. Everywhere else in the Empire, it seemed, was immeasurably better than where they were at the moment. Lucius wondered if they would all get nostalgic about Germania when they were eventually finished here and sent somewhere else.

Lucius was half listening to Pullo's story when he had a flashing impression of something dark in his peripheral vision. Before he could work out what it was, a double headed axe appeared as if by magic, embedded in the centre of Pullo's back.

The man gave a choking gasp and fell to the side, knocking over his companion. For a moment, the world seemed to stand still in silent shock, then the barbarians attacked.

Ahead of Lucius, three figures leaped from the trees and dragged Gaius Maximus from his horse. Half a dozen spears flew through the air onto the unprotected soldiers. Lucius saw one man go down with his throat impaled. Behind him, he heard the screams of terrified slaves and oxen.

"Stay together!" Titus yelled, drawing his sword. It was useless. Those soldiers still alive after the first onslaught were too few and too shocked to react effectively.

Lucius grabbed for his sword but the scabbard was entangled in his cloak. As he struggled to free it, he became aware of a figure standing before him. The man was a good foot taller than Lucius. He was dressed only in a short skirt of some filthy animal hide and his naked chest was daubed with something that might have been dried blood. The man's filthy blond hair was matted with animal grease and twisted into two braids that hung on either side of his face. His pale blue eyes gleamed above a leering mouth filled with yellow rotting teeth. Outlined in dark blue on his left cheek were two triangles with their points touching. Even amidst all the chaos, Lucius noticed the strong smell emanating from him.

Lucius had a chance for one last futile attempt to free his sword before the flat of the man's axe came up and struck him a ringing blow to the side of the head. The smells, sights and sounds of battle vanished and Lucius collapsed in a heap.

~~~~

The seven bedraggled prisoners sat forlornly to one side of a small clearing. Lucius, Titus and the four other surviving soldiers huddled in a group. None of them were seriously wounded, but all were bruised and cut and Titus had an angry spear gash in his leg. Their helmets, armour and sandals had been stripped away and they wore only their woollen undershirts and trousers.

Gaius Maximus sat to one side, his hands bound behind him. He too had been stripped of all armour and badges of rank and the only thing that now distinguished him from his soldiers was the high-quality of his linen underwear. Despite his bruised and bleeding state, he kept his head high and stared defiantly across the clearing.

The clearing itself was small, measuring only some thirty feet at its widest. It was hemmed by heavy oak trees on three sides and by the still waters of a small lake on the fourth. Red-brown, lobed leaves lay thickly at the bases of the oak trunks and drifted down through the still air. While Lucius had been unconscious, the sun had managed to fight its way through the clouds, but it was unable to penetrate the surrounding forest and the clearing was shadowed and cold. Even out on the lake, the smooth water appeared to absorb the light, leaving only a black surface that suggested all sorts of hidden mysteries.

"Whatever happens here," Titus whispered out of the side of his mouth, "remember, lad, that you are a soldier of Rome. If nothing else, we can show these barbarians how a Roman dies."

Lucius did not find Titus's words encouraging. He had been conscious for only a few minutes and was still groggy and confused. His head felt as if it were about to explode and dried blood caked his hair where the axe had hit him. Every time he moved his head, the solid world around him swam out of focus and he felt as if he was going to throw up.

"Where are the others?" he asked.

"Dead," Titus replied shortly. "Those that weren't killed in the first attack were slaughtered if they were wounded too badly. They didn't even spare the slaves and that's not a good sign."

"Why?"

"Because these barbarians usually sacrifice just the officers to their Gods. They keep the slaves and some soldiers for themselves. I don't imagine it's much of a life, but there's always the chance of escape. This lot," Titus nodded his head at a group of about a dozen filthy warriors on the far side of the clearing, "are just a raiding party. They'll try and keep the horses and take whatever plunder they can carry, but guarding prisoners is too much work."

"Can't we escape? We're not even tied up." Lucius turned to look at the trees a few feet behind him and was overcome by a wave of nausea. He breathed deeply and continued. "There are no guards on this side of the clearing."

"I doubt if you could run anywhere in your state and this leg would slow me down. In any case, where would we run to? These men know the forests. They'd hunt us down in an hour. It would just be sport for them. We're done for, no doubt about that."

Lucius slumped forward despondently. Beside him one of the recruits was crying quietly. So much for Lucius's glorious career in the army. It had lasted three months and would end nastily before he'd even had a chance to become part of the Legion. What bothered Lucius most was that his family would never know what had happened to him. He would be just one more young soldier who disappeared into the vast unknown on the edges of the Empire.

A commotion across the clearing made Lucius lift his head slowly. The group of barbarian warriors had split in two and stood looking back at the trees and chanting monotonously. The underbrush parted and a figure draped in the stinking, bloody skin of one of the Roman oxen stepped into the clearing. Immediately, he began hurling himself about in a mad ecstasy of dance. Titus groaned.

"What is it?" Lucius asked. "Who is that man?"

"He's not a man, he's a God. These people believe that, during religious ceremonies, their priests are actually inhabited by the Gods. To those men over there, that savage is a true God, with all the power that entails."

"Which God?"

"That's difficult. Each tribe seems to have their own special Gods inhabiting the local pond or swamp—I suppose just as we have local Gods to look after our affairs. But these people are away from home on a raid. I would guess it's one of the bigger Gods. Woten's their top God, like our Jupiter, and he's a popular one as far as I can tell."

"How do you know all this?"

"I don't know much. What little I do know I've picked up from talking with the Auxiliaries who fight for us. In any case, it always pays to keep in with the local Gods. I don't think this Woten could last long against old Jupiter or Mithras, but these are his forests and I don't mind paying the odd bit of respect to keep him happy."

"I don't think you paid him enough respect."

Titus laughed bitterly. "You're right there, lad. But when it comes down to it, I don't think it matters a puff of smoke who this God is. The reason he's here is to take our souls into slavery in the afterlife."

Lucius shivered at the thought. Death was bad enough, but to spend eternity as the slave of some brutal barbarian God was a horrifying prospect.

The priest/God pranced gleefully across the clearing. He was a tall man and the bloody skin of the ox's head, complete with horns and glazed eyeballs, only served to increase the impression. The ox's forelegs were draped across the man's shoulders and blood and gore ran down his neck and chest and thickened his knotted, blond beard. He was naked, but his body was covered in a thick layer of white mud. In his right hand he carried a magnificent beaten gold mask that he held before his face as he danced. In his left, he brandished an intricately carved wooden rod.

Woten, or whoever he was, danced wildly around the clearing, moving ever closer to the prisoners. Waving the carved rod, he taunted them with shouts and gestures. Every time he came close, the prisoners instinctively shrank back. On one pass, he held the mask high and with a start Lucius recognized the pale eyes and the double triangle tattoo on his left cheek. This was the warrior who had knocked him out with an axe.

Lucius watched as the priest danced over to Gaius Maximus. With obvious difficulty, Gaius stood up and stared defiantly at his enemy. Lucius was proud of his officer. Even bound, beaten and facing a certain death, Gaius was still a Roman who refused to bow to a barbarian. The priest removed his golden mask and began screaming at the centurion. Gaius leaned forward and spat strongly into the man's face.

The priest screamed in a wild, high-pitched voice and drove his carved rod into Gaius's chest, knocking him off balance. Before he could regain his feet, two other warriors rushed over and grabbed the centurion, pulling him across the clearing to the water's edge. As the priest/God danced around the trio, a third warrior stepped forward. He carried a huge, double-headed axe and, with barely a moment's hesitation, swung it in a wide arc that cleanly severed Gaius Maximus's head from his body.

The groan of despair from the remaining prisoners was drowned out by the gleeful screams of the priest as the axe man lifted the head high by its hair. Gaius's eyes stared blindly as the man swung the head three times and then launched it in a spray of blood out over the lake. It splashed and was gone.

The priest dipped his hands in the blood from Gaius's torn neck, smeared it on his chest and began dancing toward the remaining prisoners. He never made it. A small stone shot from the trees and, with an audible crack, hit the priest on the forehead. The man's eyes widened in surprise and he pitched forward to lie still beneath the ox skin.

Before the stunned warriors could react, a volley of red-feathered arrows and stones flew from the surrounding trees, dropping most of the unarmoured men in crumpled heaps. The remainder went down beneath a wave of charging warriors.

The one-sided battle was over in seconds. Lucius's first thought was that they had been rescued by Romans, but his heart sank when he saw that the victors were dressed much the same as the men who had just murdered Gaius Maximus.

They must be another tribe and there was no reason to believe that they would be any kinder to the prisoners than their predecessors had been.

"Who are they?" Lucius asked Titus, but the old soldier merely stood and stepped forward. He stumbled as he put weight on his wounded leg and Lucius stood to help, but Titus brushed him off. One of the attackers, a powerful man with intelligent eyes and blond hair woven into a single braid that reached almost to his waist, crossed the clearing and faced Titus. He was obviously the leader of the barbarians and, although younger than the *signifer*, he met Titus's stare as an equal.

To Lucius's surprise, the man gave the Roman military salute, hitting himself on the left breast with his right fist and extending his arm in front of him, open palm down. Titus returned the gesture.

Even more surprisingly, the stranger spoke in heavily-accented Latin. "We came just in time, it seems."

"Not for Gaius Maximus," Titus replied.

The man shrugged. "Better to save some than none. You are headed for Vetera?"

"We are. I am *signifer* Titus Aquilinus of the First centuria of the IXth cohort of the 19th Legion, Scorpio, and I am bringing recruits, supplies and horses for the Legion."

"I am Arminius of the Cherusci and a citizen of Rome."

"You're Roman?" Lucius blurted out.

The blond man laughed. "There are more Romans in the Empire than rude boys from the provinces."

Lucius blushed violently. "I'm sorry."

"Never apologize, young man," Arminius said, placing a hand on Lucius's shoulder "but think before you speak and be certain of your words."

Lucius nodded. As he did so, he noticed a dark tattoo of a vertical line that split into two tightly curved spirals on the man's upper arm. Arminius noticed his glance.

"This is my mark. It says I am Cherusci." Arminius hit his chest with his fist. "This is my heart. It says I am Roman. I fight beside the Legions and I have been to Rome itself. The scum who attacked you were a raiding party of the Sicambri. They are savages who do not wish the benefits of Roman civilization.

"Come," Arminius said turning back to Titus. "We must be on the road if we are to make any distance before night."

"No," Titus said authoritatively. "There are dead who must be given an appropriate send off into the afterlife."

For a moment, Lucius thought that Arminius was going to argue, but he simply shrugged. "As you wish. What do you need for the ceremony?"

As Titus rattled off a list of instructions for the funeral pyres, Lucius examined Arminius. Close up, he was not at all like the Sicambri attackers. For a start, despite being clothed similarly in animal skins, he was much cleaner and wore Roman light armour like Lucius's beneath his bearskin cloak. The cloak was gathered at the waist by a leather belt from which hung a Roman sword, a long dagger and a quiver of arrows. On his feet he wore sturdy Roman marching sandals.

He stood with his weight on one leg with the other slightly bent. Lucius had the impression, despite the man's relaxed posture, of a cat poised to spring.

As Titus finished giving instructions, another figure appeared beside Arminius. The warrior was short and slightly built, but he walked with an arrogant swagger. Beneath the dirt and grease, Lucius could see that his hair was a deep red. He carried a long braided sling and three blood-stained arrows, which he handed to Arminius. Lucius couldn't help staring. He had never seen anyone like these wild barbarians. For all their savagery, they were obviously very good soldiers and Lucius could feel admiration growing.

The newcomer turned in response to Lucius's stare, flashing him a dismissive look that made him feel as important as a worm. The look was brief, but it was long enough. Lucius gasped audibly as he continued to stare. The short warrior was a girl about Lucius's own age. The barbarians used women in battle? It was unheard of in the Roman world.

The red-haired warrior spoke to Arminius in a guttural language that Lucius didn't understand.

"Speak Latin in the presence of our Roman companions," Arminius said with a smile. "It is only polite."

The girl thought for a moment and then, with obvious difficulty and with many hesitations and mistakes, she said, "Revered Uncle Arminius, I bring arrows of yours."

"Thank you, Freya." Arminius said. Turning back to Titus and Lucius, he went on. "It was Freya who fired the stone that hit the Sicambri priest. It was difficult to make a good shot with so little of the man's face exposed."

"It was nothing, Uncle," Freya said, but Lucius could see the pride in her eyes at Arminius's praise.

"In any case," Arminius went on, "now we must attend to *signifer* Titus's wishes." Saluting again, Arminius and the girl turned and went over to the rest of the band who were busy stripping the dead of anything of value. Lucius noticed that they didn't strip the fallen priest, but simply dragged his limp body into the trees.

"All right, you lot," Titus said. "On your feet. Just because you're not dead doesn't mean you can sit around all day. There's work to do. Lucius, see if you can find the wagons and if any of the oxen are still alive. The rest of you bring in the horses and the bodies of our comrades. We have a funeral and a camp to organize."

Lucius went off to do Titus's bidding, pondering what a strange few hours it had been. He had almost died, met a barbarian chieftain who was also a Roman citizen and a girl who was also a warrior. He shook his head in wonder and almost collapsed under fresh waves of pain.

~~~~

The funeral pyres on the shore of the lake were smaller than they should have been. It had been difficult to find dry wood in the forest, but the Sicambri raiders had broken up one of the transport carts and Titus made use of its seasoned wood. The larger of the two pyres carried the bodies of the six slain soldiers and the smaller, that of Gaius Maximus. The dead slaves and Sicambri had simply been dragged into the forest and left for nature and the local animals and birds.

"It should do," Titus said. The survivors of the attack stood beside the pile of wood on which Gaius Maximus's headless body lay, wrapped in his centurion's cloak. Their armour and clothes had been found in a pile in the forest and they were once more dressed as Roman Legionaries. "No relatives to close his eyes and say a eulogy," Titus reflected so quietly that only Lucius, who stood closest, could hear, "but then, that's a soldier's lot. Besides," he gazed out over the black lake, "it's difficult to find his eyes."

Rummaging in the leather purse on his belt, Titus produced a *dinarii* coin and laid it on Gaius's chest. "Same problem with a tongue to place the ferry fare to the afterlife under."

"Let us hope," he added in a voice loud enough for all the gathered soldiers to hear, "this is enough to get him to Elysium." He stepped back. "I knew Gaius Maximus, First centurion of the IXth cohort of the 19th Legion, for a long time. He came from an old and honourable family and he fought in many battles and acquitted himself well to the honour of the Legion. He always treated me and my men well and I was glad to be his *signifer.* I hope and pray that Mithras has reserved a place for such a fine soldier in the fields of Elysium."

Titus seemed to run out of things to say and stood looking at the body in silence. Eventually, he added, "he was a worthy Scorpion." He gave a formal salute and gestured to one of the recruits who handed him a burning torch. Hobbling slowly on his wounded leg, Titus circled the pyre, thrusting the torch into the wood. By the time he had returned to Lucius, the flames had taken hold and dark smoke was beginning to curl over the lake. "That should do it," he said, turning away. "The rest of you, say what you have to for your friends and light the other pyre."

When both funeral pyres were well ablaze, the soldiers drifted over to their tent, close to where they had sat as captives. Behind them, the horses were tethered and on the far side of the clearing, the Auxiliaries had gathered mats of branches to sleep on. Between the two groups, a large fire blazed and chunks of the ox slaughtered by the raiders hung over it, dripping fat and giving off a delicious smell.

Lucius was surprised to find his mouth watering after the horrors of the day. He had cleaned up his axe wound at the lake, but still had a splitting headache and became dizzy if he moved too fast. He shuddered if he stopped to think about Gaius being beheaded or the fear he had felt when he thought he was going to be sacrificed to the barbarian Gods. So this was what living history was like—and what he could expect from life as a soldier.

"Here," Titus offered Lucius a jug of wine from the supplies. "I've sweetened it with honey. Take a good long drink, pass it on to the others and get yourself some meat. You'll be amazed how much better things look with a full stomach."

Lucius drank and handed the jug to the nearest recruit.

"I don't feel too bad," he said.

"It was a nasty knock you took from that axe," Titus said. "I expect your head'll hurt for a few days yet, but you've got a thick skull. That's a good attribute for a soldier."

"I don't mean that. If I was back home and had seen the things I've seen today, I'd be a wreck. My mother would have sent me to bed and fussed over me for days."

Titus smiled. "You're a Scorpion now. The 19th's your mother. She doesn't fuss over you too much, but she does give you something larger than yourself to be a part of. You're only a tiny part of the Legion, and you and I, and poor old Gaius Maximus, don't matter a jot. Gaius has gone to a better place, but the Legion goes on, just as it will long after you and I are dust. That puts life in perspective and you seem to have grasped that already. If you live long enough, you'll make a fine soldier."

"I hope so." Lucius paused, thinking for a moment about Titus's words. He almost hadn't lived long enough. The afternoon's events returned to his mind. "What was that mark on the Auxiliary's arm?" he asked.

"That was his tribal mark," Titus explained. "I'm told it represents a tree and marks him as a Cherusci warrior. The Sicambri have those triangles on their cheeks. Each tribe has its own mark—the Marsi have a bear's tooth, the Chatti three wavy lines for water, the Bructeri a complex knot, and so on. It's primitive, but they hold much store by them.

"But enough of this! You will learn plenty about these peoples soon enough. Now go and fill that stomach before the barbarians finish everything."

Lucius hesitated. Every meal he had eaten before he joined the Legion had been prepared in his mother's kitchen and served to him by slaves. Even in the past few weeks on the road, the slaves, under Titus's critical eye, had cooked and prepared the food. Lucius stared at the large hunks of charred meat balanced on forked sticks above the flames.

"What's the matter?" Titus asked with a smile.

"Nothing," Lucius said hurriedly as he picked up his bronze plate, unsheathed his knife and went to the fire. He selected a large hunk of meat skewered on a sharp stick, dripping fat and blood into the flames. It smelled good, and Lucius's stomach growled appreciatively, but he had no idea how to retrieve the meat without burning himself. Was this how the barbarians ate? He poked ineffectually at the meat with his knife. Flames flared up as the fat fell on the glowing red coals. The meat teetered precariously over the fire.

"Here, Roman. Eat meat, so."

Lucius glanced round to see Freya beside him. Her sling was tucked into her belt beside a pouch of stones. With a broad grin, she reached through the flames, expertly flipped the meat out of the fire and caught it in a fold of her leather cape. Holding one end of the skewer in the leather, Freya raised the joint and tore off a large piece of meat with her teeth and began chewing. She offered the skewer to Lucius.

Lucius took it and attempted to rip off a chunk. He ended up with a much smaller mouthful than Freya had managed. The hot fat and blood dribbled down his chin and burned his lips, but he was determined to continue and not show weakness in front of a barbarian, and a woman.

As he chewed, Lucius stared at Freya. Despite her slight build, Lucius could see knots of muscle move beneath the skin of her bare arms. Her face didn't look Roman at all. It was flatter and Lucius found the small nose that almost turned up at the end far less attractive than the prominent nose that was a traditional sign of beauty in Rome. Still, there was a wild sort of beauty to the face surrounded by the halo of extraordinary red. Everyone Lucius was used to seeing had dark brown or black hair. Fair hair was occasionally seen in Rome on slaves from the far north lands, but red hair was unheard of. Standing in the flickering light, dressed in animal skins and messily chewing a large hunk of meat, Freya perfectly fit Lucius's image of a wild barbarian. But there was something about her that Lucius found intriguing. It's the eyes, he thought. They were a slate grey that sparkled in the firelight, and they were continually moving, flashing this way and that, taking in everything from the tiniest detail to the overall picture. Lucius would have wagered that not much of importance was missed by those eyes, which was odd. Barbarians were not supposed to be intelligent. They were only good as slaves or auxiliary soldiers. They weren't as smart as Romans, everyone knew that, but this girl looked smart. Freya's gaze came to rest on Lucius and he looked away guiltily, suddenly afraid that she could read his thoughts.

Freya laughed and took back the meat. "Good. Good. Now come sit. Talk. I need learn."

Freya turned away before Lucius could answer, selected a large oak at the edge of the clearing and settled herself with her back to the trunk. Lucius joined her.

"You have, what name?" Freya asked in her halting Latin.

"I am Lucius Quinctillius of the Claudianus family."

"So many names you Romans have. I am Freya of Cherusci."

"We need so many names," Lucius explained, "so that we know who we are. There are many Romans called Lucius."

Freya snorted. "Cherusci need only one name. The Gods know me."

"But you need tattoos to tell who you are," Lucius said pointing to the mark on Freya's arm.

"That is tree of—" Freya hesitated, "not death."

"Life," Lucius said.

"Yes. Yes. Life. Tree of life. For Cherusci is where all began. Tree from earth, holds up—" Freya waved a hand vaguely above herself.

"Sky," Lucius prompted.

"Sky," Freya agreed. "All animals and us fell from tree like nuts in cold time."

Lucius smiled. He liked the idea of people falling from trees.

"Where you Romans begin? Tree?" Freya asked.

"No. Long ago, two babies, Romulus and Remus—the sons of the God of War, Mars and a Priestess, Rhea Silvia—were in a tribe where Rome now stands. As was the custom when a Priestess gave birth, the babies were cast into the River Tiber. But they didn't die. Their lives were saved by a she-wolf and they were brought up by a shepherd and his wife. They grew to be great heroes, killed the tribe's king and decided to build a city on a hill. Unfortunately, they couldn't decide which hill so an argument broke out and Romulus killed Remus. Romulus became the first king of Rome and that's how Rome began."

Freya looked thoughtful. "That's how *Rome* began, but there was a tribe there before the twins. Perhaps they fell out of trees."

"Perhaps," Lucius agreed with a smile.

"So," Freya went on, "you Romans come out of war and murder. I think a tree is better."

"The leader of the tribe who attacked us," Lucius said, trying to change the subject, "the Soc—"

"Sicambri," Freya said. "Their leader, one I shot with sling," she added proudly, "was Arnulf, son of chief."

"He had a mark," Lucius scratched the double triangle in the dirt and touched his left cheek.

"Axe," Freya said. In a few lines, she turned Lucius's scratch into a double-headed war axe like the one that had killed Pullo. "They are savages. Sicambri fought, like Cherusci, against your great

—" Freya struggled to find the right word, "Chief of battles."

"War chief. General. Do you mean Julius Caesar?"

"Yes, Julius Caesar. Sicambri betray Cherusci and we were defeated. Many died. We do not forgive."

The pair sat in silence for a while, passing the meat back and forth.

"You are Arminius's niece," Lucius asked, eventually.

Freya nodded.

"Is he the chief of the Cherusci?"

"He is general, like Julius Caesar."

"He's very young."

Freya laughed loudly. "You Romans do not learn fighting before you are men! We Cherusci learn battle at our mother's breast. I was," Freya held up seven fingers, "this many years when I killed first enemy—a Sicambri."

Lucius was shocked. At seven he had been busy playing with his spinning top.

"But you're a girl!" he said. "Why are you a warrior?"

"Roman girls not fight?"

"No. War is for men." Lucius tried to imagine his sisters as warriors. It was impossible. He remembered them running away squealing whenever a pig had to be butchered for a feast. "Women stay home."

"Roman women weak?"

"No." Lucius struggled to explain. He had never thought of his mother as weak. When Lucius's father was away, she ran the farm and could stand up to the roughest trader or travelling merchant who thought he could pressure her into selling the crop cheap. "It's just not a woman's job to fight."

Freya nodded thoughtfully. "But what if attacked?"

"The soldiers of the Legions will protect them."

"Cherusci women don't have to rely on men soldiers. I am good soldier and can protect self. I am better fighter than Irmin."

"Irmin?"

"Arminius," Freya explained. "Irmin is his Cherusci name. Now he is Roman, he use Roman name. But why only Arminius and men fight? If Cherusci lose battle, Arminius dies as all do. I raped and sold as slave. Rather die, so fight.

"Also," Freya's eyes gleamed with pride, "I am very good." She touched the sling hanging from her belt.

"Did you use your sling to kill your first Sicambri enemy when you were seven?" Lucius asked.

"No. Sling learning is many years. He chased me up cliff and I drop rock on head." With obvious glee, Freya made a gesture to suggest that the man's head had been squashed flat.

Lucius decided to change the subject. "Are the Cherusci a large tribe?"

"Not large, but brave. Our elders tell we defeat all when attack—Marsi, Chatti, Bructeri. You saw today, how we kill Sicambri. They beat you Romans."

"I did see, but you took them by surprise, just as the Sicambri took us by surprise."

"War surprise is good," Freya said, tearing off another piece of meat before passing the hunk back to Lucius.

The roast was cooler now and Lucius found it easy to hold and bite.

"Why do the Cherusci fight on the side of the Legions?" Lucius asked after a while.

"You do not wish us?" Freya said with a smile.

"No. I mean, yes. I mean—" Lucius stumbled over his words. "It's good that the Cherusci fight for Rome."

Freya's smile turned to a frown. "We not fight for Rome. We fight for Cherusci."

"But on the same side as Rome," Lucius said hurriedly, afraid he had offended this strange girl. "We fight the same enemies."

"Yes," Freya agreed. "The Romans are strong and Cherusci have many enemies. Also," Freya's brow furrowed as she searched for the right words. "You have civiliation?"

"Civilization," Lucius corrected.

"Civilization. Yes. It brings many good, Arminius thinks."

"It does. My family's villa has running water—hot and cold—baths, kitchens, gardens with water fountains, heating in the winter." Talking about his home gave Lucius a twinge of sadness, but he hurried on. "Walls and roofs protect us from the sun in summer and the rain in winter. We have beds so we do not have to sleep on the ground, lamps to light the night, couches to sit on, manuscripts to read and tablets and scrolls to write on. We have everything."

"But if have everything," Freya said thoughtfully, "why struggle? I think not only Roman women soft in this life?"

"Our soldiers are the best in the world," Lucius said, indignantly.

"But not all fight. Others weak? Not carry water from lake. Slaves do all. I have seen. Cherusci work and are strong—even women." Freya laughed and flexed the muscles in her arm.

"The Legions protect those who are not strong so that they may be farmers, senators, philosophers and historians."

"I have heard this, but not understand. Every Cherusci can do all."

"What do you mean?"

Freya thought for a moment. "In war, every Cherusci a soldier. In peace, all farmers or hunters or builders. You soldier only. Can you hunt or grow crops?"

"No," Lucius admitted, "but if soldiers had to do all those other things, the Legions could never leave Rome and come here."

"Perhaps one day," Freya said, "I go to Rome and see. When the Cherusci fight well for Rome, we all become Romans. Then we have civilization."

Lucius smiled at the thought of Freya and Arminius, dressed in their animal skins, walking through the Forum in Rome amidst all the immaculately dressed and manicured senators and high-born ladies.

"But," Freya looked puzzled, "if Rome so good, why come here to fight?"

"Because." Lucius hesitated. The obvious reason was that the farther away the Legions could keep the barbarian border from Rome, the safer the city would be. But he didn't think Freya wanted to hear that he was in Germania to keep her and Arminius away from Rome. "To bring civilization."

"But why? What does Rome get?"

"Rome gets trade. In the city it is possible to buy grain from Africa, olives from Hispania, wine from Gaul, horses from Parthia and silk from even farther east. There are things you cannot imagine." Lucius warmed to his topic. "Tin, lead, gold, pepper, spices, precious gems, amber, ivory, pearls—from places few have seen on the very edges of the world."

Freya wiped the grease from her mouth with the back of her hand and stared at Lucius thoughtfully. "If Rome get all this, what do others get?"

"Trade—roads, towns, ports, farms, money, peace. The civilization you and Arminius want."

"But if someone not want civilization?"

"Everyone wants civilization."

"Sicambri don't."

"They should," Lucius said. "With the Roman peace, everyone can live in safety and comfort without being afraid of the next raiding band to come through and burn their village. That's good, isn't it?"

"Yes," Freya acknowledged, "but no choice."

Lucius struggled to understand. To him, it was inconceivable that anyone would not want the benefits of Roman civilization. Rome was the best place in the world, the greatest empire the world had ever seen; Roman citizens had the best of everything. Why would anyone *not* want to be a part of that?

"It is odd," Freya said, breaking the lengthening silence.

"What?"

"Roman soldiers fight for peace, even if people don't want it."

"You and Arminius want Roman peace and civilization, and you fight with us against the Sicambri," Lucius said.

"We do," Freya agreed. "But is this why you become soldier? To fight wars for peace?"

"Not exactly," Lucius said, relieved that Freya had changed the subject. "My father was a soldier and his father before him."

"A whole family who fight for peace." Freya smiled. "My father soldier too, but he fight for glory and plunder. Your father died a great death in battle?"

"No. He's still alive. He has a farm and trades all over the world."

"I am sorry. My father died a great death. I was much young. Just baby. It is said he took seventeen Sicambri with him to the next life. Our bard made a song of his battle. One day I shall have a great death like him.

"What your name mean?" Freya changed the subject again.

"Lucius means light," Lucius said. "What does Freya mean?"

"Freya mean 'important women,' but I am called for Goddess Freya."

"Who is she?"

"Goddess of love, but also, with Woten, keeper of dead souls from battle." Freya stood up abruptly and dropped what was left of the meat in Lucius's lap. "But now I sleep. I like talk," she said. "We talk more. Good night."

"Good night." Lucius watched Freya's retreating back. What a strange land, he thought as he stared out over the cooking fire and the funeral pyres. A place where death and chaos strike from nowhere and where people feel sorry that my father is still alive. A place where a beautiful girl is a killer and named for the keeper of dead warriors.

Lucius took another mouthful of meat. Most of what had happened today had confirmed his belief that the barbarians were savage, dangerous and uncivilized. But Freya was different. Lucius smiled to himself. She was more civilized than some Romans he had met, and despite her struggle with the language, she was intelligent. She had argued cleverly and made him think about things he had always taken for granted. That was something he had never expected from a barbarian. Already, Germania was more complex than he had expected.

Lucius stood and stretched his aching limbs. It had been a strange day indeed, but now sleep seemed like a good idea.

Freya

Freya selected a sharp sliver of wood and began picking pieces of meat from between her teeth. This boy, Lucius, was just what she had been looking for. Of course, he was arrogant, like all Romans, and couldn't understand why not everyone would want to be a Roman, but at least he was about her own age and was prepared to talk to her. Freya wanted to learn. Already she knew the Cherusci lore and she was becoming proficient in the ways of a Roman Auxiliary, but she wanted more. Her Uncle Arminius, who had raised her like a son after her father died in battle, had taught her to respect and fear the Romans, but Freya wanted to understand them. This was only her first season with the Auxiliaries and today had been her first fight.

"That was a good shot with your sling, today." Freya turned to see Arminius approaching. "You are becoming very skilled."

"Thank you, Uncle. But it would have been easier to kill him."

"That's what made it a good shot. You hit him hard enough to make him sleep for as long as it would take to get him into the trees."

"Why did you not let me kill him? He is Sicambri, our enemy."

"He is also Arnulf, son of a chief, and it is foolish to make more enemies than you need. Arnulf is a hot-headed fool who led this raid without his father's permission. But if you had killed him, word would have reached his father and he would have declared a blood feud between us. As it is now, Arnulf is being escorted back over the river with a very sore head, and his father does not need revenge for a dead son."

Freya nodded. It made sense. "I have a question."

"Ask."

"You always tell me the Romans are wonderful soldiers. Yet today, the Sicambri, whom we can beat every time, easily overcame them. They would all be dead now if we had not come upon the sacrifice."

"The Romans are different from us. Their armour and weapons are very good—"

"Yes," Freya interrupted, "but their armour is heavy. It slows them down, and their short swords are no match for a Sicambri battle axe or a well-handled sling. You are fond of telling me that, if the Romans are well led and can choose the place of battle, their Legions are unbeatable. How can that be if our warriors, man-for-man, are better then them?"

Arminius looked thoughtfully at his niece. "Let me tell you a story. A wise Roman general once had an army who thought as you do, so he assembled them in the middle of his camp. He brought forward two horses, one a magnificent stallion, the biggest and strongest horse in the camp, the other a poor, sickly, weak beast, close to the end of its life. Then he brought forward two men, one the biggest, strongest soldier in the camp, the other a short, scrawny slave, not even powerful enough to carry a legionary's armour and weapons.

"The general ordered the strong soldier to approach the weak horse, grasp its tail and pull as hard as he could. He told the weak slave to go to the magnificent stallion and pull out its tail hairs one by one. In time the strong soldier collapsed with exhaustion and the weak horse kept its tail. Eventually, the weak slave completely removed the tail of the strong horse.

"A Roman Legion is like the tail of the sickly horse. The individual hairs are bound together by something our warriors have yet to learn— discipline. That is what makes them strong."

"How?"

"A Roman soldier is a soldier and nothing else. The army is his life and he trains to become better every day. When a Legion is formed up in open ground, every Roman soldier fights, not only for himself, but for his companions on either side, and he knows that his companions will fight for him.

"Our warriors are farmers and hunters. They fight well when they have to or want to, but then they go back to their village and family. They practice fighting, but they do so individually, not in a unit like a Legion. We are like the individual hairs on the strong horse. However strong each hair is, it cannot match the strength of all the hairs together, even on a weak horse."

"But the Romans can be beaten; I've heard stories."

"Yes they can, but only if the Legion breaks down —if it is badly led or poorly trained, if it is attacked by overwhelming numbers, or if the terrain does not allow it to become organized. But in open country, a well-led Legion is invincible."

"Lucius, the Roman boy, told me that the Romans fight for peace. Is that true?" Freya asked.

"In one way. The Romans are a nation of traders. They want peace so their merchants can trade safely."

"We trade with our neighbours, but we don't try to conquer the world."

"But we are small, Freya. In Rome alone, there are ten times as many people as there are Cherusci in the whole world. I have seen them. They live so close together that no one can grow anything, keep any animals or find room to hunt. They need the rest of the world to supply food, cloth and wood."

Freya thought for a long moment, then shook her head. "That's not good. If Rome needs the Legions to keep the peace so that the traders can get the things citizens need to survive, then if Roman soldiers are defeated and the Legions destroyed, Rome itself will wither and die."

Arminius laughed. "One day, Freya, your curiosity will get you into trouble. Why must you question everything?"

"Because I want to learn. I want to know everything."

"That's an admirable goal, but I don't think it is possible."

"Why not?"

"Because the world is too complicated. Listen, my great grandfather lived to be a very old man and he knew everything. He knew the Cherusci were chosen by the Gods and that the way we had lived forever was the way we should live. For him it was that simple. He was as certain that the Cherusci were the greatest people on earth as your young friend is certain the Romans are."

"They cannot both be right."

"Maybe not, but you see the difficulty. Life was much simpler before the Romans came."

"Why do we fight beside the Legions? Can we not beat them?"

"We are Cherusci," Arminius said, seriously. "If there were enough of us we could beat the Legions. But your question is more complex than that.

"As long as anyone can remember, the Cherusci have lived in these forests. We have hunted and farmed and fought when we had to. We have sacrificed to the Gods and life has been good, but the world changes. My grandfather lived in a simpler world, a world without Romans. The Romans came in my father's time. He and your father, fought against the Romans, just as the Sicambri did."

"But we are better warriors than the Sicambri! My father killed seventeen of them in his last battle."

"He did," Arminius agreed, "although some of the seventeen may have been added by the bards." He held up his hand to stop Freya's protest. "Whatever the number, it was a small battle, a squabble over something no one even remembers. The big battles had already been fought and lost, and the Sicambri fought against the Romans as well as we did. Beating the Sicambri is one thing, beating the Romans another.

"We had to choose: keep fighting the Romans as the Marsi and the Chatti do, or accept the change and try to adapt. It was a hard decision and not all agreed. Tribes split. Many Sicambri and Cherusci moved west to try to live like Romans. Others, including my own brother Lothar and his family, still live the old way on the traditional lands to the east."

"Why did you decide to accept the Roman way and fight for them? Do you admire them so much?"

"I do admire them, especially their soldiers, but that would not be enough. Even though I fight in the Auxiliaries, part of me, deep down, is still Cherusci. I fight for the Romans and wish us all to become civilized, because I believe we have little choice.

"Freya, I have seen Rome. You cannot imagine what it is like. They have streets of stone on which ten horsemen can ride abreast, buildings that are taller than the tallest tree in the forest, and stadiums where tens of thousands of people can sit and watch entertainments. And they are as numerous as ants! It is possible to beat some Romans, but not all. One day, all the world will be Roman. When that happens, those who are not Romans will be lost. I fight for the Romans so that one day, when all the world is Roman, the Cherusci will be Roman too.

"But this is enough for one night!" Arminius slapped Freya on the back. "We need to sleep if we are to take these Romans to safety tomorrow. And I must go and see the guards to make sure there are no more Sicambri raiders in the area. We would not want to be surprised like the Romans."

Arminius walked away and Freya settled by the fire, wrapped in her cloak. But she lay awake for a long time, thinking over what Arminius had said. There was a difference between herself and her uncle. She wished to become Roman because she admired them and wanted to be like them and know everything they did. She was making a free choice. Arminius wished the Cherusci to become Roman because there was no alternative—no choice.

Freya shrugged. What difference did it make why anyone wanted to be Roman? She was glad the Romans had come into the Cherusci lands, not least because they had brought her new friend, Lucius, with them. Freya closed her eyes and tried to imagine the wonders of Rome. She couldn't, they were too different from anything she was familiar with. She would ask Lucius about them. That would have to do until she had a chance to go there and see for herself.

Herculaneum

That was my introduction to Germania and to Arminius, Freya and Titus. All would play important roles in my life in the years to come but my immediate future was one of hard work and learning.

The one thing I remember most from the years immediately following the ambush and my arrival at Vetera is how dull the ordinary life of soldier in the Legions can be. After I learned my duties—how life in camp worked and what my role was to be— one day was much like any other and all ran together in a haze of sameness. We marched, drilled, trained, built barracks, mended roads and marched some more.

Titus had been right: I was a part of the greatest army of the largest Empire on earth; I was a member of one of the elite Legions commanded by our best general, and yet my world encompassed little more than the other seven men in my *contuberium*. I remember them now as well as if they were in the next room: Drusus, a giant of a man with the temperament of a child; Quintus, a small, rat-faced man with a cruel streak; Appius, the scholar of the group, who was always hunched with a glass over some old manuscript; Sextus Livius and Sextus Vipsanius, the inseperable pair of friends; and my own closest friend apart from Titus, Herod the Judean.

Of our general, Germanicus, or of Varus, the Governor of Germania, I saw nothing except as distant figures on festivals and feast days. Titus was much more of a presence in my life as he taught me the roll of *signifer*.

The camp at Vetera was like any other Roman fortress—a sturdy rectangular wall protected by double ditches and enclosing a small military town laid out along both sides of a grid of streets. When not on campaign, the Legions lived within the walls, while the Auxiliaries camped outside, either close to the walls or, more commonly, farther off in the forest.

Vetera was located on the western bank of the Rhenus River. The Rhenus offered a route for supplies and messages to pass between Vetera and the frontier's other river fortresses, and our camp possessed a considerable dock facility. It was also located opposite where the Lupia River joined the Rhenus from the east and thus provided the beginnings of a route into the heart of Germania's wild lands.

Because of its important position at the confluence of rivers, Vetera had an air of permanence not seen in many of the frontier forts and it was surrounded by a ramshackle town of local traders eager to serve the Legions. It was my home for almost four years with the exceptions of the times I was out on campaign.

Germanicus was determined to take the battle to the enemy and led us, always accompanied by a strong force of Arminius's Auxiliaries, on many raids across the Rhenus River. We pushed east along the Lupia, building a wide road and constructing forts as we went. At first the forts were manned only in the summer and allowed to lie empty in winter, but they were intended to become permanent bases as the land was pacified.

We defeated everyone we came against. But even the fighting was not exciting. The barbarian tribes were so primitive that they were continually squabbling amongst themselves and could not cooperate enough to field an army that could threaten the Legions sent against them. Often because of the scouting done by the Auxiliaries, we caught the tribes piecemeal when we had overwhelming superiority and either destroyed them or chased them back where they came from.

In my first battle, a large raid the summer after I arrived at Vetera, I was needlessly terrified. The engagement lasted less than an hour and my centuria never even came to grips with the enemy. All I saw were glimpses of the ragged tribesmen through clouds of dust as I stood with Titus beneath the standard awaiting orders that never came. I heard the clash of battle and the screams of the wounded, and saw the carnage after, but I came no closer than a long spear throw to the action. Many times it was like that. The problem with the Scorpions' position of honour at the rear of the march was that, if the forward Legions came unexpectedly upon the enemy, as they often did in the thick forests, the battle was frequently over by the time we arrived.

Oddly enough, the most violent fight I was in in those years was against fellow Legionaries. The 18th Legion, Taurus, was named for their habit of barging forward through all obstacles in a battle. Thus they were often at the front of a column and saw much of the hard fighting.

One evening at Vetera, the soldiers of Taurus began taunting some Scorpions, saying that we were lazy and cowardly, always arriving late at battles. It began in jest, but soon got out of hand and resulted in a general brawl. I joined in to protect the honour of our name, and received several hard blows and a broken finger for my pains.

No one died, but the following day, both Legions were formed up outside the camp and castigated most fiercely by the two Legates who walked among the soldiers beating them randomly with their staffs. We all suffered a fine from our pay which Titus administered for our *centuria*.

Gradually, I grew both physically and in experience from a naive youth into a seasoned soldier of Rome. As well as learning how to march and fight my comrades, I became proficient in throwing the *pilum*, our soldier's spear, and in fighting with the *gladius*, our short sword. I also spent a considerable amount of my spare time with the Auxiliaries, where Freya taught me the use of the sling, although I never approached her remarkable talents with that weapon. I once saw her knock a sparrow off a branch at near fifty paces.

I learned that battle is not the worst part of a soldier's life. The anticipation before a battle is far more trying. At that time, my imagination could run riot and I would foresee the most bloody disasters and hideous wounds. Once action was joined, my companions and I were fine; we acted and reacted with no time to imagine anything or feel fear.

Of course, the fighting was not absolutely one-sided. Occasionally, small parties of our men were ambushed, as Titus and I had been, but these were isolated incidents and the work of pacification went on relentlessly. The barbarian raids across the Rhenus ceased completely and more and more chiefs came to submit to the power of Rome.

Arminius and the Cherusci were invaluable in our work, acting as scouts, negotiators and shock troops in battle. Many times his archers and sling men, led by Freya as she grew older, would emerge unexpectedly from the forests and set the enemy fleeing.

Arminius's knowledge of the forests and of the habits of the other tribes helped us greatly and he became an important advisor to both Germanicus and Varus, although as a barbarian, neither accepted him as an equal. Arminius's advice was flawless and many times allowed us to out-fox the enemy or saved us from walking into an ambush. Although I did not think of this at the time, Arminius was as noble a Roman as any I have met, and it was cruelly unfair that, after a day spent crafting one of Germanicus's victories, he had to return to the Auxiliary camp while the Governor and General dined in luxury.

During this time, I saw much of Freya. At first she sought me out simply to practice her Latin, but as time passed, we grew to be close friends. She had an insatiable curiosity about all things Roman and would sit by me for hours as I described my home villa and the places I had visited. Her particular favourites were tales of Rome itself. She would sit next to me by the fire in the evening and beg to have described, yet again, the forum, the temples, the Senate house and the steps where Marcus Antonius made his plea for action over Julius Caesar's bloody corpse and began the years of civil war.

I think it was in talking to Freya that my desire to write history crystallized. She was so enthralled by the stories I told that I immediately saw the power of history to captivate even someone from a totally different world. Freya also held writing as something magical and regarded it with the simple awe of someone who has never learned the craft. Even though, over the years, I taught her to read my beloved Herodotus and to write down her thoughts, she never lost that wonder at the written word.

I remember her telling me once that her dream was to stand in a vast library, surrounded by the thoughts of great men and women and the tales of countless unknown worlds. I have never since been able to visit a library without recalling Freya's wish.

I know what you think, dear reader: that I took Freya as my country wife, as many legionaries did with the local women on the outposts of Empire. But it was not so. I felt an affection for Freya as strong as I did for the companions of my *contuberium*, upon whom my life depended in battle. I freely admit that had Freya been Roman and we back at Pisanus, I might well have courted her, but I did not. A soldier will willingly die for his companions and there is no stronger bond between humans than that. I was content to let that be the bond between Freya and myself.

I enjoyed telling Freya my stories and many of them had a special resonance for us at Vetera. Germanicus was a grandson of Mark Anthony and a grandnephew of Caesar Augustus, and Governor Varus's father had been one of Julius Caesar's assassins. He fell on his sword in disgrace after Brutus and the others were defeated at the battle of Philippi. Thus the ancestors of both our leaders were part of the history I was teaching Freya.

As for our leaders themselves, Varus must have been a clever man. He managed to successfully transfer his own allegiance from Julius Caesar's assassins to the Emperor Augustus and rise to prominence, even marrying into the Imperial family. But he was a politician not a soldier and had led a soft life. I have never been impressed by his talents, but I admit I am prejudiced by the history I saw.

Germanicus, on the other hand, was the perfect soldier. Tall, striking and always with the interests of his soldiers to the forefront of his mind, he was a great favourite with all the Legions he commanded. When Augustus died, Germanicus's Legions even mutinied to try and force him to become emperor in Tiberius's place. It is characteristic of the man that he refused.

By the thirty-third year of Augustus's reign, as I approached my seventeenth year of life and as Germanicus was planning a major assault to establish Roman dominance on the eastern bank of the Rhenus once and for all, news arrived at Vetera of a rebellion in Illyria to the south. The plans for Germania were shelved and the following year Germanicus led several Legions, including the 19th and Arminius's Auxiliaries, down to quell the revolt. Varus remained as Governor at Vetera with our two companion Legions, the 18th, Taurus, and the 17th, Capricorn.

The winter trek to Illyria was a long and tedious affair, three months of marching along the edge of the Empire, twelve miles every day and a fortified camp every night. After a few weeks, I craved the relative comforts of life at Vetera, however, we arrived safely and—

The strongest earthquake of this strange day has spilled my ink and almost thrown me to the floor. As soon as the uncertain earth finished its quivering, Pallas rushed through and refilled my ink so that I might continue this story. I wonder if I shall have time to finish? The earthquakes are becoming more frequent, although none are close to the power of the great earthquake of sixteen years ago that caused so much destruction. Perhaps this last one was the climax and it will all die down and my companions soon return sheepishly.

Whatever happens, I shall continue writing as long as I can. It is hard work for my stiff old hands, and yet I find it strangely satisfying. I have thought back on those long ago days many times, but to put my thoughts down in words gives my memories a solidity they have not had before. Why did I not undertake this many years ago when I had ample strength and time? Freya would say that I should have enshrined my experience in the magic of words long before I became an old slave to this untrustworthy mountain.

But I ramble. I must return to Illyria.

Mithras

The reign of Augustus Caesar: Year 34
14th Junius

"Today you are eighteen years of age?" Titus asked.

"I am," Lucius replied, puzzled.

"Then tonight you will be initiated into the mysteries of Mithras."

Lucius's heart leapt. At last. In the five years since he had left his father's villa, Lucius had changed from a skinny, uncertain boy of thirteen with dreams but no knowledge of the wider world, to a tall, broad-shouldered man who had experienced life in the farthest reaches of the Empire. He was fit and strong enough to march in full armour carrying his personal possessions from dawn to late afternoon and still have the energy to dig an earthen ditch around a fortified camp. He could hurl a *pilum* the length of a stadium with enough force to impale a man to a tree and he could wield a *gladius* against the strongest opposition for hours. Using Freya's sling, he could also hit a target the size of a man's palm at thirty paces, nine times out of ten. He had developed from a raw recruit into an efficient member of a disciplined fighting force, a soldier in the Imperial armies of Rome. He need fear no living thing in the known world, but there was one thing he craved above all: acceptance into the soldier's religion, Mithraism. Now he had proven himself and he was old enough. Tonight he would become a *corax*—a raven—in the ancient cult of Mithras, the bull-slayer.

Lucius knew that Mithras had been introduced from the east and was rapidly becoming a favourite God with soldiers, especially those manning the remote fringes of the Empire. Mithras was the perfect soldier's God, symbolizing truth, honour and courage and demanding rigid discipline from his adherents. This much was common knowledge, but the ceremonies of Mithras were another matter. They were conducted in secret places and only by initiates. No one other than those deemed worthy to join the cult knew what went on.

"Thank you." Lucius struggled to control the idiotic grin on his face.

"Do not thank me," Titus replied, his voice serious. "You have earned it and lived long enough. If you are going to thank anyone, thank Mithras. But don't do it too hastily. Mithras does not accept initiates lightly. Your journey tonight will not be easy."

"I know," Lucius said, brushing off Titus's warning. "But this is what I have always wanted."

"Very well then. I shall bring you to the Mithraeum when the sun sets. Be ready."

Titus walked off to the treasury to check on his beloved standard, leaving Lucius in a turmoil of emotions. To calm himself, he walked along the Via Principalis, past the headquarters complex where

Germanicus was planning the summer campaign, and climbed the walls above the East Gate.

Carnuntum was nowhere near as sophisticated, permanent or luxurious as Vetera, but it was a world away from the rough, temporary camps the Legion had been living in on the road. As befitted one of the headquarters of a military campaign, Carnuntum was well-defended. The outline of the large rectangular camp was defined by a beaten earth wall surmounted by a palisade of wooden stakes and surrounded by two deep ditches. For almost half a mile in all directions, the trees and underbrush had been cleared so that no enemy could approach unseen.

Inside the walls, wooden officers' quarters, barracks, storerooms, workshops and a hospital were precisely laid out along straight roads of beaten earth. Outside the perimeter, down by the river bank, two bath houses—one for officers, the other for men—had been constructed from local stone and were kept warm by a host of slaves who fed the fires beneath them.

Carnuntum had been built for much the same reason as Vetera—to protect a river crossing, in this case the Danuvius, that led east into the hostile barbarian wilderness. Unfortunately, it was the tribes to the west and south of Carnuntum, all across the supposedly pacified lands of Illyria, that had erupted in revolt the year before. And they were proving difficult to subdue. The Illyrians were a warlike people who had been originally defeated three and a half centuries before by Phillip of Macedon, the father of Alexander the Great. Many of the Illyrian tribes had also been Auxiliaries of Rome for years and had learned a great deal about how the Romans waged war. They were disciplined and proficient with sword, axe and bow.

On Augustus's orders, Germanicus had assembled a vast army of ten full Legions, seventy cohorts of Auxiliaries and fourteen cohorts of Auxiliary cavalry. This he had spread throughout the country with orders to mount coordinated summer attacks on the rebels. The Scorpions were to leave camp in two days time, rendezvous with two other Legions and a force of cavalry, and march south to attack the Bruesci under their leader Bato. Many Illyrian tribes had risen in revolt, but Bato and his Bruesci had been the first. If they were crushed, the revolt would be seriously weakened.

Lucius stood on the platform and peered over the wooden palisade. Below him, the vast Danuvius River flowed past on its way to the Pontus Euxinus. A cargo ship, two banks of slaves labouring to row it against the current, struggled upriver with supplies for some even more remote Legionary outpost. A Roman officer on the raised stern deck saluted briskly as they passed. A much smaller boat, probably carrying messages or an important passenger, shot past on the current, its small sail billowing in the breeze.

Lucius smiled to himself. On that boat, he could sail down the Danuvius, across the Pontus, past Byzantium, legendary Troy and ancient Greece, and back home to the port at Pisanus. Did he want to? No. There were things from his old life that he missed—most strongly, seeing his sisters and the rest of his family—but Titus had been right. The Legion was his family now and his home was wherever it went. And that was fine with him. The soldiering was often boring and Lucius sometimes wondered if he could stand a lifetime of it, but he had learned such a lot. He also loved the feeling that he was part of history in the making. What better training for a historian than that?

"Feeling homesick, Roman?" Freya appeared by Lucius's side and punched him companionably on the shoulder. The pair had talked often over the past five years as Freya had eagerly learned Latin and about all things Roman.

"You know, Freya," Lucius replied, taking his friend's hand by the wrist in greeting, "I'm almost growing fond of all these trees you worship."

"We don't worship trees. We worship the Gods who live in them. You should know that by now."

"I do. I'm just teasing you," Lucius said with a smile. "Do you worship the same Gods as these barbarians in Illyria?"

"Why do you call us barbarians?"

"It's just our name for someone who is not a Roman."

"But Uncle Arminius is a Roman, yet he is still called a barbarian."

"That's different."

"How?"

Lucius struggled to form his answer, stumbling over his words. "Well, because... Look, barbarian just means someone who doesn't speak Latin, whose language sounds like babble, *bar-bar-bar-bar*."

"I speak Latin almost as well as you now, yet I am still a barbarian."

"Freya," Lucius felt flustered, "it's just a name. It doesn't mean anything."

"Does it not? You say it is this and that, but if we non-Romans are neither this nor that, we are still barbarians. I wonder, maybe, if the word means more than you think."

"Enough!" Lucius's discomfort turned to anger. He usually enjoyed Freya's relentless curiosity and debating, but this was different. He felt defensive, cornered; forced to explain something he really couldn't explain. "I said it was just a name."

Freya smiled broadly. "I'm just teasing you."

Lucius returned her grin, but a trace of his anger lingered. He wasn't sure she was teasing him. Freya had seemed serious and this was not the first time she had brought up the subject in recent weeks. Still, he wasn't going to let anything ruin this day. His smile broadened. "You've always been able to joke better than me. You can keep such a straight face while you do it! I would not wish to gamble with you. It is impossible to tell what goes on in your mind by looking at your face. But I *am* interested in the Gods down here."

"They're a strange lot as far as I can tell from talking to the few Auxiliaries from around here," she said, looking out toward the trees. The main one seems to be a Goddess, Genusus. She is the Goddess of the earth. Her husband is Ou, the God of the heavens. But there are many more, probably almost as many as you Romans have."

"There *are* a lot of Roman Gods."

"And a lot you've stolen from others, the Greek Gods, Isis from the Egyptians."

"True enough," Lucius admitted, "and all Romans respect the major Gods, but everyone has their own personal favourite."

"Who is yours?"

"Mithras, the soldier's God." Lucius felt a thrill at the thought of the initiation in a few hours.

"The bull-slayer. I've heard you stole him from the Persians."

"That may be true. It's said that there were people, even before Troy was destroyed, who worshipped bulls and bull-slayers. They were destroyed in a great cataclysm."

"They can't have kept their Gods happy then. I've heard that the ceremonies to Mithras are secret."

"They are. No one but an initiate is allowed to witness the ceremonies."

"Have you ever been to one?"

"I'm not an initiate."

"But you'd like to be one day?"

"Yes." Lucius was getting nervous. He knew it was strictly forbidden to talk about the mysteries of Mithraism. "In your talks with the Auxiliaries," he asked, changing the subject, "did you find out why Bato started the revolt? Illyria has been peaceful for many years."

"I did talk to one man. He is a Bruesci and knew Bato. He said that Bato made a big speech last year at a council of all the tribes. Bato is an impressive man, very large and with a commanding presence. He told the council the whole history of his people from the creation and the wars with the Greeks to the arrival of you Romans. He described his years as an Auxiliary of Rome, the campaigns he had fought in and the battles he had won.

"Bato said that the Bruesci used to be like bears, taking what they wanted and ravaging the lands and peoples around them. But, just as some years the bears can find no fish in the rivers or berries on the hillsides, there were lean times when there was nothing to steal. In those times it was hard to watch the children suffer with swollen bellies and die while all the warriors could do was rage against the Gods.

"When the Romans came with their armies and defeated the Bruesci, the Bruesci became like sheep. They no longer took what they wanted, but the children didn't die and the men could fight to their hearts' content—as long as they did it for the Romans.

"But the well-being of sheep depends on the shepherd, Bato said. For many years life was good for the Bruesci. The local governors were like good sheepdogs, they looked after their flocks and kept them in order and everyone prospered. But things changed. Now the shepherds aren't like sheepdogs, they are like wolves looking after the flocks. Wolves who demand too much in taxes, who live in luxury while their sheep starve once more, and who laugh at the sheep when they show them the children crying out for food. Bato says it is time the Bruesci became bears once more."

"So the rebellion is because the Bruesci have had bad governors?"

"And because a proud people like the Bruesci can only be sheep for so long."

"But as Bato said, with a good governor, the children don't die. Surely all Rome need do is replace the governor."

"That would help, but while life may be hard for bears, at least they are masters of their own destiny."

"But look at all the suffering Bato's rebellion has brought and will bring on his people! Would it not be better for the Bruesci children if Bato negotiated with Rome for a better governor?"

Freya stared long and hard at the dark forests across the rushing river. "Perhaps," she said at last.

The two friends stood in silence, each deep in their own thoughts. Eventually, Lucius noticed that the sun was almost touching the western horizon. It was nearly time.

"I must go," he said.

Freya nodded. "Be careful not to be a sheep, Lucius."

Lucius turned back to face his friend. "I'm not a sheep."

"Of course not," Freya said. "You're a Roman. Roman's can't be sheep, right? Only barbarians can be sheep."

"I didn't mean that."

"Didn't you? Lucius, you take too much for granted. You're a Roman, born to rule. You accept that without question, it's the way the world is supposed to be. But what if the world is more complicated than that? If you don't question and simply follow, then aren't you being a sheep?"

Lucius frowned. What was she getting at? The Romans *did* rule the world, and hadn't Freya once said she wanted to become a Roman? Hadn't Arminius become one?

"It doesn't matter," Freya went on, "if a Roman governor is a sheepdog or a wolf, he will always be in charge. That is what Bato is fighting against."

"That's silly." Lucius felt his earlier anger returning. "Someone has to be in charge."

"Yes, but must it always be a Roman?"

"Yes," Lucius blurted out, louder than he intended. "We're civilized."

Freya smiled sadly, "And I will always be a barbarian."

"I didn't mean that," Lucius struggled to explain. "I just—"

"Lucius!" Titus's voice rose from the compound below. "It is time."

"I have to go."

Lucius stumbled hurriedly down the steps to Titus, his mind swirling. He didn't understand what had happened with Freya, but he felt instinctively that it was important. Something had changed between them, but he would have to think about it later. Now Mithras was calling and the God demanded undivided attention. Lucius pushed Freya far back in his mind as he followed Titus to the barracks.

~~~~

"Are you ready?" Titus wore the wolf skin of the *signifer*, the head with its bared teeth sitting atop his helmet and the skin draped over his shoulders and hanging down his back. Where it showed, his armour gleamed in the setting sun.

"As ready as I'll ever be," Lucius replied. As required for the ceremony, he was dressed only in a plain woollen tunic and sandals.

Titus turned and led the way along the Via Principalis. Watching soldiers nodded as they passed. To Lucius's surprise, he and Titus left the fort through the East Gate and headed toward the river. Almost at the trees, Lucius twisted his head to look back at the fort. He thought he saw the silhouetted figure of Freya on the battlements, watching. He wanted to wave and see her wave back. He desperately wanted her to take pleasure in the significant events of this evening. But he kept his hand by his side. Too many people were watching.

At the river, Titus and Lucius turned south along a rough path that led into the trees. As they progressed, the river bank beside them steepened until it formed a low cliff of the rough white stone that was common hereabouts. The cliff wound about, sometimes so close that it almost forced them to walk in the shallows of the river, sometimes so far away that it was invisible through the trees.

Eventually, Titus found some sign that Lucius missed and turned into the trees and headed toward the cliff. Through the thickening twilight, Lucius could see a collection of flickering lights. The pair emerged into a small clearing at the foot of the cliff. Lining the clearing were soldiers in full uniform, every second man holding a flaming torch.

Lucius recognized some men from his *contuberium*: Drusus, Quintus and Appius were there. With a pang of disappointment, Lucius noticed that Sextus Livius, Sextus Vipsanius and Herod were missing.

"Welcome, initiate Lucius Quinctillius Claudianus." The soldiers spoke in unison and clashed their fists to their chests in salute. "Are you ready to undertake the first rites and begin your journey into the mysteries of Mithras?"

"I am," Lucius replied.

"The road to Mithras is hard," Titus stepped forward and spoke softly. "Mithras does not accept the weak and he will test you to the utmost. You will see and hear things that will terrify you. You will wish you were once more an infant safe in your mother's arms. But you must not falter. You must either go forward or die in the undertaking. If you are not ready to undergo the ordeal and to die for Mithras, you may turn back now. No one will think the worse of you."

"I will go on," Lucius said, although he was far from certain. Titus's unusual formality and the talk of death unnerved him. And distracting thoughts of Freya and their argument kept popping into his mind.

"Good," Titus said. "We shall continue. Be aware, initiate, that you may never speak of the mysteries you are about to learn to any living soul who has not undergone them. If you do, Mithras will strike you dead."

"I understand."

"Now, remove your tunic and sandals."

Lucius did as he was told and stood feeling vulnerable and uncomfortable in only a loin cloth. Titus placed a soft red peaked Phrygian cap—the symbol of Mithras and freedom—on his head. It was almost completely dark now and the torches cast weird, flickering shadows on the ground and on the faces of the soldiers.

"Mithras the bull-slayer lives in the dark places of the earth. To discover him, you must enter his lair blind," Titus handed Lucius a short dagger, "but not unarmed."

Two soldiers at the far side of the clearing stood aside to show a leather curtain hung against the cliff face. One of them pulled it aside, revealing a black hole. The hole was close to the ground and large enough for a man to crawl through.

"Enter the lair of Mithras," Titus said, portentously, "and learn the mysteries or die."

"Learn or die. Learn or die," the soldiers chanted in unison.

Lucius could feel sweat begin to prickle his skin, even in the cool evening air. Slowly he edged forward toward the hole.

"Learn or die. Learn or die."

As he reached the opening, he crouched down and peered in. The feeble light of the torches showed a floor, sloping downward, but it soon disappeared in darkness.

"Learn or die. Learn or die."

Taking a deep breath, Lucius crawled inside. Immediately, the chanting stopped and the heavy curtain fell behind him, plunging him into total blackness. Lucius waited but, strain as he did, there was no light for his eyes to adjust to. Cautiously feeling about, he discovered he was in a low tunnel, just high and wide enough for him to crawl through. He edged slowly forward on his knees, feeling the floor with one hand and waving the other in front so that he didn't hit a protruding rock.

As he struggled forward, Lucius felt a cold draft of air that chilled the sweat on his bare skin. He shivered. The tunnel must be widening out a bit. What was going to happen? What was he supposed to do? Then he heard a noise. It was a soft scraping sound, like a piece of bronze, or a claw, rubbing on rock. What if he had crawled into a wolf's lair or a bear's den? He had little to protect himself with. Was that what "Learn or die" meant? He clutched his dagger tightly. It seemed pitifully inadequate to fight off a wild beast.

A violent, glancing blow caught Lucius on the hip and knocked him against the rough wall, painfully scratching his arm and side. Lucius flailed wildly with the dagger but met only empty air.

"Who enters the realm of Mithras?" the voice was deep and rough and seemed to come from everywhere at once. "Do you know the mysteries?"

"I come to learn," Lucius stammered.

Gruff laughter echoed through the cave. "Then come forward and let us see if you are worthy."

Lucius scrambled back onto his knees and struggled blindly forward. All thoughts of Freya had vanished. Every nerve in his body was straining to overcome his fear and to understand what was happening in the surrounding blackness.

"Hurry!" Another blow caught Lucius on the opposite hip. Four more times, blows struck out of the darkness, catching Lucius somewhere on his body, but he kept going. "Stop!" The voice commanded

Lucius froze.

"What are you prepared to do to learn my mysteries?"

"Anything," Lucius replied.

"Anything?" The echoing laughter returned. "That is a lot to offer. Let us see if you tell the truth."

With a shudder of horror, Lucius felt a hand on his shoulder. Another was on his arm, and two on his sides. Before he could work out what was going on, the hands grasped him strongly and threw him upwards. Lucius gasped, convinced that his skull was about to be crushed against the tunnel roof, but it met only air. As the hands let go, Lucius struggled to balance on his feet.

"Step forward."

Lucius found it more frightening to walk forward in the total dark and it was all he could do not to fall to his knees and crawl. Again he felt hands on him, but this time they held his arms softly. From all around him, but close by, a low animal noise sent shivers down his spine.

"Are you worthy to follow the bull-slayer?"

"I hope so."

"Hope! Do not hope. Be certain."

Lucius cleared his throat. "I am worthy," he said as firmly as he could.

"Good."

Something long, cold and living landed on Lucius's shoulders and began to writhe frantically, twisting itself around his neck. Lucius screamed in utter panic and grabbed at the beast. He felt fangs sink deep into his wrist. Whipping his arm forward, he dragged the snake off his neck and hurled it away.

I'm dead, Lucius thought. He groaned out loud, imagining the snake's venom racing up his arm. Already his fingers were numb and his arm was tingling.

"Have you failed Mithras?" the voice asked.

"No!" Lucius yelled into the darkness. He was angry now—none of this was fair! He was being taunted and teased, but he wouldn't let them win. He hadn't come this far only to give up. He clenched and unclenched his fist and the numbness seemed to ease. Lucius stepped forward. Somewhere in the darkness he heard a dog bark.

Hands in the middle of his back thrust him forward. He fell painfully to his knees on the cold stone of the floor but his chest and face came up against something warm. Something living that moved as Lucius hit it. A loud bellow echoed through the cave.

What now? For a moment, Lucius stayed on the ground, shivering with terror and gasping for breath. He wondered what happened to initiates who didn't pass the test, who gave in to their nerves or fear? He pushed the thought from his head. Go on! He had to. "Learn or die."

Fighting his way to his feet, Lucius used his empty hand to explore the creature before him. It was large—Lucius could feel its spine at the level of his chest. The animal moved restlessly and grunted and bellowed, but it was obviously hobbled and could not escape. Lucius's hand found a strong neck, broad head and a pair of wide horns. Of course! If this was the lair of Mithras, there would be a bull.

And suddenly, it all made sense. Lucius remembered Titus taking him to the temple of Vetera to see the statue of Mithras. The God rode a bull and wore the Phrygian cap of freedom. His helpers, Canis the dog and Hydra the snake, were at his feet. Now Lucius also knew what the dagger was for.

Clambering up, Lucius settled himself astride the animal's back. He grabbed a horn and held on tight, leaning forward until his mouth was beside the struggling creature's ear, Lucius whispered to it. "Easy. Easy." Gradually the bull calmed. "We are both servants of Mithras. We have our roles to play. I have mine and you have yours. It cannot be changed."

The bull was completely quiet now, listening to Lucius's voice and waiting. Lucius stretched the hand that held the dagger down the side of the bull's neck. He felt the artery pulsing with blood and life.

"I have learned," Lucius whispered. "This is for you Mithras." With a short, swift movement, Lucius sliced the dagger deep into the bull's neck. The creature shuddered and a warm flow of blood washed over Lucius's hand.

Lucius kept his grip on the horn and continued talking softly as the bull's blood pulsed out onto the floor of the cave. Gradually, the shuddering eased and the creature sank onto its knees. Then, with a deep sigh, it settled to the ground and was still. Lucius sat up on the dead beast's back.

A flint sparked in the darkness and a single torch struggled to life. Others followed until the cave was as brightly lit as the clearing outside. The cave was not as large as Lucius had imagined, but there was enough room for five soldiers to stand around the edges. Unlike the men outside, these soldiers weren't in uniform and just wore their woollen tunics. Lucius recognized three of them: Sextus Livius and Sextus Vipsanius stood to one side smiling and Herod stood in front of Lucius grinning sheepishly.

Beneath Lucius, the bull lay dead, a large pool of blood shining in the torchlight by its head. A skinny dog lapped at the blood and the snake writhed beside it. The scene was identical to the statue Lucius had seen in Vetera's temple—Mithras the bull-slayer in a Phrygian cap, astride the dying bull with a dog and a snake lapping the blood. The Phrygian cap was freedom, the dog loyalty and the snake the earth. The cave was the cave of the heavens and Lucius had just re-enacted the primeval battle for the world between the forces of Good, himself, and Evil, the bull.

"Congratulations," Herod stepped forward and reached out to help Lucius from the bull's back. "Good has triumphed once again."

Lucius's knees were weak and he was shivering with the cold. Sextus Livius stepped forward and draped a cloak over his shoulders. "You did well, Lucius Quinctillius," he said.

"The snake," Lucius said, looking at the serpent writhing on the ground.

"That was me," Herod said, his grin broadening into a smile. "I was worried that I would miss you completely."

"Worried that you'd miss me!" Lucius exclaimed, horrified. "The thing bit me." He held out his arm to show the two angry red puncture wounds on his wrist. "I've been poisoned!"

"Calm down," Herod said. "I learned an old trick from my mother for emptying the poison sacs. You get the snake to bite a ball of moss and then squeeze gently behind the head. Most of the poison comes out."

"Most!"

"Don't worry. At worst your wrist will itch for a while. But come on, we can't stand here talking all night. We have to get this bull out of the cave so we can have the feast. At least it should be easier getting a dead bull out than a live one in. We would never have managed if my mother hadn't taught me the recipe for a salve that calms the wildest beast."

~~~~

With much puffing, grunting and swearing, the six soldiers managed to haul the dead bull to the mouth of the cave. When Lucius pulled back the curtain, he was met by a completely changed scene. The clearing was packed with soldiers from his centuria who cheered lustily as he emerged. A large fire had been built in the centre and soldiers swarmed to the cave entrance to drag the bull out, skin it and carve it into pieces to roast on the fire. The path to the river had been widened and a small cart, loaded with amphorae of wine, pulled in.

One by one, Titus and the others in Lucius's *contuberium* stepped forward and embraced him.

"Welcome," Drusus said as he enveloped Lucius in a bear hug.

Quintus's embrace was perfunctory and cold, but Appius wouldn't let go and launched into a scholarly history of Mithras and the origins of the cult.

"Let the boy go," Titus ordered. "He's learned enough for tonight."

Titus led Lucius to one side where his uniform lay. While Lucius dressed, they talked.

"Well done, lad," Titus said. "You are now an initiate into the Mithraic mysteries. You're a true soldier now."

"I was terrified," Lucius admitted. "All that chanting about learning or dying almost scared me to death."

"Fear is the one thing that can destroy us. Conquer that and you can be like Alexander and conquer the world."

"I would never have made it if I hadn't remembered the statue of Mithras you showed me in the temple at Vetera."

"And why do you think I showed it to you?" Titus's weather-beaten face wrinkled into a broad grin. "I knew you wouldn't fail. You've a long way to go and a lot to learn, but the first step is always the hardest. Now you are one with thousands of soldiers in the Legions and, if you ever need it, they will help you without question. All you need do is ask."

"How will I know which soldiers are initiates?" Lucius asked, worried about revealing the mysteries to someone undeserving.

"Show this." Titus handed Lucius a small silver medallion on a leather thong. Lucius examined it carefully. One side showed Mithras slaying the bull while the other was engraved with the words, *Ille vir debet fidelitatem ad Mithrum—This man owes loyalty to Mithras.*"

Lucius felt a rush of emotion as he pulled the thong over his head and tucked the medallion under his armour. Now he truly belonged. "Thank you," he said.

"You keep doing that!" Titus said, cuffing Lucius on the arm. "It's Mithras you have to thank. Now let's go eat. Even the simplest food may taste like an Imperial banquet if the hunger is sharpened by fear and exertion."

Lucius's *contuberium* sat in a rough circle around the fire, eating, drinking and joking.

"They do say," Drusus said through a mouthful of half-raw meat, "that in Egypt some people worship cats."

"That's true," Appius replied.

"Well," Drusus went on, "I don't agree with that."

"But it makes some sense," Appius said in a serious voice. "Cats are very intelligent and independent. Many cultures have cats as Gods. It's even said that there is a tribe, far to the east, where the priests can change into cats at will. Now if you ask me, I don't think—"

"No." Drusus interrupted, ripping off another mouthful of meat. "You're very learned, Appius, but you're wrong here. Cats don't make good objects of worship."

"Why not?"

"No meat on them. Not near as good eating as a bull."

The others around the fire collapsed in laughter. Appius looked indignant for a moment, but then he started laughing too. He was used to being teased and he knew it was all in fun. He also knew he was the first person the soldiers came to when they really needed to know something.

The only one of the group who didn't laugh was Quintus. He sat picking at his food, his eyes darting from one of his companions to another.

"Come on, Quintus," Drusus said, heartily. "Laugh for the sake of the Gods. Young Lucius has passed a great test, we should all be celebrating."

"I will not mock the Gods with coarse humour as you do, Drusus," Quintus said severely. "The Gods control our destinies and demand respect. If they don't get it, dreadful things will befall us all."

"Doom and gloom!" Drusus said. "I've been the way I am all my life and no harm has ever come of it. The Gods put good food, fine wine and beautiful women on this earth and, if you ask me, we insult them by not enjoying these things to the full."

Quintus stood up. "The Gods have not received the respect they deserve since that upstart Julius

Caesar destroyed the Republic. And look! That led to years of bloody conflict and now we have an Emperor who rules all our destinies. People are even talking of making him into a God. What nonsense! He's a man, like you and I. It's arrogant and presumptuous and the Gods will not stand for it for long. No good will come of this degenerate world we live in, you mark my words.

"Now, I am going to pray."

Flinging his cape theatrically over his shoulder, Quintus stalked off into the darkness and the group lapsed into a silence broken only by the crackling of the fire and the murmured conversations of other groups.

"No one can throw a wet blanket onto a happy occasion like that man," Drusus said eventually. "I know the Gods have to be taken seriously, but by Mithras himself, a man needs to have fun as well."

The talk continued for a while, but Quintus's gloom had dampened the spark. One by one, the soldiers drifted back to their barracks. Eventually, only Lucius and Herod were left by the dying fire, although a group of soldiers by the cart were taking the fact that there was still some wine left in the last amphora as a personal challenge.

"You're not turning in?" Herod asked.

"Not yet," Lucius sipped at the dregs of wine in his goblet. "My mind's still whirling. I don't think I could sleep. Was it like this when you were initiated?"

"Much worse. You were lucky to have Titus as the one to lead you to Mithras. He's an old soldier who understands things. I had Quintus."

"By all the Gods, that must have been dreadful."

"It was. The man is utterly devoid of a sense of humour."

"But the initiation was the same?"

"Broadly. It wasn't in a cave. We were in Egypt at the time, down near Alexandria, and it was in an old tomb outside the city. That was fine, but Quintus felt that to do honour to Mithras, he had to find the largest bull on the Nile. The beast was huge. I managed to clamber onto its back, but then it broke it's hobble and started crashing around the tomb, beating itself and me against the walls. I was hanging on to the horns with one arm and frantically stabbing at the neck with the other."

Lucius laughed at the image of Herod in his red Phrygian cap, clinging to the rampaging bull for dear life.

"Eventually, I must have hit something vital with the knife, because the beast slowed down and collapsed. When they lit the torches, the place looked like a slaughterhouse. There was blood over everything. I was bruised and bleeding almost as much as the bull and Sextus Livius had broken his leg trying to get out of the way in the dark. To top it all, the dog had fled and the snake had been trampled to death by the bull."

Lucius was laughing so hard that tears were coming to his eyes. "I bet Quintus wasn't happy," he choked out.

"Quintus is never happy, but you're right, he was absolutely wild. He ranted on for the rest of the evening about respect for the Gods and how it was somehow my fault that everything had gone wrong.

"But I think Mithras has a sense of humour, because he's always looked after me since then. All the battles I've been in—and not all of them against barbarians; some of the most violent places in the world are the taverns down by the docks in Ostia—and never a single scratch! Drusus thinks I'm a charm and worries like crazy if he's not standing beside me in the ranks."

The pair lapsed into companionable silence. Apart from Titus, Lucius was closer to Herod than anyone else in the *contuberium*. Herod was unusual in the Legion. He was half Judean and looked different from most of the other soldiers who were from Rome or the northern provinces. His skin was darker and his nose more arced. His mother was from Hierosolyma and had caught the eye of a Roman Legate during the civil wars. When the Legate returned to Rome he took his new wife, who was pregnant with Herod, with him. Herod was as much a Roman citizen as Lucius, despite his looks and his Judean name.

Lucius thought back to his earlier conversation with Freya about Bato and the Illyrian revolt.

"Are you happy being a Roman?" he asked.

"Happy? As happy as anyone else, I suppose."

"No, I mean, you're half Judean and Judea is province of Rome. Isn't there a part of you that would like to be part of a free Judea?"

"You mean like the Zealots who dream of throwing out the Romans and recreating the Kingdom of David? I don't know. I've never been there. I've been close—Egypt, Syria—but never Judea itself.

"My mother told me stories about it," Herod continued. "She loved the desert and the bare hills and I must admit, sometimes they do seem preferable to these forests with a barbarian behind every tree. Maybe some day I'll go and take a look, but as for going back and fighting to free the land of my ancestors, forget it. I like being a soldier and I like being a Roman.

"Oh, sometimes, when I'm not in uniform, someone calls me a barbarian or tries to push me around, but they only do that once. *Civis Romanus sum*—I am a citizen of Rome—really does mean something."

"Are you sure?"

Herod looked hard at Lucius. "What do you mean?"

"Well," Lucius said, carefully, "I know you're not a zealot."

"By all the Gods, no," Herod interrupted. "They're a bunch of scruffy fanatics imagining some impossible world."

"But the ones who aren't fanatics—can they ever truly be Roman citizens?"

"Of course they can. Look at me."

"Yes," Lucius acknowledged, "but you're lucky. Your father was a general and you were born in Rome itself. What if we're talking about a peasant who grew up in the Judean hills, or an Auxiliary? Can they ever truly be Roman?"

"You have to take the long view. The Roman Empire is the greatest the world has ever seen and it's growing every year. One day everyone will be a part of the Roman Empire, and then your peasant will be the same as everyone else."

"Will he? Freya would argue not."

"So, we're talking about your Germanic friend! Her uncle's already a Roman citizen."

"And a great general, but he cannot dine with Germanicus."

"Of course not!" Herod sounded shocked at the idea. "Germanicus is Rome's greatest general and a noble. He's married to the Emperor Augustus's granddaughter—"

"But Arminius has won more victories than Governor Varus, who dines with Germanicus at Vetera every night. He should be given a triumphant procession through Rome, should he not?"

"Don't be ridiculous," Herod's shock turned to annoyance. "Give a barbarian chieftain, however useful he's been, a triumph in Rome? It's unheard of! That friend of yours is a good soldier, but she's putting some strange ideas in your head, Lucius. Be careful."

Lucius knew he should stop now. He had argued with Freya earlier in the day, and now he was on the verge of arguing with another close friend. But he couldn't stop. He had to sort things out in his mind. "So, what you're saying is that there are two kinds of Romans—those who are born Roman and those who are thrown Roman citizenship as a meaningless award for being useful?"

Herod stood up and brushed off his cloak, glaring down at Lucius. "I don't understand what your problem is. Everyone knows that barbarians are different from us."

"But lots of true Romans are different from each other, too," Lucius said as calmly as he could. "Look at the eight of us in the *contuberium*. No one could ever say that Drusus and Quintus are the same."

"That's entirely different," Herod said, angrily. "These German barbarians have a completely different culture from ours. They don't think the same way we do."

"But why is that such a bad thing?" Lucius persisted. "Freya is one of the smartest people I know. She is continually questioning everything, trying to learn more."

"And you have picked up the habit," Herod said, accusingly. "There are things that should not be questioned. Everyone knows that. A Roman is a Roman and a barbarian is a barbarian."

"Your mother was a barbarian." As soon as the words left his mouth, Lucius regretted them. He had said them to make a point, but he had been angry and thoughtless. Herod worshipped his mother and would be badly hurt by any insult to her.

"I'm sorry," Lucius said, standing up to face his friend. "I didn't mean it that way. I was just trying to make a point. It's all so complicated!"

"It's *not* complicated," Herod said, coldly. "It's very simple, and the sooner you realize that, the better."

Herod turned and strode off pushing past the last of the drunk soldiers, weaving their way to bed.

Lucius slumped back down by the dying embers of the fire, reflecting ruefully on the day. In only a few hours, one of his dreams had come true and he had managed to have major arguments with both of his closest friends. Lucius flung his goblet into the fire, raising a shower of glowing sparks. Turning his back on the cave of Mithras, he trudged miserably back to camp.

Freya

As Freya watched Titus and Lucius head for the trees by the river, she felt a pang of envy. She knew Lucius was to be initiated into the mysteries of Mithras tonight; it was common knowledge around the camp. Not that Freya wished to be a follower of Mithras—she had her own Gods—but it was just another sign of something that, as a barbarian, she could never be a part of.

At the edge of the trees, Lucius hesitated and looked back. Freya almost waved—she knew tonight was important to him and wanted to wish him luck—but she hesitated and the moment was gone. Lucius disappeared between the trees.

Freya felt miserable. She hadn't intended to argue with Lucius, but it was happening more and more these days. Sometimes she yearned for the early days of their friendship. Things had been so much simpler then and they had both been content to learn from the other. Now Lucius seemed much more set in his ways, more sure that he was right and unable to see any point of view other than the Roman.

But maybe it's I who have changed, Freya thought glumly. Perhaps I've learned too much to see the world as simple anymore.

There was a time when Freya had unquestioningly worshipped her uncle, Arminius. He was everything she wanted to be, strong, brave, admired. When he had been granted Roman citizenship and gone to Rome, Freya had been ecstatic. That was her dream too, and Arminius was proving it was possible. She had wanted more than anything to be Roman. As a child she had sat for hours watching the Legions drill, awed by their gleaming armour, waving, colourful plumes and massed, ordered ranks. To be a Roman soldier, she'd imagined, must be the best thing in the world.

Now she wasn't so certain. Partly it was because she knew more about the soldiering life and it had, consequently, lost some of its glamour. But mainly it was because she was no longer certain that being Roman was the best thing in the world.

She still wanted many of the things the Romans had, like their knowledge, power and confidence, but she no longer believed blindly that gaining Roman citizenship would achieve that. Partly it was Arminius who had changed her mind.

"Are you glad you became a Roman?" Freya had blurted out one evening during the march from Germania.

"Of course I am," Arminius had answered automatically. "Why do you ask?"

"It's just," Freya began tentatively, "you are a great general."

Arminius laughed. "I cannot argue with you there."

"You command more men than there are in a Legion. You know more about Rome's enemies than Varus or Germanicus. You have won countless battles for Rome." Arminius nodded slowly. "But you're not a Legate. You're not invited to the meetings to discuss strategy. You don't dine with the other officers. Sometimes it seems as if you are just a barbarian in charge of some Auxiliaries."

"Enough!"

Freya cringed at the sudden anger in her uncle's voice. "How dare you presume to call me a barbarian? I am a citizen of Rome *and* I am a Cherusci war chief. You are just someone who happens to be good with a sling."

Arminius glared at his niece, but Freya refused to flinch. She took a deep breath. "Uncle, please don't be angry. I didn't mean to insult you. I'm sorry."

Arminius grunted, but his expression softened, encouraging Freya to go on. "I'm just trying to understand. It doesn't seem fair. You're a better soldier than Varus. You should be his equal, at least."

"Governor Varus is a high-born, noble Roman," Arminius began to explain.

"And you are a high-born, noble Cherusci," Freya interrupted.

Anger flashed across Arminius's face again, but vanished as soon as it had appeared. Freya kept silent as her uncle wrestled with his thoughts. When he eventually spoke, his voice was soft and slow and he stared off into the distance, not at Freya.

"I was angry," he said, "because you expressed something that I have been thinking. Becoming a Roman citizen is not what I thought it would be. You are right, Freya. In many ways, I am still a barbarian."

Freya opened her mouth to argue, but Arminius held up his hand to silence her.

"And I am proud of being a barbarian," he went on. "What you say is true: I am not accepted as an equal. I suppose if I cut my hair in the Roman style, dressed more like a Roman and affected Roman manners, I might be accepted more, but I will never completely be one of them. I was naive to think I could be and, for a time after I realized I could never be fully accepted, it angered me, but not any longer."

Arminius looked at Freya and smiled faintly at her puzzled expression. "For all my denial and bluster, I *want* to be a barbarian. If Varus and Germanicus came to me tomorrow and said, 'Cut your hair and dress like us and you can eat at our table, attend our strategy meetings, even go back to Rome and become a Senator,' I would say no. Even if it were possible, I would not, could not, completely exchange being a Cherusci for being a Roman."

"When we are finished in Illyria, you could cross the Rhenus and live the old way like Lothar," Freya suggested.

Arminius shook his head sadly. "I don't think so. What I have always thought is still true. The

Cherusci cannot defeat the Romans. One day, the world will be Roman and the sooner we adjust to that the better."

"But it's not fair."

"The world is not fair, Freya. Do not think I like living between two worlds, half Cherusci and half Roman but fully neither. I pray every day that I never have to choose one over the other."

As Freya stood on the battlements at Carnuntum, far from home, remembering her conversation with her uncle, she realized that what Arminius had said on the road from Germania was the reason she kept arguing with Lucius. She was jealous of his certainty about all things Roman and of the simplicity of his life. He had no choice to make—he was a Roman and that was that. So she needled and taunted him, trying to make things as complex and difficult for him as they were for Arminius and herself. It wasn't fair but, as her uncle had pointed out, the world wasn't a fair place.

Freya was about to return to her camp when a movement in the deepening shadows to her left, caught her eye. As she squinted, she made out a figure heading into the trees. It was Arminius. Puzzled, Freya climbed down and, with a nod to the guards, left Carnuntum by the East Gate.

Arminius was easy to follow. He wasn't making much noise, no Cherusci did when travelling through the forest, but neither was he keeping totally silent. Stopping to listen occasionally, Freya followed her uncle for almost a full hour, by which time the sun had set and the only light came from the full moon that was playing hide-and-seek with the tattered clouds.

Eventually, Freya spotted a flickering light through the trees ahead. Crouching, she worked her way forward until she could see into a small clearing. There were three men there: Arminius, a torchbearer and a tall, heavily-built warrior wrapped in a thick bearskin cloak. The warrior and Arminius were deep in conversation.

Why was Arminius meeting a stranger in the middle of the forest? She crawled forward, trying to get close enough to hear what was being said.

A foot crashed into Freya's back, bruising her spine and forcing the air out of her lungs. Arms grabbed her by the shoulders, hauled her to her feet and dragged her into the clearing.

"I found 'er creepin' 'bout in the forest," her captor said as Freya gasped for air. Arminius and the other man turned to see the source of the commotion. "Want me to send 'er to the Gods?" Freya could understand what the man was saying, although his accent was very guttural and several words were unfamiliar.

"No," Arminius said. "She is my niece."

The other man nodded and the hands let go of Freya, who sank to her knees. "As you wish," her captor said and returned to the forest.

"Your niece has some strange habits," the big man said. His voice was less harsh than the other, but there were still words Freya couldn't follow. "She could get herself into trouble."

"Don't worry, Bato," Arminius said. "She's young, and her curiosity sometimes gets the better of her. I'll deal with her later."

"Bato?" Freya gasped.

"If you wish not to compound your foolish, youthful error," Arminius said, sternly, "you will sit by that tree and maintain a silence befitting your presence in the company of your elders and betters."

Chastised and in pain from her bruised back, Freya crawled over to where she had been directed and got as comfortable as she could. Her mind was racing. What was her uncle doing, meeting secretly with the leader of the Illyrian rebels? Freya studied the stranger. He was the same height as Arminius, but more heavily built. Beneath his cloak, Freya caught glimpses of armour glinting in the torchlight. Bato was hatless and his wild hair was almost black. His face was square, swarthy and very expressive as he argued with Arminius. At first they spoke quietly and Freya could only catch the occasional word, but gradually, the conversation became more animated and their voices rose.

"You know as well as any what it is like to live under the Roman yoke," Bato said, his face twisted in anger.

"I live under no one's yoke," Arminius replied. "I am the equal of any man."

"That may be. I know of none who are your superior, and the fame of the Cherusci warriors has spread far and wide, but it is not your opinion or mine that matters. Can you bathe with the Roman officers, your equals?"

"I do not wish to bathe in the Roman manner."

"That does not matter. Should you wish it, could you?"

The pair stood in silence for a minute, then Bato went on, "I shall answer for you. You could not. If you tried, you would be told to leave, like the common rabble."

"It's not so."

"Perhaps not. Perhaps you dine with the Legates. Perhaps Germanicus consults you on all campaign matters. Perhaps you wear a toga and discuss the world in the Senate house in the forum in Rome."

"Enough! You are perilously close to crossing the line into insult."

Bato tilted his head in a mock apology and half bowed in supplication. "I meant no insult. But the Bruesci have been 'the equals' of Rome for many years. We are offered much when our soldiers are needed to fight Rome's battles, but given little when peace returns. Now we have chosen to take our destiny in our own hands and I am asking that you join us. With the Auxiliaries on our side—and you could persuade them—we could destroy these Legions."

"Perhaps," Arminius said, "but what of the other Legions in Illyria?"

"A victory such as you and I could win here would unite every warrior in Illyria. We could throw the Romans out."

Arminius turned away and stared hard at Freya. In the flickering torchlight, his face was a mask of concentration, but his thoughts were unreadable.

"I have taken an oath," he said at length, turning back to face Bato.

"An oath must be upheld by both sides," Bato said. "The Romans have made many oaths to us and kept not one. Now I take oaths with my sword."

"That may be fine for you, but a Cherusci oath binds the giver regardless of what anyone else may do. I cannot join your rebellion."

"So be it," Bato sighed. "I believe you, and perhaps I will live to regret that decision, but I promised you would come and leave here in peace and I will abide by that. You are free to go. When next we meet, I fear it will be on the battlefield, and that will be a tragedy. We should be standing side by side, facing our common foe."

Bato held out his hand. Arminius took it and held on for a long moment. Then the pair parted. Bato let out a low whistle and half a dozen men appeared from the forest around the clearing. Led by the torchbearer, the party disappeared into the trees, leaving Arminius and Freya blinking as their eyes adjusted to the near dark.

"We must return before we are missed," Arminius said. The pair walked back to Carnuntum in silence. Freya had expected Arminius to berate her for following him, but he was obviously considering much more weighty matters.

At the edge of the open area around the camp, Arminius stopped. Torches burned all along the walls, casting a wavering, eerie light over the scene.

A small tent city had grown up around the camp, full of the people who always seemed to appear from nowhere whenever a Legion stopped for more than a few days. Vendors sold everything from trinkets and fortunes to wine and roast boar. Blacksmiths forged weapons of all descriptions and gamblers organized games of chance around small fires. Legionaries wandered everywhere and the air was filled with laughter, curses and the shouts of groups of women accosting passing soldiers.

"Did I do the right thing?" Arminius asked.

Freya looked at her uncle, surprised by the question. Arminius was always so decisive and certain. He had never asked her advice before. She answered loyally. "Of course you did. You cannot go against an oath."

"I have taken no oath."

"Then why—?"

"I had to give Bato a reason he could understand. Otherwise he would have killed us both in that clearing. I am a mercenary who works for pay— and for the chance at civilization." Arminius paused. "Maybe Bato's right. Maybe it is better to die as a man on your feet than live as a sheep of Rome."

Freya was shocked. She understood the thoughts he was struggling with—she had tried to explain them to Lucius earlier—but she had never heard Arminius talk this way before. "I don't understand."

Arminius looked at his niece. "I'm not certain I do either. All I know is that it used to be more straightforward.

"When I first led our warriors to become Auxiliaries of Rome, I had a horrible argument with Lothar. He called me a traitor and said I was selling out the Cherusci's proud heritage for a few trinkets. I tried to reason with him, to tell him that I honestly believed it was best for all if we accepted the Roman way. He spat in my face and told me I was being blinded by Roman discipline, which he called a lack of imagination, and by their technology, which he dismissed as unimportant. Lothar told me that the things I admired about Rome were only worthless trappings, covering an empty heart. Only the traditional Cherusci way of life and honouring our ancient Gods were significant and I was throwing that away like a madman who, in a violent fit of insanity, destroys everything that is precious to him."

Arminius paused for a moment, staring at the Roman camp bustling with activity. "We both said things that night that cannot be unsaid and created wounds that will never heal. But for all that and despite the countless fine speeches I have made on the benefits of Roman civilization, there has always been a corner of my mind that whispers—in the darkness of a midnight storm in the forest, and from the bloody bodies of Rome's enemies after a battle—'Lothar was right. Arminius, you are a traitor.'"

Freya stood in horrified silence, barely able to take in what she was hearing. Arminius—her uncle, her hero, the person whose opinion she admired and respected most in the world—had always had doubts about the most important thing he had ever done?

Arminius's face was unutterably sad in the torchlight. "Freya," he said eventually, "that dark voice that I have pushed into the deep recesses of my mind is getting louder. It is Bato's voice now, asking me to choose once and for all between Roman and Cherusci."

"But you refused to join Bato's revolt," Freya pointed out.

"I did," Arminius agreed, "but I did so for practical reasons. Bato's rebellion is doomed."

"Doomed?" Freya was surprised to hear Bato's chances of victory dismissed so firmly. "But he's a great leader and he has most of the Illyrian tribes with him."

"Yes, and he will win battles, but he is destined to lose, nonetheless. Maybe not this year or next, but whatever victories he wins, there will always be more Legions. Illyria is too close to Rome for Caesar Augustus to allow a rebellion here to succeed. Do you know the story of Hannibal?"

"Of course. He led his army, complete with war elephants, over the mountains to the very gates of Rome, where he destroyed the Roman armies at the battle of Cannae. Everyone knows that."

"And he won other victories, too," Arminius added. "Hannibal destroyed every army the Romans sent after him."

"He was a great general."

"One of the greatest, but he lost the war and had to retreat back to Hispania. Why?"

Freya thought for a moment. "Because he was so far from home, he couldn't get reinforcements."

"But why did he need reinforcements if he had already won every battle?"

Freya's brow furrowed in concentration. She'd never thought of that. "I don't know."

"Because the Romans never gave up," Arminius said. "By any logic, they should have surrendered after Cannae, but they didn't. Every time Hannibal destroyed a Roman army, the Romans got another one together and went after him again. Of course, they had little choice. Hannibal was fighting them a few days march from Rome itself—it was either keep fighting or surrender—but that is the great Roman strength. They don't give up. Attacking Rome is like stepping on an ants' nest. The ants will keep coming and attacking your foot, however many you squash.

"Hannibal went into the heart of the ants' nest and the ants defeated him," her uncle continued. "Bato will have the same problem. He's not attacking Rome directly, but Illyria is very close. The Romans cannot afford to have a victorious enemy on their doorstep. However many victories the Illyrians win, the Romans will keep coming at them until Bato is led in chains through the Forum in Rome."

"So the Romans are unbeatable."

"I didn't say that," Arminius explained. "What happens when you step on a column of ants foraging far from their nest?"

Freya thought back to the games she had played as a child, taking a stick and poking at long lines of ants on the forest floor. "Some of the ants will attack and others will spread out and look for another place to forage."

"Exactly. The ants will fight back, but, eventually, they will stop and forage elsewhere. The Romans are the same. Meaningful victories against them can only be won on the far edges of the Empire where the outcome cannot worry the Senators in the Forum."

"And Germania is much farther away from Rome than Illyria," Freya said.

A half smile crossed Arminius's face. "You're a very intelligent girl, Freya. So?"

"A rebellion far from Rome *might* succeed." Freya was a little frightened by the course this conversation was taking. Was Arminius suggesting that the Cherusci fight Rome?

Arminius nodded "You're right."

"Are you saying the Cherusci should rebel?" Freya asked, nervously.

"No, of course not!" Arminius said, turning to face his niece. "I'm just croaking on. Pay me no mind! I am far from home and lonely. Bato asked for a meeting and I went to see what this great warrior who defies Rome had to say. In truth, I liked him. But tomorrow, or the next day, or the day after, I will kill him if I meet him in battle. I hope the Roman peace comes soon."

Arminius nodded goodnight and walked off between the tents.

Freya followed more slowly. The evening had been long and tiring. She had been scared half to death, her back still hurt where the Bruesci guard had stood on her, and her mind reeled with thoughts of Arminius. It was the first time she had seen her uncle uncertain about the path he had chosen for their people. Was he considering rebellion? The very thought terrified Freya, but if she was honest, it excited her too. She had admired Bato's strength and his certainty in the rightness of his cause. Wouldn't it be so much simpler just to stop trying to be Roman? To scream from a mountaintop that you were a Cherusci warrior, pure and simple, and live with the consequences of that? But if they chose that path, and if a revolt in Germania were successful, she would *have* to live a traditional life, like the one Lothar had chosen.

Did she want that?

No. But nor did she want to give it up for life in a Roman world she suspected would never truly accept her. She was living in two worlds: half Roman, half Cherusci. She wanted both, but it could never be. She prayed she would never have to chose one over the other, but the conversation with Arminius had left her with an unsettled feeling that she might have to.

Freya kicked at a clod of dirt, wishing something would happen to make the decision easy. It all depended on the Romans. If they left Germania for good, she would have no choice but to live the Cherusci life. If the Romans made everyone in Germania citizens and accepted them as equals, she would be Roman. Freya wondered if she could talk to Lucius about her dilemma. Probably not. Lucius didn't question. He was a Roman and that was that. Freya sighed. In a day or two there would be a battle with the Bruesci—at least that would be simple. What she needed now was sleep.

Ilyria

The reign of Augustus Caesar: Year 34
31st Julius

Two days after Lucius's initiation into the mysteries of Mithras, the 19th Legion left camp and marched south into the heart of the Bruesci lands. The men marched in full armour, with their shields and weapons, and carried their personal effects, cooking gear, digging tools and five days food, strapped to a cross-shaped pole over their shoulders. It was a heavy load and marching over the rough roads and tracks of Illyria was gruelling, but Lucius and the others were hardened by years of rigorous training and fighting and were superbly fit. Even the scholarly Appius, who was the smallest and lightest of them all, had enough energy left at the end of the day to compare their expedition to previous great campaigns of the Roman army.

On the way they had been joined by the 15th, Appollinarius, and the 20th, Valeria Victrix— Legions totalling almost 18,000 men. In addition to the three Roman Legions there were 10,000 Auxiliaries from Germania, led by Arminius and his Cherusci warriors, and 4,000 cavalry. It was a formidable force and Lucius felt secure to be a part of such an imposing host.

For six weeks, the Legions marched deep into the Bruesci heartland. Bato retreated before them, harassing the invaders whenever he could, using fast, lightly armed cavalry and raiders who seemed to appear from nowhere and disappear just as mysteriously. For the most part, the Auxiliary troops kept the raiders away from the Legions, but any small party that ventured too far from the main body was in grave danger of being ambushed. The cavalry sometimes found small patrols or wood-cutting parties, stripped naked and butchered in a clearing, often with their heads mounted on nearby tree branches. These small, grisly scenes wore on the soldier's nerves and, almost every night, somewhere along the line of march, the smoke of a funeral pyre rose in the summer air.

Late in the afternoon of the 30th day of Julius, word came back to the Scorpions at the rear of the column that the Bruesci had decided to stand and fight. The front Legion, Appollinarius, had marched into a clearing to see the Bruesci gathered on the upper slopes of a low hill, blocking the way forward. It was too late for battle that day, so the Legions withdrew and set up camp for the night.

"These barbarians will run away as soon as they see us," Drusus said cheerfully as the men settled around their fires after they had dug defensive works, established camp and eaten.

"Don't be so sure," Appius responded. "If you had read Caesar's Commentaries on his campaign in Gaul, you would know that these barbarians are capable of putting just as big an army together as we are. At Sabis, Caesar's six Legions were outnumbered almost two to one by the Nervians."

"But Caesar won?" Drusus asked.

"Of course," Appius replied. "Caesar always won."

"Then we shall win and end this rebellion," Drusus said, confidently. "A host of barbarians, however many there may be, are no match for three disciplined Legions."

Lucius agreed with Drusus, but he noticed Titus sitting silently with a small smile on his face.

"You don't think we'll win?" Lucius asked his old friend.

"Oh, we'll win. We always win in the end, but I doubt it will be as easy as Drusus hopes. The Illyrians are good soldiers and Bato is a fine leader."

"What's that?" Herod asked the group, tilting his head to one side.

The men fell silent and Lucius became aware of a deep, throbbing, rhythmic sound, more felt than heard.

"Drums," Titus volunteered. "The barbarians do love their drums."

"They must be huge," Drusus said in awe. "We must be two miles, at least, from their camp."

The *contuberium* sat in silence contemplating the coming battle. Gradually, they drifted off to try and sleep. Even though they were secure behind their ditches and earthen walls, and the Auxiliaries roaming through the woods would give ample warning of any approaching danger, no one slept well.

Lucius lay in his tent, thinking about the coming battle and about Freya. He hadn't talked to her since they had left Carnuntum, both had been too busy marching and scouting, but their conversation still played in his mind.

At first Lucius had been angry at her—how stupid not to see the benefits of becoming Roman! But he had gradually begun to see at least some of her points. He watched how the Auxiliaries were treated. It wasn't badly—they weren't beaten or punished any more than regular Roman soldiers—but there was a distance. If an Auxiliary warrior came up to talk to a Roman, he was often kept waiting, whereas a Roman soldier would not have been. If Auxiliaries were walking along a road, it was always they who had to step aside when they met a group of Romans going the other way.

And Lucius listened. Many of the soldiers thought, like Herod, that the Auxiliaries were just barbarians. Few were cruel in what they said, but many made jokes or disparaging comments about the Auxiliaries. Lucius had to admit that he had told his share of these jokes and laughed at ones the others told about how stupid the barbarians were. Now, though, he was finding the jokes less funny. He wished he could have a talk with Freya. Maybe it would be possible after the battle.

Tired and nervous, Lucius was up well before dawn. He found the others sitting around a new fire talking, sharpening already razor-sharp swords and polishing and adjusting equipment.

"They say the Illyrians were part of Alexander the Great's army," Appius volunteered.

"Let's hope they've forgotten what they learned back then," Drusus observed. "I'm happy enough to fight barbarians, whether they come from Illyria or Germania, but I don't want to fight Alexander the Great."

"He's been dead for over three hundred years," Lucius contributed as he sat down. "I don't think we'll have to worry about him."

"Some say he's buried in Egypt," Herod said, "in a tomb out in the desert west of Alexandria."

"Everybody gets buried in Egypt," Drusus said. "Burning's much cleaner if you ask me. I don't want my body to lie in a hole and rot."

"You don't need to worry," Herod said, cheerfully. "Nobody will want to dig a hole big enough to put you in—far too much work. We'll just leave you out and let the animals have the feast of their lives."

Everyone laughed as Drusus hurled the sandal he had been repairing across the fire at his companion. Herod caught it easily.

"There'll be a lot of fires tonight," Quintus said, flatly.

The laughter died and the group lapsed into silence at the reminder that some of them might not be alive in just a few hours. "Funeral pyres after a battle are good news," Titus said.

"Good news?" Drusus asked.

"Of course! Look, soldiers die in battle, that's the nature of war and a soldier's job. We knew that when we joined up. But only a victorious Roman army gets a chance to build funeral pyres. I don't know what these Illyrians do with their prisoners or enemy dead, but I'd rather have my body on a pyre while my comrades celebrate a great victory around me."

There were nods of agreement all around.

"Build me a big pyre," Sextus Livius said. Everyone looked at him.

The two Sextuses rarely joined in the general conversation. They weren't related, but they were inseparable, marching together in column and sitting side by side in the evenings. They were from the far south of Italy, where the people were more Greek than Roman, and both had dark olive skin and black hair. They had joined up on the same day, five years before Lucius, and had been together ever since. The joke was that they were twins who had been separated at birth. When they did talk around the fire, it was mostly one telling stories about how the other had saved his life in some almost-forgotten skirmish or battle.

"What are you talking about?" Lucius asked, annoyed that the conversation was still on the subject of funeral pyres.

"I've been having a dream, lately," Sextus Livius said. "In it, I am a scorpion."

"We're all scorpions," Drusus said.

"But I am a giant scorpion, and I am standing in the centre of the temple of *Mars Ultor*—the Avenger—in the Forum of Augustus. A bull and a goat are with me, but something is wrong. I am in terrible pain. I look down and see that my body is covered with red ants, and they are biting me ferociously. The same is happening to the other animals. I sting the ants, the bull stamps on them and the goat butts them, but for every hundred we kill, a thousand more spring from the ground. I look around for help, but the only person I see is

Lucius, standing by the alter to Mars. I cry for help but none of you come and Lucius just stands there without moving. I am alone with my agony. Then I wake up." Sextus looked around at his companions. "I think it means that I, and the other two, whoever they are, will die in the battle today."

"It could mean anything," Drusus said as cheerfully as he could manage. "We're not the fastest lot, you know. Maybe we're on our way and a little slow, so you always wake up before we arrive to fight off the ants."

"Perhaps," Sextus Livius said without much conviction. "But if not, then be sure to build my funeral pyre high." He gazed morosely into the dying embers of the fire.

"Well," Titus said, standing and stretching, "I've had dreams both good and bad in the days before battles and each fight has ended up being just as confused and just as bloody as all the others. If the dreams meant anything, only an Oracle could tell me and I never did find one of them on a battlefield. But Drusus is right, we're not the fastest. The sun's about a finger from coming up over that hill, and if we don't get a move on, we'll miss the battle altogether."

Scratching and stretching, the men collected their weapons and armour and packed their personal belongings for storage in the baggage train. By the time the sun was an hour into the sky, Lucius and his centuria were arranging themselves with the rest of the 19th Legion in the centre of the Roman front line.

Lucius looked around him. Every time he saw a Legion arrayed for battle, he felt a lump rise in his throat. The sun gleamed off the polished armour and weapons, red helmet crests waved in the morning breeze and standards stood up proudly above the packed mass of soldiers. The officers' horses stamped and snorted impatiently and a pale steam rose from the mass of sweating, breathing men.

The Scorpions formed the centre of the line today, with the 15th to their left and the 20th to their right. Each Legion was arranged the same, six of the ten cohorts formed the front line, with the elite Ist, twice the size of the others, taking the position of honour on the extreme left. The other four cohorts stood behind the front lines and the reserves and legionary archers took up the rear. The cavalry was spread through the trees on either side of the army to act as scouts.

Lucius's IXth cohort was positioned third from the left on the Scorpions' front line. As a veteran cohort, they were there to strengthen the VIIth cohort of mostly new recruits which stood restlessly between them and the solid Ist.

The six centuria of each cohort were arranged three to the front and three to the back. Each centuria was arranged ten ranks deep and eight wide. Lucius's First centuria was on the left of the front row and Titus, holding the centuria's standard, was in the centre of it with his *contuberium* around him.

Arminius's Auxiliaries were not present. Confident that the Legions could handle the

Bruesci alone, Germanicus had sent them off before dawn to swing around Bato's army, find the enemy village and destroy it. They were to wait there for the Legions to drive the beaten Illyrians on to them. The enemy would be caught between two forces and crushed once and for all. Lucius touched the medallion around his neck and murmured a prayer to Mithras to look after Freya.

Most of the men in the Roman army stood silent, staring grimly ahead, although one man in the raw cohort to Lucius's left was on his knees vomiting with fear. Lucius raised his eyes to examine the enemy on the hillside.

Bato had chosen his ground well. It was one of the few open areas in the forest where two armies could engage and the Bruesci, at least 20,000 Titus estimated, were assembled in a dark mass half way up a low rise. Wisps of mist rose from a narrow stretch of boggy ground at the base of the hill. The Legions would have to wade through the bog and march up the slope to reach the enemy. The distance wasn't far, about two hundred paces Lucius guessed, but it would be hard work and slow going, and the soldiers would be tired before they even reached the enemy.

The drums, which hadn't ceased their maddening rhythm all night, were much louder now and the pounding noise seemed to vibrate in Lucius's bones. He could see the drummers—huge men dressed in wolf skins—lined along the hilltop in pairs, beating the taught skins ferociously. Crude horns were set between them, screeching a high-pitched counterpoint that set Lucius's teeth on edge. The closest barbarian warriors added to the infernal noise by screaming wild, guttural insults and curses at the Romans and clashing spears and axes against their round shields.

The Illyrians had camped where they stood on the hillside and smoke from their fires rose in thin streams all around. The smell of wood smoke reminded Lucius of a thousand peaceful mornings awakening in camp. Many of the Illyrians were either almost naked or wore a variety of animal skins, but quite a lot, Lucius was disturbed to note, wore pieces of Roman armour.

To Lucius, the Bruesci looked like a huge dark living carpet, covering the slopes. His first assumption was that this was a typical structureless barbarian horde that would crumble when faced with the disciplined Legions. But the more he looked, the more he began to see an organization in the mass opposite. The front ranks consisted of rows of warriors eight or ten deep and, Lucius guessed, stretched for nearly half a mile. Behind the front ranks, other masses of troops— including, Lucius was surprised to see, considerable numbers of women—milled around. And the army had been intelligently deployed. To Lucius's left, the barbarian lines stopped at the edge of a wide swamp and to his right, they reached a thick stand of large trees. It would be impossible for the Legions to swing around and catch the enemy from the side or from behind. The battle would be won in a brutal frontal assault by the side that could break the other's lines.

Along the barbarian front, the soldiers were divided into what Lucius assumed were tribal groups. There was little about their clothing to distinguish the groups, but each possessed a tall pole draped in animal skins and topped with an animal head. Lucius recognized a wolf, bear, boar and some kind of large cat. To his disgust, Lucius saw that one pole was decorated with half a dozen human heads.

"Odd," Appius, who was standing to Lucius's right, spoke thoughtfully.

"What?" Lucius asked.

"Well, I've read that the Illyrians wear a distinctive uniform—a simple helmet, like an inverted cooking pot, a chain mail shirt and a skirt of leather flaps. They're supposed to carry brightly painted shields, oval like our own or circular, like the ones in Germania. And the officers should stand out because they wear black and white plumes on their helmets."

"Dammit, Appius," Drusus said. "Only you could discuss books as we're about to go into battle. Maybe the Illyrians haven't read the same books as you! We're here. They are over there. It's simple and the sooner we get on with it the better."

"It's good to be distracted at moments like this," Titus offered. "There will be hard enough work to do soon. Me, I imagine a feast—every dish you can think of on an endless table."

"And a host of beautiful women," Drusus interrupted.

"No," Titus explained patiently, "only me, reclining on a couch like the Emperor Augustus and with enough servants to bring me whatever food my heart desires."

"I wish I'd had breakfast," Lucius said.

"That's a mistake, lad," Titus admonished. "I've told you before, if a soldier looks after his stomach, everything else will look after itself."

Titus fell silent and Lucius continued his examination of the enemy. The Illyrians, whatever they were wearing, carried a variety of dangerous-looking weapons, long spears, axes and swords. The axes were smaller and lighter than the ones Lucius had seen the Germanic tribes use, but the swords were longer and heavier than the Roman ones.

"The spears are not a problem," Titus said, as if reading Lucius's mind. "Can't use them in close quarters. Watch out for the axes, they're light and they can swing them short and quick. Still, if you catch them on your shield they won't do much damage. Appius tells me that the Illyrians don't use their swords for stabbing as much as we do. They're longer weapons and they swipe sideways with them to cut at an enemy. So be careful of that, don't expect a stab if there's enough space to swing."

Vibrius Servillius Balbus, who had replaced the unfortunate Gaius Maximus as centurion, stepped forward. He came from a wealthy family and looked magnificent in his spotless uniform. His bronze breastplate was moulded to his chest and decorated with a relief scene of lions bringing down a deer. Along with his helmet, leg armour and sword scabbard, it was polished so highly that the reflected sun hurt Lucius's eyes. The red, horsehair crest on his helmet was tall and positioned sideways to distinguish him from the more junior officers, whose crests ran front to back. He carried a knotted wooden stick, which was both a symbol of his authority and a useful encouragement to any men who didn't charge into battle as enthusiastically as Balbus wished.

All along the Roman lines, centurions were addressing their men. "Soldiers of the First centuria," Balbus said in a high pitched voice that didn't suit his martial appearance, "before you, you see the enemies of Rome. We shall defeat them this day, of that there can be no doubt, but what I require of you is that you lead our cohort and our Legion in that defeat. You are like my children."

Drusus snorted quietly and drew a stern look from Titus.

"And like my children I require that you do well. I will honour those who are victorious and mourn those who fall. For Germanicus, the Scorpions of the 19th Legion, the First centuria and for Rome, let this be a glorious day."

The centuria let out a ragged cheer which was echoed all along the front and the advance began.

Weapons, armour and equipment clanged, banged and rattled, and men grunted with exertion as they trudged forward across the swampy ground. But the progress was inexorable. Lucius wondered how anyone could stand and face such an impressive advancing force. But the Illyrians held their ground, some men even darting close to the Roman lines to taunt the soldiers slogging forward.

Now that the advance was underway, Lucius's mind was wonderfully focused. All he could do was concentrate on keeping his position in the ranks and avoid getting his equipment tangled up with the men closely packed around him. Lucius carried his wooden shield strapped tightly to his left arm. It was almost as tall as he was and heavy, but its size and curved shape meant that he only had to crouch to be almost completely protected from enemy arrows or rocks. In his right hand, he carried his spear, a three-foot long wooden handle surmounted by a two-foot iron spike. The spike ended in a small pyramidal point that the weight of the weapon could force through even the toughest shield. The iron was softened where it attached to the wood, so that, as the point drove into an enemy shield or body, the spear bent. This made it awkward to dislodge and prevented it being thrown back.

Lucius sweated under his mail shirt and the coarse wool of his tunic itched against his skin. He was glad it was still early in the morning and not yet too hot, but the slog over the soft ground and up the slope was hard work.

The Legions came to a halt some twenty paces away from the Illyrians and the two armies regarded each other carefully. The barbarians were still hurling insults and curses and, occasionally, a warrior, wishing to show his bravery, would dart forward and hurl a spear or an axe at the Romans. These were easily caught on upraised shields.

"*Testudo!*" Balbus yelled.

Moving like a well-oiled machine, every man in the centuria crouched low, raised his shield and overlapped its edge with that of the man beside him to form an impenetrable wall—the shell of the *testudo,* or tortoise. Almost immediately, Lucius felt his shield vibrate as arrows thudded down onto it.

"Up." The order sped along the lines. As a man, the Legion stood and lowered their shields. Lucius glanced around. No one in his centuria was hurt, but several soldiers in the formation to his left had been too slow and were being helped back to the rear.

"Forward." Before he had taken a single step, Lucius heard a swish as Roman arrows launched from behind the Legion flew over his head.

The Illyrians who had shields raised them, but many didn't and a lot of arrows found targets. A cacophony of screams filled the air.

"Spears." The Legion halted, arms stretched back and a forest of the heavy spears flew forward. Lucius snatched his *gladius* from its scabbard and charged.

It was a slow charge, uphill by heavily laden, tired men, but the impact of the two forces coming together was frightening. As thousands of shields clashed, a thunderous sound rolled along the front. The ordered ranks compressed and Lucius found himself sandwiched between Quintus in front and Drusus behind. Only the front two ranks of either army was within reach of the other's weapons. Just two paces in front of him, the battle raged and men died. Lucius could see axes and swords rising and falling and hear the screams and groans of the wounded, but all he could do was push.

But pushing was having an effect. Step by step, Lucius was moving forward as the Illyrian lines sagged back. Lucius stumbled over the body of a dead barbarian and, suddenly, felt Quintus fall to his knee before him. Lucius hoped he was all right, but it was forbidden to stop, even if there had been time. The rule was simple—keep fighting, regardless of what's going on around you.

All at once, Lucius was staring into the face of an Illyrian warrior. The man wore a neatly trimmed beard and would have been handsome except that his face was distorted in a grimace of rage. Lucius was fascinated to notice that the man was missing both of his front teeth.

Lucius pushed forward, knowing that he had to get close to the man to use his short sword, but Quintus's slumped body got in the way. The man screamed something guttural and swung his axe. Lucius just managed to catch it on the top edge of his shield. He stabbed blindly forward, but was too far away to make contact.

The Illyrian had almost succeeded in releasing his axe from Lucius's shield when Lucius heard a roar and Drusus's arm reached over his head. Drusus grabbed the axe and hauled. The man refused to let go and his arm was dragged over Lucius's shield. Frantically, Lucius hacked at the exposed flesh. The hand came away at the wrist and the blood-stained stump withdrew.

Lucius stepped over the prone Quintus and pushed on with Drusus shoving from behind.

Lucius was in the killing zone now, but all he felt was a wild thrill. Another face appeared before him and Lucius stabbed upward through the screaming open mouth. The face disappeared. There was no time to think, no time to understand. All Lucius could do was be pushed forward, to either kill the man in front of him or be killed. It was primitive and bloody, but he had no choice. Besides, the adrenaline was coursing through his body, overwhelming all other emotions. With an insane grin distorting his face, Lucius hacked and stabbed his way forward.

He had lost all sense of time. He had no idea whether he had been fighting for five minutes or an hour. Gradually, he noticed the pressure in front of him lessening. He could see gaps opening in the Illyrian lines. With a deep roar, the Legion surged forward. Almost magically, the Illyrian lines broke and the Romans swarmed through toward the crest of the hill. Lucius glanced around. The IXth cohort was solid as was the elite Ist off to his left, but the recruits of the VIIth had not kept up with the advance and there were Illyrians to Lucius's immediate left. He couldn't worry about that now. The momentum of the rush carried Lucius forward, over the brow of the hill and several paces down the far side.

A brief lull in the fighting around him gave Lucius a chance to look up. He stared down the slope in shock. Instead of a disorganized mass of Illyrians fleeing for their lives, he was heading toward a compact mass of disciplined troops. They wore the armour that Appius had described, and there were thousands of them.

The soldiers of the 19th Legion who had flooded over the hilltop along with Lucius, hesitated. This was not what they had expected. It was a trap. The centre of the Roman line had been drawn in by the Illyrian retreat, over the crest of the hill and onto the main body of enemy troops—troops who had been hiding on the back slope of the hill.

Frantically, Lucius looked around. The Ist cohort, centred on the Legion's eagle standard was to his left and slightly ahead, and most of the rest were to his right. There was no sign of the other two Legions.

"Charge! Keep going or we die." Balbus yelled.

"He's right," Titus took up the cry. "If we turn back now the front will collapse and we're dead. Follow the eagle."

The IXth cohort hesitated for a moment then surged forward. They hit the Illyrian troops at the same time as the rest of the Legion and, because they were running downhill this time, the shock was even more brutal than the earlier impact. Pain raced up Lucius's arm as his shield struck a big Illyrian soldier, but the man was so surprised by the force of the Roman attack that he fell back. So did many of his comrades and the compact mass of Roman soldiers drove deep into the fresh enemy troops.

Lunging wildly with his sword and using his shield as much as a weapon as protection, Lucius fought like a madman. It was either that or die. The Illyrians swarmed around the Legion, cutting it off from the rest of the army. It was like Sextus Livius's dream—ants swarming around a scorpion. The scorpion was bigger and more dangerous, but there were too many ants. Other units breasted the hill and tried to fight through to the beleaguered 19th, but the barbarians held them back.

As the casualties mounted and men grew even more exhausted, the disciplined shape of the Legion began to fade. Soon it was isolated cohorts or centuria fighting for their lives. Lucius, Herod, Drusus, Appius, Sextus Vipsanius, Sextus Livius and about forty others from the centuria stayed around Titus, protecting the standard. They were hard pressed, but luckily, the Illyrians seemed to be focusing on the Eagle standard and were pushing their greatest weight against the stronger Ist cohort.

The 19th Legion's wild charge down the hill had confused the Illyrians and prevented the rout of the entire army that might have happened if they had retreated, but it had carried them far from any help. Lucius managed a glance back up the hill. The other Legions were reforming on the crest, but they were being strongly harassed by the Illyrian cavalry, who had appeared from the trees on either side, and by archers who poured arrows into the densely packed Roman soldiers, forcing them to keep a defensive posture.

A large soldier swung his sword at Lucius. The man was strong but he had no discipline and his sword was too long and unwieldy for close-quarter work. Lucius ducked easily and brought the edge of his shield up under the man's chin. There was a loud crack and the man fell away. Another took his place. There was always another.

"To the Eagle," Titus screamed above the chaos. "If this is the end, let it be beside the Eagle."

Gradually, the small group battled their way through the mass of Illyrians. They were all wounded somewhere. Drusus had lost his helmet and a bright stream of blood ran down from his scalp. One of Herod's arms hung useless at his side and Sextus Vipsanius was so covered in blood it was impossible to tell where he was wounded. Lucius had a deep gash in his right thigh, but he was barely aware of it. Appius was fighting like a maniac, darting this way and that, stabbing and slashing at anything that presented itself. Titus stood like a rock in the centre, his sword drawn, staring grimly from under the wolf's head of his cape and gripping the standard.

It's only a matter of time, Lucius thought bleakly. It's my first full battle and it's going to be my last. He felt a pang of regret, but he had no time to wallow in self-pity. Another Illyrian warrior was in front of him and had to be dealt with. He raised his shield to block the axe stroke, but his arms felt like lead and the shield seemed to weigh twice as much as it had at the start of the battle. Instead of blocking the axe completely and allowing Lucius to stab upward, he only managed to deflect the blow. The axe head missed him but the heavy shaft caught him a ringing blow on his helmet. Lucius gasped and sagged to his knees. The Illyrian raised his axe and Lucius cringed, waiting for the final blow. It never fell. The centuria standard flew over

Lucius's head, catching the man in the throat. The barbarian's eyes widened as he tried to suck air through his shattered windpipe before he fell sideways. The body caught the edge of Lucius's shield, still strapped to his arm, and pulled him over. Lucius floundered helplessly amidst a forest of legs.

"Come on, you lazy soldier," Titus yelled as he hauled the standard back. "No time for resting. There's work to be done."

Titus leaned forward, grabbed Lucius by the collar of his uniform and hauled. Lucius got to his knees, but his collapse and the fall of the Illyrian warrior had allowed the barbarian's fellow warrior to swing his long sword. Lucius saw the blade fly over his head and heard Titus gasp.

"No!" Lucius screamed, lunging forward and up with his *gladius*. He felt the blade slide under the attacker's ribs. The man fell away, wrenching the *gladius* from Lucius's grip.

Lucius stood and looked around. Titus was on his knees, struggling to hold the standard upright. The sword blow had caught Titus on the left shoulder, shattering his collar bone and biting deep into his chest. Already the entire right side of his body was soaked in blood. As Lucius watched in horror, his friend's eyes glazed over.

"The standard, *signifer*," Titus managed to choke out before he collapsed.

With tears blinding him, Lucius grabbed the standard with his free hand and turned to face the enemy. Lucius felt detached. It was almost as if the battle were happening to others and he was just an observer watching his friends fighting around him. Exhaustion had finally overcome the adrenaline surge he had felt at the battle's start. Now he just felt like weeping. Titus was dead.

What was left of the Lucius's centuria had almost reached the Ist cohort but it was no use. However hard they fought, they would never make it—there were too many Illyrians. Then, above the clashing weapons and screaming men, Lucius heard a cheer. He turned his head to look. Were the barbarians celebrating victory already? His eyes narrowed as he tried to take in the action. It wasn't the barbarians who had cheered. It was the Ist cohort. The Illyrians in front of him hesitated and several glanced back over their shoulders. One man collapsed with a red-feathered arrow protruding from his neck.

"*Testudo!*" Lucius yelled.

Those who were able raised their shields as arrows clattered down. Screams echoed across the battlefield.

When the noise of the arrows stopped, Lucius lowered his shield and looked around. The pressure on the centuria had eased and many of the Illyrian warriors were pawing at arrow shafts that had found gaps in their armour. Lucius saw the Ist cohort pushing forward down the hill. The Illyrians before it were breaking formation and struggling to get away. Coming up the hill, beneath a forest of rising and falling battle axes, Arminius's Cherusci warriors were carving a path through to the beleaguered Legion.

Lucius's sadness vanished, replaced by a sudden surge of joy. "Come on," he shouted, thrusting the centuria's standard into the air. "It's not over yet."

Revitalized by the sight of the fleeing enemy, Lucius's centuria surged forward to join the Ist cohort.

The battle was over remarkably quickly. Lucius leaned on the standard, utterly drained both by the fighting and the strength of his emotions. Now he felt strangely calm. He was surprised to see that it was only mid-morning. The hillside was covered with bodies and their distribution told the story of the fight. Where a cohort had kept its shape there were few Roman dead, but where the discipline had collapsed, sad little groups of bodies told the story of frantic, hopeless last stands.

Everyone in Lucius's *contuberium* was wounded, the worst being Herod, who had a broken arm and Quintus, with a deep sword wound in his side. The rest had varying cuts and bruises and even Sextus Livius, who was convinced he had foreseen his own death, was walking around, grinning stupidly. Titus had been the only death.

Lucius unstrapped his shield from his arm and trudged back up the hill to where Titus lay. The *signifer* lay on his back, his face almost peaceful. Lucius swallowed the lump in his throat and forced back rising tears.

"So, we've saved you again, Roman."

Lucius squinted against the glare of the sun. Freya stood above him, a bloody sword in her hand and her sling hanging from her belt. Despite his happiness at seeing her again, Lucius felt a rush of bitterness. "And too late, again."

Freya shrugged. "I am sorry for your friend. He was a good soldier, but he rests with the Gods now." Freya bent and wiped the blood off her sword on a nearby body. "You Romans are good fighters, but you are not flexible. You did exactly what the Bruesci wished and fell into their trap like a drunk man into the arms of a woman. You would have been crushed had we not come along."

"Why did you come along?" Lucius asked. "Didn't Germanicus send you south to search out the Bruesci village?"

"He did, but we captured a party of Bruesci who told us, after some persuasion, of Bato's plan. Arminius decided we would be of more use if we doubled back and surprised them in the rear. As you see again, surprise is everything in war."

"Well, I should thank you. I would be as dead as poor old Titus had Arminius not disobeyed orders and come back. Is Bato captured? Is the rebellion put down?"

"Bato is defeated but not destroyed—he and most of his warriors escaped. This rebellion will not be as easy to put down as you think. Bato is not the only leader and the Bruesci not the only tribe, and they have nothing to lose. Will they be forgiven if they surrender?"

"Of course not! They rebelled against Rome."

Freya nodded and smiled ruefully. "And that is the worst possible crime, to not see the benefits of Roman civilization, even if it is offered on the point of a sword. It is not an easy time to be a barbarian."

Lucius wanted to say something, to begin the discussion he had imagined since their argument at Carnuntum, but he was too tired. He was having trouble forming ideas or expressing them coherently.

"You there." Lucius looked past Freya to see centurion Balbus, striding over the corpses toward them. Lucius struggled to his feet and saluted. Balbus returned the gesture, but spoke to Freya.

"What are you barbarians doing here?"

"Saving your Roman lives," Freya replied, bitterly.

Without warning, Balbus swung his stick and caught Freya a sharp blow to the side of the head. She gasped and staggered but managed to keep her feet. Lucius instinctively took a step forward, but Balbus's cold voice stopped him.

"I will not tolerate insolence from a German barbarian. You should be pursuing Bato. And why did you disobey Germanicus's direct order to search out the Bruesci camp?"

Freya stood in sullen silence, a bruise already discolouring her cheek.

"Answer me."

"I cannot answer for Arminius," Freya said quietly.

"One barbarian hiding behind another," Balbus said dismissively.

"Arminius is a Roman citizen," Freya said.

"He has been honoured for his usefulness to Rome, but he is still, and always will be, a barbarian. Now go. Take your rabble and pursue Bato."

For a moment, the future balanced on a knife edge. Lucius was shocked by the utter contempt and cold hatred in Freya's eyes. He saw her knuckles go white on her sword hilt. If she reacted she was dead.

"Centurion Balbus," Lucius said, taking another step forward. "The *signifer* of the First centuria of the IXth cohort was killed defending the standard."

For a long moment, Balbus and Freya continued to stare at each other. Then Freya swung around and strode down the hill.

Balbus looked at Lucius as if seeing him for the first time. "And you rescued the standard?" he asked.

"I did. I am the apprentice *signifer*."

Balbus glanced down at Titus's body. "You are the *signifer* now. See that your comrades' wounds are attended to."

Balbus saluted and turned away. Then he hesitated and looked back at Lucius. "What is your name, *signifer*?"

"Lucius Quinctillius Claudianus," Lucius responded as he saluted again.

"A good name," Balbus said, thoughtfully. "I saw you react when I hit that barbarian. I neither know nor care what your relationship is with that woman, but never forget, Lucius Quinctillius Claudianus, you are a Roman among Romans, the rest are just barbarian rabble.

"We would have won today without the Auxiliaries," Balbus continued. "The Ist cohort stood firm and the other Legions were coming to our aid. If Arminius had done as he was instructed, he would have found the Bruesci village and Bato and his army would have been caught between our Legions and the Auxiliaries. As it is Bato has escaped to fight again. The rebellion will be longer and more Romans will die because of it. Remember that."

Balbus strode off, leaving Lucius with his thoughts. Perhaps the centurion was correct and the battle would have been won without the Auxiliaries. Lucius didn't have the experience or the overview to judge. What was certain was that had Arminius, Freya and the Cherusci not disobeyed their orders and come to help the Scorpions, Lucius would now be as dead as Titus.

Lucius shook his head and looked around. Far down the slope he could see Freya talking with Arminius. Even through his battle weariness, Lucius had a sense that something important had happened. All the discussions he had had with Freya about what it meant to be a Roman or a barbarian had crystallized around Balbus's sudden, unthinking violence and the hatred of Freya's look. It felt as if an uncrossable line had been drawn.

Which side am I on? Lucius wondered. His instinctive reaction had been to help Freya, but Balbus was his centurion and represented everything Lucius was striving for. What could he do?

Lucius sighed with exhaustion and let his gaze wander. All across the hillside, Cherusci and Romans were moving around, looking for comrades and dispatching wounded Illyrians. Drusus and Sextus Vipsanius were standing nearby.

"Keep busy." Lucius heard Titus's voice inside his head. "There's plenty to do after a battle and busy hands prevent idle minds getting into trouble."

Lucius looked down at his friend's body. "I will build you the biggest funeral pyre the Legion has ever seen," he promised, his voice shaking. He took out his medallion and stared at the picture of Mithras on the bull. "Thank you," he said.

Lucius replaced the medallion beneath his armour, took a deep breath and looked at his nearby companions. "Drusus, Sextus," he shouted. "Help me get Titus back to camp."

~~~~

Lucius stared into the flames that licked around Titus's body. As Quintus had predicted, there were a lot of funeral pyres burning throughout the Roman camps. The 19th, because it had been cut off and surrounded, had suffered most and many of the pyres were large and had a number of bodies on them, but Lucius had insisted that Titus have one to himself.

The rest of the *contuberium* stood beside their new *signifer*. They were all tired and bruised, and most had salves covering cuts and scrapes. Quintus was in the infirmary having his wound attended to, but Herod had had the broken bones of his forearm pulled back into position and strapped in place. Despite the pain, he had insisted on coming to the funeral. Everyone had said a few words to accompany Titus on his journey to the afterlife and convince Mithras that their friend was worthy of pride of place in the Elysian Fields.

They would all miss Titus, but Lucius most of all. Not only had Titus been his teacher since he joined the Legion, but because he had known Lucius's father, he was also a link to family and the past. Lucius was honoured to be taking on Titus's role as *signifer*, and the others seemed quite happy with his appointment, despite his youth.

"Scipio Africanus was not much older than you when he led his first army against Hannibal," Appius had pointed out.

"Welcome to it," Drusus had said. "I've not the mind to keep all the numbers in my head. Just make sure I have enough savings to enjoy myself when we get back to civilization."

"Well," Lucius said, tearing his eyes away from the fire, "we have launched our friend as well as we can on the journey we must all take. I think we can only honour him by always remembering his life and his deeds."

The others nodded.

"And by finding and enjoying the finest foods wherever we go," Drusus added.

"Indeed," Lucius agreed with a smile. "I learned as much about good food from Titus as I did about how to look after you sorry lot."

"You have it wrong there, *signifer* Lucius Quinctillius," Drusus said in a mock formal tone. "It is we who look after you. All you have to do is stand around holding up the standard. We do all the hard fighting to protect you."

"And for that, infantryman Drusus Meridius," Lucius copied his friend's formal tone, "I give you my future thanks."

Drusus bowed deeply and groaned.

"What's the matter?" Lucius asked.

"Nothing," Drusus replied. "I think I've cracked a rib, that's all. It's not the first time, nor, I should think, the last. It will heal in time."

With last looks at Titus's pyre, the group drifted back to the hearth outside their tent. Lucius accompanied Herod, who looked grey and winced with every step.

"How are you?" Lucius asked.

"I've been better," Herod said. "It hurt like Hades when the surgeon reset the bones, even with the crushed Mandrake root to deaden the pain."

"At least you'll get a spell off guard duty and a ride in the wagons when we move on."

"The wagons! I'd rather walk. Those things are death traps, and on these roads, every jolt would near kill me."

The pair sat by the fire. Drusus and Appius left to stand guard duty and the two Sextus's sat together, deep in conversation.

"We did win the battle, though," Herod said.

"We did," Lucius agreed, "although Bato and most of his men escaped."

"True, but it was a close-run thing. If Arminius and his Cherusci hadn't shown up when they did, Titus's pyre would not be the only one from this *contuberium*."

"Balbus thinks that Arminius shouldn't have come to our aid," Lucius said. "He says we would have won the battle without their help and if the Cherusci had obeyed their orders, Bato would have been trapped between our two forces."

Herod thought for a moment. "He's right. True, if that had happened, you and I would most probably be dead, but you have to consider what's best for Rome."

"You have to be alive to consider what's best for Rome! Balbus was very angry. I was talking with Freya and he came up and struck her."

"That is his right."

Lucius frowned but kept silent.

"You don't think so?" Herod asked. "Why did Balbus hit her?"

"Freya spoke back."

"Well, there you are. It's simple. I would expect to be struck if I spoke back to a centurion."

"I know. I know," Lucius said, resignedly. "But I am a Roman, fighting in the Legions for my homeland. Freya, Arminius and the others are Auxiliaries. They fight for us for pay, not love of their homeland."

"Exactly. They are barbarian. Surely you are not suggesting they be treated better than the soldiers of Rome?"

"No, of course not." Lucius shook his head. Herod was right, but Lucius wished he was talking to Freya instead.

"It's only difficult because you've befriended a barbarian," Herod said.

"Those barbarians saved my life and Titus's when we were captured by the Sicambri on the road to Vetera," Lucius responded angrily.

"And they did so once more this morning. That is their job, but they are still barbarians. Listen," Herod hauled himself painfully to his feet, "I must go and rest now, but I will leave you with some advice. Don't get too close to Freya. She's not like us and your loyalties lie with Rome and your Roman friends."

"I know where my loyalties lie," Lucius said, indignantly.

"I do not doubt that you do. But if you befriend a barbarian too closely, one day a conflict will arise and you will have to choose. Think on it. Good night."

Herod retreated slowly to the tent, leaving Lucius with his thoughts. With Titus gone, Lucius felt close to only two people, Herod and Freya, and they stood squarely on opposite sides of the line Balbus had forced him to see earlier. Neither could help where their Gods had placed them at birth, but did that mean they could never understand each other? Was it absolute that to be a Roman was to be better than everyone else? Herod would not hesitate to say yes, but Lucius wasn't as sure as he had once been. He was proud to be a Roman. Rome had given most of the world peace, prosperity, civilization, roads, government—the list was endless. How could anyone not want to be a part of that? But if Lucius had been born a Cherusci, would he see it that way?

Lucius swore out loud in frustration.

"What did you say?" Sextus Livius asked from the far side of the fire.

"Nothing," Lucius said. "You're still alive," he added with a smile. "Old Titus was right about your dream."

"I suppose he was," Sextus said. "And Drusus was right about the ending. The Scorpion was almost overcome by the ants, but I woke up before I could see help come into the temple. And I thank Mithras for that."

"I do too," Lucius said, standing and rubbing his aching limbs. "But I must rest now. We will have work to do tomorrow to clear the battlefield."

"And then I suppose it will be more marching after the rebels," Sextus Vipsanius said.

"That's a soldier's lot," Lucius said. "Marching, fighting and being bored. Good night."

"Good night," the pair answered.

Freya

Freya stood beside Arminius amidst the carnage of the battlefield. She could barely speak she was so angry. The bruise on her cheek sent a dull ache down into her jaw.

"We're fighting the wrong people," Freya snarled, giving the dented Roman helmet at her feet a vicious kick that sent it clattering down the hillside. "Bato was right. We're nothing but barbarians to these arrogant invaders!"

"Hold your tongue," Arminius ordered. "Do you want the entire Roman army to know we have had words with Bato?"

Freya took a deep breath. "Of course not," she said, lowering her voice, "but had we fought *with* Bato today instead of against him, we would have destroyed these Legions."

"Possibly," Arminius agreed, "and then what? That would leave seven other Roman Legions and the Gods only know how many other Auxiliaries. Unlike Bato, we would be far from home and, persuasive as Bato is, when things go bad he would sacrifice us before his own men. Bato is not the leader to defeat Rome."

"Why not? He almost won today."

"Almost is not good enough against the Romans. You drive them off the field and they will keep coming back. Bato has two serious problems. One we talked about already, Illyria is too close to Rome. Like Hannibal, Bato will never be allowed to win here. The Bruesci revolt cannot succeed."

Even through her anger, Freya could see the logic of her uncle's argument. "You said there was a second problem?"

"Bato is not a great general."

"His tactics today were clever," Freya said.

"Oh, he is clever, but he made a mistake. He chose to fight the Romans on their own terms, in open ground. Even if his clever tactics had worked, many of the Legions would have escaped to fight again. If you are going to defeat the Romans, you must do it in such a crushing way that none survive. You must choose the time and place to your own advantage and destroy the Romans so thoroughly that they are shocked into leaving you alone. Bato cannot do that."

"Who can?" Freya asked.

Arminius said nothing.

Another thought crossed Freya's mind. "Why did you disobey Germanicus's orders today and come back to the battle?"

"To save the Legions," Arminius said.

"But the arrogant centurion was right: the Romans would have won even without us and then Bato would have been trapped between the Legions and the Auxiliaries. He would have been destroyed, the revolt ended and we could have gone home. Instead, Bato can claim a victory, persuade other tribes to join his revolt and keep fighting, possibly for years."

Arminius smiled encouragement.

A new, frightening idea flashed into Freya's mind. "That's what you want!" she exclaimed. "You didn't want Bato to be defeated too easily! You didn't return to save the Legions—it was to allow Bato to escape so his rebellion would go on."

"That's an interesting idea," Arminius said quietly. "You're using that brain of yours again. You're good at putting things together."

"And you," Freya said, "are good at suggesting things but never saying anything concrete."

"A good leader will always beware of saying too much, too soon."

Freya's mind went back over all the conversations she had had with Arminius. "You explained to me after the meeting with Bato why he could not win," she said, thinking out loud, "and why only a rebellion much farther from Rome could succeed. Today you say that Bato is not the right general to defeat Rome and yet you deliberately threw away an opportunity to end the revolt quickly."

Arminius shrugged.

"It almost seems," Freya expressed the thought that had been hovering in the back of her mind, "as if you are planning a revolt in Germania and want the Romans to remain distracted here in Illyria."

Freya's brow furrowed in thought. "But that makes no sense. How can you lead a revolt in Germania if you are here fighting Bato?"

"Your mind is devious, Freya," Arminius said. "Be careful it does not get you into trouble. I did not say any of what you suggest, I merely made observations. A good leader must keep every option open so he can make decisions that are best for his people. But we should not talk of this now. We have work to do. Look." Arminius swept his arm wide to encompass the battlefield where scattered Cherusci warriors were collecting weapons, stripping armour from the dead and dispatching the wounded. "Our warriors need to be collected so we can pursue Bato as the Romans wish. We will reform at the base of the hill. Please spread the word."

Arminius turned and walked down the hill. "I forgot to tell, you," he said over his shoulder. "Germanicus has decided that, after this campaign season, the 19th Legion and the Auxiliaries will no longer be required in Illyria. We're to return to Germania."

Freya opened her mouth to say something, but Arminius was already striding away, leaving her with her thoughts. Was her uncle simply keeping his options open, as he said, or was he really planning a revolt? If he was thinking of a revolt, win or lose, nothing would ever be the same again. There would be no more living with one foot in the Cherusci world and one in the Roman.

Freya reached up and touched the tender bruise on her cheek. Anger flared up at the memory. If all the Roman were like the centurion, the decision would be easy: be a Cherusci and damn the consequences. But there was Lucius. He had defused the situation with the centurion when it could have exploded into violence. He was naive and sometimes annoying, but if all Romans were like him the decision to remain loyal would be much easier.

But Arminius was right—it was enough for one day. There was work to be done. Freya began shouting to the nearest warriors to head down the hill. Arminius was waiting.

Herculaneum

The reign of Titus Caesar: Year 1
24th August, 8:00 p.m.

Pallas has just brought me some olives, dates and a lamp to light against the growing dusk. The dates are not of a quality to have made old Titus's mouth water, but they suit my needs. The earthquakes continue, although not with the ferocity of earlier. Pallas tells me that the ash over poor Pompeii has become, if anything, darker while the sun setting out to sea is painting the cloud the colour of dried blood.

Pallas has just asked me what it is I am writing and, when I told him I was setting down events of long ago, he said would I not be better to set down what is happening here this day as, surely, people in the future would be interested in such things. Perhaps he is right. My past is of much greater interest to me than my present or brief future, but one day, this too will be the past for others. So I will briefly describe the events of this day so far.

It all began this morning, a little before the noon hour. Pallas was reading to me when I was almost thrown off my couch by a tremendous explosion. Pallas, and all others of the household who could, rushed onto the roof. There they saw, as he told me later, a terrifying sight. Our friendly companion, Vesuvius, whose peak is but six miles from where I now lie, has betrayed us. I know she has been an uncertain companion of late and the olive farmers on her slopes have reported springs drying up, odd bulges in the ground, cracks opening to belch steam and other odd and worrying occurrences, but no one expected the like of what happened this morning.

Above the mountain, many miles high and growing with frightening speed, stood a vast column of smoke and dust, roiling and twisting like a hideous living thing devised by the inhabitants of Tartarus. Pallas could not see clearly, but he was convinced that the entire top of the mountain was gone. The noise was like the roaring of a thousand beasts, and this I can vouch for even from my cot.

Fortunately, for us at least, the wind was toward the southwest and it was in that direction that the cloud stretched. It seemed that the weight of the material within the cloud could not support itself once it moved away from the frightful updraft spewing from the top of the mountain, and the countryside was rapidly being blanketed in ash and rocks. I do not envy our neighbours in Pompeii, which is directly beneath the cloud.

As I have said, we have remained in sunlight all day, but this did not reassure Calpurnia, the mistress of the house. She is of a nervous disposition by nature; the least disturbance to her dull, daily routine and she predicts the most dire consequences. By the time we had finished our hurried mid-day snack, she had convinced herself and many others that the end of the world was at hand and that all should flee along the coast to Neapolis. I did wonder what good going to Neapolis would do at the end of the world, but I held my peace. Calpurnia somewhat resents my presence. I think she considers me an inconvenience who makes an unnecessary mess of her pristine villa. When I die, she will tidy my room before my ashes are cold and it will be as if I never existed.

In any case, at my age and with my physical infirmity, I cannot stagger far, let alone join the nervous crowds on the highway to Neapolis. But this tiny complication did not stop Calpurnia hurrying on with the evacuation. She promised to return for me at the earliest opportunity and, although it does me little good when I am confined to my cot, gave me free reign of the villa. I think she was mightily relieved when loyal Pallas insisted that he stay and attend to my needs.

So, Pallas and I are here and the others gone. Pallas updates me on the goings on in the world with frequent visits to the roof. He says there is a steady stream of people on the road out of Herculaneum and entertains me with tales of the oddities of our fellow man. There is little panic among the refugees, although one ragged soothsayer wanders back and forth proclaiming that the Gods are punishing us for all manner of debauchery and for not recognizing some strange, many-armed eastern God that is his personal favourite. The rest have a sort of resigned air, like mules that are being asked to carry too much too far. And many are so laden down that they resemble mules in other ways, too.

I suspect it tells much about a person to see what they will attempt to save in an extremity. High-born ladies travel in litters with slaves carrying their finest garments and cosmetics, the slaves of men of business drag carts of bills and loan documents, and the supplier of beasts to the circus gets much of the road to himself as his slaves attempt to drag and herd his collection of terrified, exotic animals around the bay. Pallas said that he saw Publius Sextus, the cynic philosopher, struggling along, laden with a pack overstuffed with scrolls.

For all that Pallas sees of passing human foibles and frailty, the flow of folk from Herculaneum is light and many must still reside in the city or wait on the shore for relief from Misenum by boat. Certainly, none flee to the south where the ash still falls most thickly over Pompeii and is now accompanied by sizeable boulders that can be seen rolling down the open slopes of the mountain or splashing into the waters of the bay.

I can offer no explanation for what is happening. Those of a religious bent will say that Vulcan has stoked his forge beneath the earth too high, but that can only be a parable for the simple or for children. What we see, feel and hear this day must be an occurrence of nature as certainly as the winds or the change of seasons. But what occurrence can possess such power that an entire mountain explodes with a fury the like of which we are witnessing, I cannot begin to imagine. Obviously, there are forces at work in the world that we puny mortals do not yet begin to understand. Maybe the Gods are as good an explanation as any.

In any case, these few words should satisfy Pallas for the time being and I shall endeavour to insert updates into my tale as seems fit. Now I must return to the past.

After the battle in which Titus died, we spent many weeks marching hither and yon to little obvious effect. Bato and his armies avoided us, although the other Legions fought battles elsewhere. As I understand it, all were as inconclusive as our own engagement.

Herod's arm and our various cuts and bruises healed in time, but Quintus's sword wound became infected and, late in the month of Augustus, he succumbed. We mourned him as a comrade and fellow Mithrian, but if the truth be told, he was a cold, solitary man and Titus's loss was felt more sharply by us all.

As winter approached, Germanicus decided that the Scorpions were no longer needed to complete the pacification of Illyria and would be better employed adding to Varus's forces in Germania. So we had yet another winter journey back to Vetera, followed by a summer season of the small raids we had become so used to in previous years. However, as the summer of the 36th year of Augustus's reign began, it became clear that something different was in the offing.

Alterium

G ermanicus is still fighting in Illyria," Herod pointed out. "My guess is that they'll march us back the way we went two years ago, but this time they'll take the 17th and 18th as well. They can't let the rebellion drag on forever, it doesn't look good."

"If they take the three Legions from Vetera," Appius pointed out, "who will defend the frontier here in Germania?"

"The frontier's quiet this side of the Rhenus," Lucius observed. "With Arminius and the Cherusci loyal, the forces at Mogantiacum, Batavodorum and Arenaclum will be more than adequate to hold the frontier until we return victorious."

It was late in the month of Maius and signs of spring were everywhere. Birds were singing, trees were budding, and even the cold rain that seemed to have been constant all winter was easing. As usual, the camp at Vetera was alive with rumours of what the coming campaign season would hold.

Lucius, Herod and Appius sat in the *tepidarium* of the baths. It was mid-afternoon, the time when the soldiers were allowed to bathe, and the large room was crowded. Most sat in loose linen tunics, on benches around the walls, but some splashed or sat quietly in the large warm pool in the centre of the floor.

This was Lucius's favourite part of the daily bathing ritual. He enjoyed the feeling of his skin opening up and sweating out all its dirt in the hot *caldarium* room, the smoothness of the oil being rubbed in, the freshness of being scraped clean, and the plunge into the cold pool of the *frigidarium* awoke every nerve in his body, but the time in the *tepidarium* was the most relaxing. The warmth from the floor and walls was just right and promoted easy, casual conversation among those who sat along the benches.

"Drusus heard from a friend of his in the Ist cohort," Lucius said, "that Varus is planning a major summer campaign along the Lupia to subdue the tribes once and for all and extend the frontier to the River Weser or even the Albis."

"And Drusus's friend is in the habit of taking wine with Publius Varus?" Herod asked.

"But it makes sense," Lucius said, ignoring his friend's sarcasm. "Germanicus led an expedition to the Albis many years back. It would make as good a frontier as the Rhenus, and it would explain why Varus has been increasing the taxes all winter. He needs to supply us for the campaign."

"When Germanicus reached the Albis," Appius contributed, "Mars appeared to him in a dream and told him he was being overly presumptuous to bring his armies so far. Disaster awaited if he did not turn back."

"Mars is a good excuse for a commander who has overextended himself," Lucius said. "But I must admit, three Legions is not a lot to pacify a whole new province. Would it not make more sense for Varus to await the return of more Legions from Illyria next year?"

"Three Legions is more than enough," Herod said, dismissively. "Look how many times we have gone far to the east with only one Legion. Have the tribes ever come close to defeating even such a small force?"

"No, but—"

"Exactly," Herod carried on. "The barbarian tribes would much rather fight each other than cooperate against us, and no single tribe can threaten our forces. The most powerful are the Cherusci and they are fighting for us. Don't you agree, Appius? You're the historian! Have the tribes in Germania ever been organized enough to threaten a force of three Legions and Auxiliaries?"

"Not recently, no. When the Legions first arrived, it was hard going, but things have changed. The road and the forts along the Lupia mean we can travel far to the east in safety. It should simply be a matter of extending the forts and the roads until we can go anywhere whenever we wish."

"See," Herod said, "our scholar agrees."

"Not exactly," Appius went on. "Away from the road and the forts, the land is still wild and untamed. A Legion would have trouble keeping formation there and that would make it vulnerable to attack."

"But it would need to be an overwhelming attack," Herod said, "and the tribes here, even if they wished it, aren't capable of collecting and organizing enough men to do that. They live in scattered little villages of only a few families. Even if there are four or five men who could be soldiers in each village, it would take thousands of villages to supply an army that could threaten even one Legion, and we are talking about three. We have nothing to worry about."

"True, if we don't make mistakes."

"Mistakes! What mistakes?" Herod asked.

"I don't know," Appius admitted, "but Varus's reason for an expedition to the east bothers me. He doesn't want to wait because he wants all the glory for himself. He's not a military man. He made a name for himself in Syria and is close to Augustus, but here, as a general, he's overshadowed by Germanicus. If he can win a significant victory before Germanicus returns from Illyria, he will be awarded a triumph in Rome and maybe even a consulship. If Varus leads the Legions east this summer, it will be for personal advancement and that will cloud his judgment."

"Clouded judgment or not," Herod said, standing and stretching, "I say we should take the Legions east and teach these barbarians a lesson."

"And when Publius Varus asks me who he should consult in planning the campaign," Lucius said, "I'll be certain to give him your name."

"Thank you," Herod said with a smile. "And when he does ask my advice, I shall be certain to recommend you for the most dangerous missions so you can die heroically and achieve everlasting fame and glory."

The three friends laughed and headed for the *frigidarium*.

"As an historian," Appius said, "I am certain of one thing. Wherever we go and whatever fame and glory we win, we'll do it like soldiers marching on tired feet."

"Or freezing," Lucius said, throwing off his tunic and plunging with a gasp into the cold pool.

~~~~

After he had dried himself off and dressed, Lucius strolled down to the docks on the river bank where amphorae of oil and grain were being off-loaded from a wide cargo vessel that had made the journey along the coast and up the Rhenus from Gaul. The docks had been extremely busy lately, and that fit with building up supplies for a summer campaign to the east.

Lucius strolled among the piles of food and equipment that dozens of slaves were working to organize and move up to the granary and storehouses. He loved the complex, rich smells—the strong, concentrated fish paste that flavoured so much of his food, the honey that sweetened his wine, and the olive oil that did everything from fuel his lamps to preserve his food. The smells reminded him of home and created a sharp pang of nostalgia. Not that he wanted to be anywhere other than with his comrades in the 19th, wherever that might take him, but he was a Roman and could never escape his childhood.

Lucius had begun a leisurely return to the fort when he spotted Freya by the riverbank away from the docks. She was talking with a tall warrior who had his back to Lucius. Lucius waved but Freya was too immersed in her conversation to notice, so he strolled down to talk. He was within an arm's length of the stranger when Freya spotted him and abruptly stopped talking in mid-sentence. Seeing Freya's expression of surprise, the stranger spun around.

Lucius almost collapsed with shock. The greasy hair in two braids, the pale blue eyes, the double-headed axe tattoo on the left cheek—it was the Sicambri warrior priest who had so nearly killed him so many years ago!

Lucius's heart raced and his breath came in short gasps. The man sneered at Lucius and turned away. He said something to Freya before stalking off into the trees.

"Who was that?" Lucius asked as soon as the initial shock passed.

"Nobody," Freya said, dismissively.

"I swear he was the Sicambri who led the raid that captured Titus and me years ago. You killed him with your sling."

Freya laughed, but Lucius thought he noticed a slight hesitation. "You Romans think all barbarians look the same. If I killed him years ago, how could he be here today?"

"I suppose so," Lucius said, doubtfully. It had been a long time and this man's nose had been broken and skewed to the right. Yet the eyes looked so familiar, and he did have a half-moon scar on his forehead that could have been from Freya's sling. But Freya was right—many barbarians did look very similar.

"But why were you talking to him, anyway? I thought the Cherusci and Sicambri were sworn enemies?"

"Not always. Even enemies cannot fight forever. Let's walk. I have a gift for you." Freya dug into a leather pouch at her belt and pulled out a four-foot length of pleated hemp. One end was knotted and the other ended in a braided loop. Midway along, a diamond of leather had been tied on.

"A sling," Lucius said, taking the weapon and examining the tight weave. "It's beautiful. Thank you."

"Let's see how well I have taught you." Freya led the way to the riverbank. "Can you reach the far side?"

"The *far* side? It must be four hundred paces! I've never thrown that distance."

"Try." Freya bent and picked up a small, round stone and handed it to Lucius.

Lucius placed the looped end of the sling around the middle finger of his right hand and grasped the knotted end between his thumb and forefinger. He set the stone in the leather pouch and let it hang. He tried to remember everything Freya had told him: turn sideways to the target, release on the first swing and, most importantly, use your entire body to throw.

Lucius relaxed and let the sling swing slowly from his hand. The weight felt good. He picked a point on the far bank and visualized the stone hitting it.

Taking a breath, he leaned back. Tensing every muscle in his body, he pushed forward, at the same time whipping his right arm in a wide arc. When his arm reached the vertical, Lucius released the knotted end of the sling. The stone flew horizontally over the water and splashed in just short of half way to the far bank.

"Not bad," Freya said, "but you did it the wrong way. Overhand, the way you threw, is good for accuracy, but that only matters at close range. Imagine the far bank was an army, packed ranks of soldiers like one of your legions, coming toward you. You're not trying to hit any individual. What is important is to get your stone into them when they are as far away as possible. It will probably hit someone. For distance throw underhand."

Freya pulled her own sling from her belt. It was stained and worn and the leather diamond was polished so smooth it shone in the afternoon sun. She bent and selected a stone and loaded the sling. In a movement so fast Lucius had trouble following it, Freya stepped forward, launched her body onto her forward leg and whipped her right arm forward and underhand. The stone flew in a high arc and landed on the far bank.

"The higher it goes, the farther it goes," Freya explained. "You try."

Lucius took half a dozen underhand throws, but the best he achieved was a splash about three quarters of the way across.

"It takes practice," Freya encouraged. "Let me show you a trick." She held out the knotted end of her sling for Lucius to examine. It wasn't actually a knot, but a braided lump, and it was heavy.

"There's a stone inside for weight," Freya said.

"Does that make the stone go farther?"

"I don't think so. Here's what it does."

Freya bent and carefully searched out five stones of the same size, shape and weight. Holding them in her left hand, she turned to look along the bank. "See that tree? The dead one leaning out over the river?"

Lucius nodded. The tree was small and about a hundred paces away.

Freya loaded her sling with the first stone and stood staring at the tree for a long moment, then she fired. The sling was a blur, but Lucius heard five stones thud into the tree trunk in less than the time it would take him to count to ten. "That's impossible."

"I know a man," Freya said with a smile, "who can fire into a rotted stump at twice that distance and hit the first stone with the other four."

"How do you do it?"

"That's what the weight is for." Freya demonstrated in slow motion. "After the first stone is released and while the leather is still moving, I place the second stone in the leather with my left hand. This swings the weighted end around and I catch it in my right hand, drop the leather and I am ready to fire again."

Lucius tried and got completely tangled up, hitting himself painfully on the forehead with the weighted end of the sling.

"It does take practice," Freya said with a laugh.

Lucius tried a few more shots and then the pair headed back up towards the camp.

"Thanks for the sling," Lucius said. "Now that I have my own I can practice much more."

Freya nodded acknowledgement. "Most of the Legions seem to be getting presents," she said, swinging her arm to encompass the activity on the docks. "I think it will be a busy summer."

"There are many rumours flying about."

"I'll tell you one thing that's not a rumour."

Lucius heard a change in the tone of Freya's voice and glanced over at his companion. Her brow was furrowed in sudden anger.

"It is not you Romans who are paying for all this."

"What do you mean?" Lucius asked.

"Varus has increased the taxes again."

"That is his right as Governor."

"Maybe, but last summer was hard. The crops did not do well and so many young men are in the Auxiliary that there are not enough to hunt. It is said that some villages are close to starvation."

"There is grain being brought in from Gaul and Hispania," Lucius said, pointing at the amphorae on the docks.

"Do you think that is for the barbarians?" The way Freya spat out the last word startled Lucius. He had seen her angry before, but he was taken aback by the violence in her voice.

"The Cherusci are not starving," he said defensively.

"Those of us who are paid and fed as Auxiliaries do not starve, but many have families still living in the Cherusci homelands east of the river. And many other tribes starve. That is what the Sicambri came to tell me."

"What do you care about other tribes? I thought the Cherusci looked down on them all."

"We can defeat any in battle, but we do not fight women and children and it is they who are starving. Those who are starving are more like the Cherusci than you Romans who let us starve."

"The Roman's don't let people starve."

"Who are you to say? Are you Varus? Do you see into his heart?"

"No, but he is an honourable Roman."

"That may be—to other Romans. And I dare say he will not let Romans starve, but why should he care about a few Chatti or Marsi children? He is planning to go to war with them soon anyway. Perhaps the hunger is to his advantage."

"That's not fair."

"Is it not? How well will a Chatti warrior fight if he knows he should be out hunting to feed his family?"

Freya paused and closed her eyes. Lucius waited silently, wondering what was coming next.

"The Sicambri brought more news," Freya said at last. "Arminius has a brother, my uncle, Lothar. When Arminius became an Auxiliary of Rome, the brothers fought and both went their separate ways. Lothar chose to live the traditional life across the river. He married and they had three beautiful children."

Lucius noticed a tear glint in the corner of Freya's eye, but she blinked and continued. "I used to sneak away and visit them, because I knew

Arminius would not approve. I bounced the children on my knee. I envied the family. They seemed so happy and lived such a simple life."

Freya fell silent for a long time. Eventually she continued. "The Sicambri told me that Lothar's children are dead." The tear escaped and ran down Freya's cheek.

"What happened?" Lucius asked.

Anger flashed back into Freya's face. "They starved! The children's bellies swole as their cheeks sunk and their eyes widened. They wasted away in this land of Roman plenty."

Once again, Lucius recoiled at the bitterness in Freya's voice. "I'm sorry," he said helplessly.

"Why should you be sorry?" Freya asked. "It's not your fault that children are dying. It is Rome's arrogance and Varus's greed that are to blame. You are just caught in the middle of it all. It is not you I am angry with."

Freya sighed deeply and calmed. "I like you, Lucius. You are kind and I think in other times, we could be," Freya hesitated, "close, but you are naive in the ways of war and politics—and you cannot help being a Roman. You see the world as a soldier of Augustus—a place to be conquered for its own good, a place to be civilized even if the people who have been there for a thousand years do not wish to become toga-wearing senators, and a place that can supply the food and taxes Rome needs to remain powerful."

"Didn't you and Arminius want to become civilized, to become Roman?" Lucius asked.

"We did," Freya said, sadly. "But we are not allowed. As your friend Herod would say, 'Once a barbarian, always a barbarian.'"

Lucius opened his mouth to deny Freya's claim, but he couldn't, he knew it was true. That was exactly what Herod would say. "You're wrong," he said weakly, knowing it was a lie.

Freya smiled bitterly. "I hope so," she said, "more than you can imagine."

Freya strode off toward the Auxiliary camp outside the walls of Vetera.

Lucius kicked at the ground. Freya had saved his life twice and in return Lucius had taught her Latin and everything he knew about Rome and Roman history. Freya had been eager to learn and soaked up the information like a sponge. She had wanted more than anything else to be as Roman as Lucius, but things had changed. Now it seemed that every time Lucius talked with Freya, they ended up arguing. Seeing Freya talking with the Sicambri warrior today bothered Lucius deeply. The man's familiarity was strange and he wasn't convinced by Freya's explanation. She had skillfully changed the subject by giving Lucius the sling, and explained the man's visit by telling the story of Lothar's children. But, would a Sicambri warrior come all this way to tell her that, and why hadn't he told Arminius instead?

"Come on, we're on guard duty tonight."

Lucius looked up to see Drusus calling to him from the battlements. "If you don't stop dawdling, there won't be time to eat first."

"Coming," Lucius shouted and strode in the east gate. His doubts would have to wait.

~~~~

"Today we begin an enterprise that will live forever in the memories of all Romans."

Lucius's centuria was gathered around Balbus as he read Varus's message to his Legions. Other centuria were gathered all through Vetera listening to the same message. It was the fifteenth day of Junius and the scene had been identical the day before when the 18th Legion had mustered, and the day before that for the 17th. As always, the Scorpions were bringing up the rear on the march to the east. Already the 18th and 17th would be one and two days march away respectively.

"The auguries are auspicious and so, secure in the favours of Mithras and Mars, we shall subdue our enemies and bring the Roman peace to the barbarian hordes. There will be hard fighting but I am confident that you, soldiers of the Legions of Germania, will stick to your task, not weaken and bring undying glory to Rome and the divine Augustus. So say I, Publius Quinctillius Varus, Governor of Germania."

Balbus thumped his chest in salute and the centuria repeated the gesture.

"I would like to echo Governor Varus's confidence," Balbus said. "I am sure each and every one of you will acquit yourselves with honour in the coming battles against the barbarians, but let me say that if you do not, you will wish you had fallen on your sword or been sacrificed to the barbarian Gods rather than face my wrath. That is all. Form up."

Lucius and his companions collected their equipment and stood in loose marching formation, waiting as the centuria in front of them marched out. Lucius, Herod, Appius, Drusus, the two Sextus's and Flavius and Servius, the recruits who had replaced Titus and Quintus, stood in the middle of the centuria around the standard Lucius carried in addition to his regular equipment. Lucius didn't mind the extra weight—it was an honour at such a young age and a significant step on the way to his goal of standard-bearer for the entire 19th Legion. Lucius was less content with his other duties as payroll officer for his centuria. He had help—young Flavius in particular was very good with numbers on the abacus and the actual coin was kept in the Legion treasury—but a lot of time each month was spent writing down figures and handing out payments. In addition, if anyone had a complaint, and some of the soldiers seemed to live for the times they could complain, it was Lucius they came to.

"Say goodbye to comfort," Drusus said, looking around at the well-established barrack buildings. "It's marching through swamps, digging forts and sleeping in wet bivouacs for us now, my lads."

"Try not to be so positive about everything," Lucius said with a smile. "If you'd wanted soft beds and a comfortable couch to lie on all day, you should have become a senator in Rome."

"I wouldn't last as a senator. I'm far too outspoken. Not political enough. I'd be on my way to exile in three weeks. Anyway, my dad's a tavern owner and I don't think there are many tavern owners in the senate."

"True enough," Lucius agreed, "but I suspect a few senators are not unfamiliar with tavern owners. Anyway, the going won't be hard for some time yet. That's a good road along the Lupia and we'll have a ready-made fort to sleep in every night."

"Look, an omen." Lucius turned his head to see Servius looking up at the sky. Although he was the same age as Lucius, Servius seemed terribly naive. He was willing enough, but he believed everything he was told and was the butt of most of the *contuberium's* jokes.

"Where?" Appius asked, squinting against the bright sky.

"There," Servius pointed almost directly overhead. "Three eagles flying east. Those are our three Legions, Taurus, Capricorn and Scorpio, heading east to subdue the barbarians. The Gods are on our side."

"Those are crows, lad," Drusus said, shading his eyes with his hand.

"Are you sure," Servius asked, his face colouring with embarrassment. "They look like eagles to me."

"They're crows," Drusus confirmed, "but crows or eagles, seeing them flying east doesn't tell us much. We all know where we're going. Me, I'd prefer to see them flying west—heading back home after a successful campaign. That would be a good omen."

"We don't need omens," Herod said. "This summer will be no harder than a walk through the Forum in Rome. It'll be a good training exercise for us. A few skirmishes against some disorganized barbarian tribes and then back to Vetera for the winter."

"Don't forget," Appius said. "Not everywhere that appears safe is so. Julius Caesar died in the Forum in Rome."

"You and your history lessons," Herod said with a laugh. "Julius Caesar was murdered by other high-born Romans. We are going up against some squabbling barbarians who can barely feed themselves."

Lucius thought back to his recent argument with Freya. "It's not their fault they're starving. The crops failed last summer, the hunting's been poor and Varus makes things worse by increasing the taxes to pay for this expedition."

"Lucius. Lucius," Herod shook his head. "Always taking the side of the barbarians. If they accepted Roman rule and lived a civilized life like we do, there would be no hunger. Instead they try and fight against us, which only means that they get beaten and starve."

"But even if they lived like us and like Arminius became Roman citizens, they would still be barbarians."

"Of course. Once a barbarian always a barbarian."

"The world is divided into Romans and barbarians," Drusus said, "and it is our duty to show them how to live and advance."

"Even if we have to do it with swords?" Lucius asked.

"Look," Drusus went on, "if it was obvious to the barbarians that our way of life is better than theirs, they would be Romans already. It's *not* seeing how they should live that makes them barbarians. That's why we have to fight them."

Lucius knew that what his companions were saying was right—Roman civilization was obviously better than living in the forest in filthy animal skins—but some of what Freya said was right as well.

He was saved from having to think of a response by Balbus ordering the centuria forward. With a clatter of equipment, they tightened their formation and marched out the East Gate toward the bridge over the Rhenus.

Lucius was surprised to see a large crowd gathered between the fort and the river to watch the Legion depart. It was mostly made up of old men, women and children, members of various tribes who lived in the forests nearby. However, there were considerable numbers of armed Auxiliaries scattered through the mass.

The crowd was eerily silent, almost sullen, Lucius thought. As he scanned the faces, Lucius spotted Freya standing near the front. She was intent on watching the soldiers pass, but Lucius couldn't help noticing the look of disgust on her face. Behind her the Sicambri warrior stood making no attempt to hide his expression of hatred.

Suddenly, a woman carrying a small, wrapped bundle broke from the crowd and ran forward. Lucius thought she was going to run straight into the centuria, but she stopped a few steps short, screamed something at the soldiers, placed the bundle on the ground and spat forcefully toward the column. A low groan issued from the crowd.

Lucius was shocked to see that the bundle was an obviously dead baby. He looked up at the woman as he marched past. He expected to see a distraught face and tears. Instead the woman's expression was one of extreme anger. Her dark eyes flashed utter hatred as she stared at the soldiers marching past. Lucius felt chills run down his spine.

"Now that's a bad omen," Drusus mumbled.

~~~~

The road to Alterium, the first of the forts on the Lupia, was wide enough for the men to march eight abreast. This kept them in a compact battle formation that could rapidly march where it was needed or swivel and fight where it stood. Balbus led the way, dressed in full uniform and mounted on a fine black horse.

The road was not paved, as those in southern Gaul or near Rome were, but it was well cleared and thousands of marching feet in heavy hob-nailed sandals had beaten the surface flat so that in summer at least the surface was almost as good.

Lucius felt happy to be on the move. To his right, the Lupia flowed, wide and calm, and to his left the trees had been cut back beyond spear throwing range.

Alterium would have been vacated by the 18th that morning. The 17th would be one fort farther on down the road. Roman and Auxiliary cavalry patrolled the road between the columns and ranged far ahead and to either side when the landscape permitted. The rest of the Auxiliary forces followed along behind.

Varus's army numbered 20,000 even before the 6,000 Cherusci Auxilliaries were counted. It was a formidable—Herod would say unbeatable—fighting force.

The plan was to follow the road along the Lupia to the River Weser. There Varus would establish a summer base from which the Legions could march even farther east, perhaps to the Albis, building roads and temporary forts as they went. There was no intention to build a permanent settlement on the Weser, at least not yet. Each summer, the Legions would return, extend the roads and system of forts, and punish any tribes who had caused trouble until, eventually, the land was quiet enough and developed enough to become a Roman Province.

Two men in front of Lucius, Servius was turning his head, looking about nervously. Drusus, marching in front of Lucius, poked the new recruit in the back. "Don't worry, lad," he said, "no one's going to leap out of the river and the trees are cut back far enough that we'll see anyone coming before they get within spear range."

Servius half-turned and gave Drusus a weak smile. Then a look of horror spread across his face and he stumbled to one side, bumping into Sextus Livius.

Drusus burst out laughing as he nimbly stepped over a pile of steaming droppings from Balbus's horse. "More important to watch where you're going than where you've been," he said.

Servius righted himself and tried to keep in step while scraping the warm dung off his sandals.

"Dung's all you'll have to worry about here," Drusus said. "Ten forts along the Lupia and each one nicely prepared and supplied for us by our friends on the river." Drusus nodded to his right where a small cargo boat was sailing up the river against the sluggish current. "I just hope those damned 18th haven't left Alterium in too much of a mess."

"We'll know soon enough," Lucius said, squinting at the sky. "It can't be far now."

The sun was still high in the sky, but it was the Roman habit to begin a day's march early in the morning and stop to camp in the afternoon. This had obvious advantages in a hot climate, but it also allowed time for a Legion to dig ditches and put up an earth wall around a fortified camp each day so that the soldiers could sleep easily. Since the forts on the Lupia were already constructed, the 19th could look forward to some time to bathe and relax.

As the marching column rounded a sharp bend in the river, they passed the Alterium docks, with two small cargo vessels being unloaded by slaves, and got their first view of the fort. Designed to accommodate only one Legion at a time, Alterium was smaller than Vetera, measuring 650 paces by 525, but it was well protected. A deep, double ditch fronted a high earth wall topped by a wooden palisade. As they approached the West Gate, Lucius could see legionaries patrolling the top of the walls, but his attention was drawn away by five objects lined along the north side of the road.

A series of tree trunks, stripped of bark and the thickness of a man's waist were imbedded in the ground, about six paces apart. Each stood some ten feet high and was topped with a smaller cross log, about six feet long. From each structure hung the naked body of a Germanic warrior. The men were supported by iron spikes through their forearms and ankles. Three were obviously already dead and fat crows sat on their shoulders cawing loudly at the passing soldiers and pecking at the dark holes where the eyes had been. The other two had been provided with crude wood blocks on which they could partly rest and take some of the weight off their suspended arms. Lucius knew that this was not done out of kindness but was simply a way of prolonging the men's agonizing death.

Each man had a wooden plaque nailed to the upright below his feet. They all read the same, although some were barely legible under the blood that had run down onto them. The plaques read: "This man is a thief. He was caught stealing grain from the Legions. So perish the enemies of Rome."

The soldiers stared at the convicts and some shouted insults as they passed. One of the survivors, with considerable effort, held his head up and stared back defiantly. Lucius noted the double axe tattoo of the Sicambri on his cheek.

"So, Varus has begun imposing his will on the barbarians already," Drusus noted.

"They were probably just trying to feed their families," Lucius said under his breath.

But Herod heard what Lucius said. "By stealing from us. Barbarians are lazy. They'll always take the easy way—stealing instead of working."

Lucius bit back a response. He wanted to point out that the hunger sweeping the land was not these men's fault and that it must be cruel to see their wives and children starve while bushels of grain were being unloaded and stored for the Legions. But Herod was set in his ways and all it would do was start an argument. This might explain why the Sicambri warrior with Freya at Vetera had glared at the Legions with so much hatred.

Lucius stared at the bodies hanging from the wooden crosses. He had seen plenty of crucifixions, but these were different. Did these men deserve this fate or had they simply done what Lucius would have done in their place? Was this the best way to transform Germania into a pacified Roman Province? But then, this was the Roman way and if laws weren't upheld and punishments meted out for crimes, everything would collapse in chaos—wouldn't it? Of course it would, but a part of Lucius couldn't help wondering if the soldiers who had nailed the thieves to the crosses were any better than barbarians themselves.

The Legion marched into Alterium and settled itself for the night. Meanwhile the Auxiliaries set up their camp outside the walls.

Freya

W e can kill them all tonight." Arnulf's face was twisted with hate. "They think themselves safe behind their ditches and walls, but you can come and go as you please. Take some men, kill the guards and hold the gate open. The Sicambri and Cherusci will pour in and the vaunted Legion will be slaughtered in their beds, as they deserve."

"Calm yourself, Arnulf," Arminius said, quietly. Freya, her uncle and Arnulf, who had been appointed chief of the Sicambri after his father's death the year before, stood at dusk on the riverbank at Alterium, looking back to the five crosses silhouetted against the darkening sky.

"Calm! You ask for calm. That is my brother hanging from a Roman tree, his only crime trying to put food in his starving children's bellies. And you ask me to be calm! You who have fed like a leech off the Roman teat while those of us with honour have struggled to preserve the old ways and pay due respect to the Gods of our forefathers. Be patient, you said. The Roman way is best. Soon we shall have all the benefits you see them enjoying. Are those the benefits you talked about?" Arnulf pointed at the five bodies outside the gate. "Once before you stopped me killing Romans, but now it is time."

Arminius ignored the insults and continued calmly. "And when you succeed and all the Romans in Alterium are dead, what then? It is early in the campaigning season and there are two other Legions within two days march of here. You will not catch the Romans by surprise twice. They will devastate every village within marching distance. Every man who cannot escape will be killed, every woman raped and every child sold into slavery. Your brother's fate will be nothing. The forests will be devastated to provide enough trees to crucify our people. Who then will rush to join your pitiful little rebellion? You, and anyone you have ever known, will die in hopeless battles or as starving refugees."

"We starve already," Arnulf said aggressively, but the fire had gone out of his words. "At least our men would die an honourable death in battle."

"So, all you want is an honourable death?"

"What else is there?"

"Victory."

Freya and Arnulf stared at Arminius. What was her uncle saying, Freya wondered. Was he suggesting rebellion?

"Victory?" Arnulf asked, tentatively. "But you have just said we are doomed if we rebel tonight."

"Then we won't rebel tonight."

Freya's heart lurched. She held her breath.

"When?" Arnulf asked, his anger replaced by curiosity.

"*If* there were to be a rebellion," Arminius stressed the first word heavily. "It would have to be in the autumn, after the crops are gathered and at the end of the campaigning season when the Romans will not be able to respond quickly. Everyone—the Marsi, the Chatti, the Tencteri—not just the Cherusci and Sicambri, would have to be involved. Even the Bructeri, who have lived in peace longer than anyone, must be persuaded to fight. There will be one chance and the victory must be total. It will have to be so absolute and shocking to the Romans that they will never wish to cross the Rhenus into our lands again."

"Would you lead us?" Arnulf asked.

Freya stared at her uncle in the dying light. She had a strange feeling that the world was suddenly spinning out of control. How Arminius responded would change everything, not just her own life but that of everyone she knew. If Arminius said yes, he would win, Freya was certain of that, and Germania would never be the same again.

After what seemed like an age, Arminius sighed heavily. "Yes," he said quietly. "Arnulf, go to the other tribes and ask their war chiefs to meet in council with me when the moon is next full where the Kalkriese Hill protrudes north into the great swamp. Travel alone. Trust this to no one else. Tell the chiefs of the Marsi, Chatti, Tencteri and Bructeri and them alone the purpose. Tell all others it is a meeting to talk of joining the Auxiliaries."

"I will leave first thing in the morning," Arnulf said. "But there is one thing I must do now that it is dark."

The Sicambri unsheathed his long sword and walked away. For a moment, Freya worried that he was going to attack one of the guards at the gate, but Arnulf headed instead to the crucified men. Freya watched as the silhouette of one man raised his head at Arnulf's approach. Arnulf hesitated for a moment and then thrust his sword up and under the man's ribs. The man threw his head back and went limp. Arnulf disappeared into the darkness.

"At least his brother won't suffer any more," Arminius said. "I fear that cannot be said for the rest of us. By all the Gods I have been a fool—but I don't know that I am any less of one now."

"I don't understand," Freya said.

"Come and let us sit by the river, niece."

The pair sat side by side on a log overlooking the dark water of the Lupia. Torches on the dock, where slaves still worked at unloading cargo, flickered orange shafts of light over the surface. A bat, hunting insects over the water, flashed in front of Freya.

"So, you *are* going to lead a rebellion against the Romans?" Freya said, when Arminius showed no signs of opening the conversation.

Arminius ran a hand over his face and drew a deep breath. "I fear I must."

Freya nodded. Here it was, final blunt confirmation of what she had wondered about and sometimes wished for. The prospect terrified her, but it excited her, too. Rebellion! Never again having to take Roman insults and live like a slave in their presence. The choice was to be made for her. Freya would be a Cherusci—and only a Cherusci.

"I have always thought we must work with the Romans," Arminius said, staring out over the black water. "My father taught me that. He said that the world is theirs and we must be the ones to adapt and change to fit. The more I saw of the Romans, the more I admired them—their power, their discipline, their conviction that the world was theirs for the taking. The day I became a Roman citizen was the proudest day of my life.

"Much good it has done me," Arminius added bitterly.

"But now the decision is made. It's simple," Freya said.

"I wish that were so. Many will die because of what I have set in motion this evening. I would rather this had not happened at all—but there is no choice. I have not come lightly to this decision. I have thought on it a long time—years. I was wrong."

"To think the Roman way is the best way?"

"No," Arminius said sadly, "I still believe that the Roman way is best. That they hold the future in their hands and that the world is theirs."

"What then?"

"I have been a fool to believe that they would share it with the likes of us. It is a future only for Romans. Even those like myself who have been given Roman citizenship cannot share in it. I will never dine with Varus, and Balbus will always be free to strike you when he feels like it. For us, Roman citizenship is only a scrap thrown to a dog to keep it quiet and happy. They would no more let me be a full Roman than they would let that dog sit at their dining table. You, I and all our people, will always be barbarians. Our only choice is to accept that, to be happy that our children will grow to be Roman slaves and their effort will only go to pay Roman taxes, which will feed and clothe those like Varus, not our grandchildren—or to fight for our past life so that our children, some of them at least, might live the free life that our grandfathers talk of around the hearth."

"Can we win?"

"Perhaps. I am certain that there will be no better time. Bato's rebellion continues in Illyria, and that must be the Roman's priority—they cannot afford to let Bato win that close to home. That means the three Legions here will not be reinforced this year."

"And we can defeat them?"

"We must do more than that. We must annihilate them. We must shock the Romans as they have not been shocked since Hannibal destroyed their army at Cannae. Not a single Roman soldier must live to cross back over the Rhenus when the leaves turn on the trees."

Freya felt a twinge of sadness as she thought of Lucius. He was one of those Roman soldiers. "If we can totally destroy the three Legions," Arminius continued, "the Romans holding the forts on the Lupia will flee back across the Rhenus. Perhaps, with Bato still a threat in Illyria, the Romans will decide that we, and our forests, are not worth the trouble of mounting a major campaign. Perhaps they will be content to leave the Rhenus as the border between us."

"Will the other tribes support us?"

"I think so. The Sicambri and the Marsi have always hated the Romans, and Varus's taxes, combined with the bad harvest last year and the hardships that the Romans do nothing to help, cause much discontent. I think there will be no better time to raise the tribes in revolt."

"There are many ifs."

"I know. We have all summer to turn some of them into certainties. For the rest we must hope the Gods have not deserted us.

"But listen, Freya," Arminius turned and looked hard at his niece. "No one can know of this. Everything depends upon total surprise. You must say nothing to anyone."

"I won't."

"You know that your Roman friend must die, too?"

"I do." Freya tried to keep her voice firm, but she couldn't stop the catch in it.

"Could you kill him?"

Freya choked back a sob and shook her head.

"Then we will lose," Arminius said, matter-of-factly. "It is easy to kill an enemy. It is killing a friend that takes real courage. You saw how Arnulf killed his own brother to stop his suffering."

Not trusting herself to speak, Freya nodded.

"In taking this step, we must harden our hearts to all but our final goal, otherwise we are doomed. Nothing can matter except our struggle—not civilization, friends or family. Even victory will bring untold suffering and hardship. I pray to all the Gods that it will be worth it."

Arminius stood. "I do not know if the path ahead is any less foolish than the one I have trod but the dice are thrown and we must live with where they lie."

Arminius strode away into the darkness, leaving Freya to struggle with all she had learned. She was confused and terrified. Would she be able to harden her heart as much as Arminius required? Over the years, she had come to hate the Romans and what they were doing to her people and her country, but what about Lucius? He was arrogant and naive, but could she fire a stone from her sling, knowing that it would split Lucius's head open and end his life? He had been kind to her and generous in teaching her about Rome. Perhaps in other times, other circumstances, they could have been— Freya felt tears welling up. "No!" she shouted, rolling over and beating the earth. She pounded the ground as hard as she could with both hands until her fists bled and her tears were for her pain.

Massacre

The reign of Augustus Caesar: Year 36
August

L ucius's home for the summer was a semi-permanent camp on the west bank of the Weser River where each Legion had its own fort, complete with ditches, walls and wooden barracks. The forts were separate, but close enough that the Legion from any one could respond quickly if either of the others were attacked. The Auxiliaries were camped in the woods between and around the forts. Supplies came along the road from the Lupia and a bridge built on floating barges led across the Weser to the east bank, where most of the campaigning was done.

The three Legions had never gone out together and it was rare for even one full Legion to cross the river, although the 18th had marched in full strength to the Albis and back. Normally only one or two cohorts, supported by a force of Auxiliaries, would head out on a fast raid to either punish a tribe or receive the homage of a local chieftain. This time, Lucius's cohort, accompanied by only a few Auxiliary scouts and Freya as interpreter, were heading north to discover what had happened to centuria Four of their cohort.

Lucius was glad Freya was coming with them, and hoped they would have a chance to talk. It almost seemed as if she had been avoiding him all summer.

Centuria Four had gone out on a routine patrol the day before to a Bructeri village where a scout had reported the presence of several Sicambri warriors. The centuria had not returned by nightfall.

"They probably discovered some good-looking women in the village and stayed to make friends," Drusus commented as the centuria formed up in marching order, three abreast on the narrow path across the bridge.

"Maybe," Lucius agreed, "but the orders not to go farther than you can return by sundown are strict. Women or not, they'll be punished when they get back."

"And meanwhile, we have to act as nursemaids," Herod added. "An entire cohort to look for a single centuria that was sent out to look for a few ragged warriors who probably either don't exist or were just passing through. It's ridiculous! We should let the Fourth centuria wander about in the forests until they find their own way back."

"Or send the Auxiliaries out to look for them," Lucius said. "They know the country and are much better suited to this kind of work."

Varus's war of subjugation had not gone as expected. The Legions had marched back and forth across the country all summer, bridging rivers, widening paths between villages and demanding tribute from every community they came to. No one had interfered with the road building, although the working soldiers were often watched by puzzled locals from the edge of the trees, and tribute had always been given without a fight. Sometimes the local chiefs had been sullen and sworn allegiance to Augustus only reluctantly, but many had been quite happy to see the Legions and sometimes even thrown a party to welcome them. The Fourth centuria would not be the first to return sheepishly a day late.

"You're just bitter," Drusus said, "because no village is big enough to entertain a whole cohort."

"I don't want to be entertained," Herod replied. "I don't trust these barbarians. We've all fought against them in past years. Why, suddenly, are they so friendly?"

"They're not friendly," Lucius said. "Many of the villages are obviously not pleased to see us and remember the crowd when we left Vetera?"

"Exactly," Herod said. "That crowd hated us because they thought we were to blame for them starving. I admit the people out here in the east seem to be better off and this season looks like being plentiful, but life is still hard. No one wants to give up what little they have in tribute. Every year that I have been out collecting there has been trouble, but not this year."

"I think they still hate us," Appius said. "They just don't show it."

"Why not?" Lucius asked.

"These people have been fighting us since the days of Julius Caesar and we're still here and still winning. Maybe they've finally realized we can't be beaten."

"Perhaps," Herod said, dubiously, "but I still think something's going on."

"Nothing's going on," Drusus said. "These people live in villages of a few families scattered everywhere through the forest. They don't have the organization to be as devious as you think, Herod. They don't have a forum or a Senate House. I think Appius is right. I think this war's over. I just hope we're not the ones left behind on garrison duty in this God-forsaken place. I've done my time here. I want a posting to somewhere warm, Egypt maybe. Even Hispania's not too bad, I hear."

"My dream has come back." Everyone looked at Sextus Livius, marching to Lucius's right.

"What dream?" Drusus asked.

"The one I had before the battle in Illyria," Sextus said. "Remember I am a scorpion and along with a goat and a bull I am being overwhelmed by ants in the temple of Apollo."

"And you thought it meant you were going to die in the battle," Drusus said, "but you're still here. Old Titus was right, dreams don't mean anything."

"Don't mock dreams," Appius said. "Many have believed that dreams are the Gods' way of talking to us. Many great events in history have been foretold in dreams."

"Then I wish the Gods would be a bit clearer," Drusus said. "It seems to me the meaning of a dream is only obvious after the thing it prophesied has happened. I would rather have a clear message *before* an event so that I could do something about it."

"Silence in the ranks!" Balbus half-turned in his saddle and shouted back at his men. The conversation died.

As he trudged between the dark trees, Lucius found himself thinking about Titus. He still missed his friend and the stories he told. It had been on a path much like this that they had been ambushed seven years before. Lucius looked around nervously, then shook his head. That had been a different time. Appius and Drusus were right—the tribes' spirit had been broken by years of war and the recent food shortages. This was going to be just another boring summer followed by a cold, wet winter.

But something nagged at Lucius's mind. Sextus Livius's dream bothered him. It wasn't that Lucius believed in dreams like some ragged soothsayer in the market. He had had plenty of dreams and none ever seemed to mean anything. It was odd that Sextus's dream should be repeated, and that it had returned after so long, but that was the mysterious nature of dreams. And, even if the dream foretold Sextus's death, that didn't affect Lucius. Still though, what did it mean? Animals being attacked by ants. Who were the animals? The scorpion must be Sextus, but the goat and the bull? Lucius missed a step and Drusus kicked his heel painfully. In a blinding flash the meaning of the dream filled his mind.

"Sextus," Lucius turned his head and whispered, ignoring Balbus's order for silence. "The dream's not about you. You're not the scorpion in it, we all are!"

"But it felt like me," Sextus said.

"Because you are one of us. You are *a* scorpion not *the* scorpion."

"But," Appius said, puzzled, "if his dream is foretelling the fate of the whole Legion and not just himself, why is he the only one having it?"

"He's not." Heads swivelled violently to look at Sextus Vipsanius. "For the past three nights, I have awoken from the same dream. I thought it had been planted by Sextus Livius when he told me that his dream had returned, but perhaps not."

"I have been having odd dreams about scorpions and ants," Servius said, shyly. "I didn't know what they meant, so I kept quiet."

"By all the Gods," Drusus said. "It's an epidemic of dreams."

Lucius ignored Drusus and continued with his explanation. "If Sextus Livius's scorpion is the 19th Legion, then the bull is Taurus and the goat, Capricorn—the 18th and 17th Legions. Think about it. The Scorpion is our symbol, the bull and the goat are theirs!"

For a moment, they all wrestled in silence with the implications. If the Scorpion, Bull and Goat represented the three Legions, then no one came into the temple to help because there *was* no one else.

"Nonsense," Drusus said, but his voice didn't carry the conviction of before. "You're like a bunch of gossiping old women! And, anyway, how could all three Legions be attacked by the ants? We're never together."

"Drusus Meridius," Balbus's voice rose in anger. "You have just drawn a double shift of guard duty tonight. If I hear one more word on the march, the speaker will find himself strapped to a wagon wheel and flogged."

The centuria marched on in silence. The road was rough but they were travelling light, carrying only shield and weapons. They were not slowed down by baggage carts, but half-a-dozen mules followed, laden with extra weapons and medical supplies.

On the narrow road, the huge trees were uncomfortably close and in places leaned threateningly over the soldiers. The route only widened out at villages, but these were few. Most of the villages were scattered through the forest, linked by a network of narrow paths. Only those that happened to be on the routes the Romans had chosen for their roads were easily accessible to the Legions.

Lucius was less frightened of the forest than he had been; after all, he had seen a lot of it over the years. The dark, mysterious lakes and black treacherous bogs still depressed him, but he had learned much about the forest and often enjoyed walking between the trees, listening to the birds call and the squirrels argue. But today, like the others, Lucius was deep in his own thoughts

Lucius was not a great believer in dreams. He believed in prophecy and omens, and that oracles could foretell the future. It was man's flawed interpretation of the messages that was the problem. The oracles of ancient Greece spoke in riddles. It was almost as if the Gods were playing games with the puny mortals who were presumptuous enough to want to know the future. But Sextus Livius's dream seemed clearer now—the three strong, large Legions were going to be overwhelmed by a small but incredibly numerous enemy that could only be the barbarian tribes. But what did the details mean?

The temple of Apollo was easy enough. Apollo represented art, culture and reason, so his temple must be a symbol of the Romans bringing order to the wilderness. Lucius struggled to remember the details. He had been in Sextus's dream, the only human. What did *that* mean? It made little sense. In any case, Lucius distrusted the simplicity of the dream message—the barbarians seemed peaceful this year and how could they organize their far-flung villages to collect enough undisciplined warriors to threaten three full strength Legions? The barbarians would need at least 40,000 warriors to have a chance of overwhelming them. To gather that many, they would need warriors from something like two-and-a-half to three thousand villages. It made no sense, but still, the dream weighed heavily on Lucius's mind.

Lucius's thoughts were interrupted by a noise from the trees to his right. Others heard it too. Heads turned and hands reached instinctively for weapons. But the figures that broke from the underbrush weren't part of a barbarian horde intent on slaughter, they were Roman soldiers—at least they had been. Now they were simply six half-naked, terrified individuals.

The strangers staggered forward and fell into the arms of the soldiers of the front rank. With a shock of recognition, Lucius saw that one of them was Julius Vulso, the centurion of the missing unit.

"What is going on here?" Balbus trotted back from the front of the column and looked down on the men. "Vulso what does this mean?"

The centurion stood straight and saluted, and Lucius noticed he had nasty gash, caked with dried blood, on his left cheek. "We were attacked by barbarians from the village."

"Where are the others?"

"There are no others."

Lucius felt a shudder pass through the standing men as they tensed at the news.

"What happened?" Balbus asked.

"We were on this road yesterday," Vulso looked about him, "It was late afternoon. We had searched the village and questioned the old headman, but there was no sign of the warriors the scout told us about. We were returning to camp when we were ambushed."

The man stopped, visibly shaken. No one said a word, the only sound was the rustle of the wind in the treetops and an occasional bird call. Vulso took a deep breath and continued.

"There were hundreds of them. We were overwhelmed in minutes. Most of my men died without even drawing a sword or hurling a javelin. A few of us formed a square and fought, but it was hopeless. I was knocked out and awoke at dusk in a clearing by a swamp. Those who had survived the fight were being sacrificed all around.

"Three of us managed to run into the trees. We wandered and hid all night. This morning we met these other three and then you."

"Could you find the clearing again?"

Vulso shrugged. "I don't know. But I am certain the village is close, down this road."

"Very well. You men," Balbus indicated the front row of the centuria. "Take the centurion and the other men back to the mules. Make sure their wounds are tended and that they are given fresh uniforms and weapons. The rest of you stay here." Balbus pulled his horse's head around and set off down the road. The men Balbus had indicated led the pitiful survivors of the Fourth centuria in the opposite direction. A hubbub of conversation broke out.

"Ants," Sextus Livius said, bleakly.

"Nonsense," Herod said. "It was a minor skirmish. I've always said sending out a single centuria is asking for trouble. Too tempting a target for some group of disaffected hotheads."

"That was more than group of hotheads," Appius said. "Vulso said there were hundreds of them. That's warriors from at least fifteen or twenty villages. That takes planning."

"Not necessarily," Drusus contributed, angrily. "That Vulso's no good. He is too fond of the wine and his men don't respect him. He can't even keep them under control in camp. I'd say he's exaggerating the numbers a good few times to make himself look better. I'll bet his centuria was straggling all along the road, not even in a defensive formation. They were probably picked off piecemeal and many of them ran off into the forest."

"I think they were allowed to escape," Lucius said. His companions stopped talking and stared at him.

"What do you mean?" Appius asked.

"When Titus and I were captured on the road when I was on my way to join the Legion, I wanted to escape. Titus said there was no point. He said that the barbarians knew the forests so much better than us, it would just be a game for them to catch us. How did Vulso and the others escape so easily, especially if there were as many barbarians as he says?"

"I told you he was lying," Drusus said, "but I agree with Lucius. It does seem strange."

As they were thinking about this, Balbus returned.

"Move out," he ordered. "We're going to the village ahead."

Lucius and the others quickly tightened their formation and set off at double time. They had been marching for barely five minutes when Lucius heard noises from the column ahead. It was a low groan that swelled as it came closer. Eventually, he saw the cause.

At first, Lucius noticed it on just one tree—a severed human head, nailed to the trunk by a long iron spike driven through the right eye. Then he noticed another and another, on both sides of the road. The heads of Vulso's Fourth centuria, sacrificed to the Gods of the forest and displayed as a warning to others.

The pace of the cohort's march quickened, as if everyone was eager to pass the gruesome display. Then they were in the open. In front of the men was a large, cultivated clearing, divided into rectangles stretching toward a moderate-sized village, backed by a large swamp. The fields grew mostly wheat and barley, which was already turning golden in the sun. Lucius's eye, trained through growing up on his family's farm, saw a good crop only a week or two from harvesting.

On the far side of the fields, surrounded by smaller patches of peas, beans and lentils, Lucius counted seven mud-walled, thatched buildings, all the same except that one in the centre was larger. Balbus ordered his centuria to spread out in a line along the edge of the fields. The other centuria were doing the same, forming a semi-circle around the village with each end anchored on the edge of the swamp. Figures were running about in confusion between the buildings.

"If anyone tries to break out," Balbus said, "kill them."

A rasping noise ran through the centuria as men drew their swords and hefted their shields. After seeing what had happened to their comrades, no one was in the mood to question an order to kill.

"Centurion Balbus!" The commander of the cohort and other senior officers rode along the line to where Lucius's centurion sat on his horse. "You will be given the honour of sweeping the village. I want a thorough search. Bring the head man and anything you find directly to me."

Balbus saluted and barked orders at the centuria. They moved forward into a loose rectangular formation, ten men wide and eight deep. The other centuria spread out to fill in the gap that they left in the line.

Lucius and the others moved forward, trampling the barley beneath their heavy marching sandals. At the edge of the buildings, they were met by an old man who gave a tentative Roman salute. Balbus pushed his horse past him.

"Search the buildings and bring me anything suspicious." Balbus ordered. Then he turned to Lucius. "Signifer, stand by me in the centre."

Lucius saluted and followed Balbus's horse to the large open area in front of the big building. Balbus dismounted and handed the reins to another soldier. The rest of the centuria split into smaller groups and disappeared into the houses.

The village was the same as countless others Lucius had seen scattered throughout the forests of Germania and had the same rich collection of smells common to a farm anywhere. Each rectangular building was divided into a communal living area where an extended family—sometimes as many as twenty men women and children—worked, ate and slept, and a barn where the livestock, a bullock, goats, chickens and sometimes a pig, lived at night and in the winter. It was a good arrangement. The livestock was protected from predators and their body heat provided warmth for the family living quarters, but for Lucius, growing up as he had where living and farming were kept separate, it seemed primitive.

Ragged women, children and old men huddled in small groups all around. Some stared defiantly at the Roman soldiers while others busied themselves tending the scattered cooking fires. Children peered fearfully from behind their mothers or older sisters. The old man who had met them at the edge of the village hovered uncertainly in front of them, wringing his hands in supplication and chattering on in the unintelligible local dialect.

"Where's that damned interpreter?" Balbus asked, irritably. "We need someone to translate this gibberish."

As if in answer to the centurion's question, Freya appeared from between two buildings, strode over and saluted.

"About time," Balbus said. "What's this old savage saying?"

Freya flashed Lucius a look of barely disguised contempt that sent a shiver through him and began talking to the old man.

"He wants to know why the honourable centurion has brought his soldiers into his village," she explained to Balbus. "He says they are peaceful farmers and want no trouble."

Balbus snorted loudly. "Peaceful farmers are they? Then ask him where all the men are. I see only women, children and old goats like him."

Freya spoke and then translated the answer. "He says they are away on a hunting trip."

"Hunting Roman soldiers, I don't doubt. Tell him I think they are out in the forest, celebrating the sacrifice of a Roman centuria."

As Freya translated, the old man became agitated, shaking his head strongly and spreading his arms in a pleading gesture.

"He says no," Freya explained. "He says he is a friend of the Romans. He doesn't know anything about dead soldiers."

"Or about heads nailed to trees, I suppose," Balbus said. "Ask him—"

The interrogation was interrupted by a commotion from the largest building. Herod burst into the open, holding a two-foot-long object in his right hand. Both the object and Herod's arms and legs were covered in, what Lucius realized as he approached, was cow dung.

"I found this in the byre," Herod said, holding the object forward and scraping some of the dirt off. Lucius was shocked to see that it was the top portion of a Roman centuria standard, like the one he held.

The old man was frantic, tugging at Freya and talking wildly.

"He says it is very old. From the wars many years ago," Freya translated as quickly as she could. "He had forgotten it had been buried in the barn."

"Old?" Balbus said with a sneer. "As old as yesterday. Bring him along," he ordered Freya. Balbus waved to the soldier holding the reins. The man knelt and Balbus stepped on his back and mounted his horse. "Signifer, remain here with our standard and collect anything else that is found." Balbus trotted out into the fields with Freya and the old man struggling to keep up.

Lucius looked around. The villagers were extremely agitated now. Those who had been working had stopped tending the fires and stared in fear at the Roman soldiers. Women were gathering their children together protectively. Quite a few of the children looked terrified and were crying, and several of the women had broken out into a high-pitched wail. Lucius felt no pity. The image of the heads of his comrades nailed to trees was vivid in his mind.

Drusus came up and dropped a *gladius* at Lucius's feet. The blade was rusted and broken. "Not from yesterday," Drusus remarked, "but it shows they've been fighting us for a long time. These people have no honour. The so-called warriors run off to hide and leave their women and children to face our anger." He spat loudly onto the dust. "We need to teach them a lesson."

More and more of the centuria were in the open now and the pile of Roman equipment at Lucius feet had grown. Much of it was rusted and it was all old and broken. None of it seemed new enough to be from the Fourth. Lucius felt a twinge of unease.

"Most of this stuff is old," he said. "Some of it must date from the days of Julius Caesar, not yesterday."

"So what," Herod said. "We've got the standard and where are all the warriors? These people are part of it, all right. By all the Gods, they're uncivilized. Nailing heads to trees. They're worse than wild animals!"

The soldiers close by mumbled agreement, but Lucius's mind flashed back to the Sicambri nailed to the wooden crosses outside the fort on the

Lupia. How was that any better than nailing heads to trees?

Balbus returned and reined to a stop in a cloud of dust beside Lucius. The soldiers looked up expectantly. "Burn everything," Balbus shouted. "If it won't burn, smash it. Kill all the livestock and the old men and round up the women and children. We'll take them back to sell as slaves. If any resist, kill them, too. Put up a post and crucify this old man as a warning."

The soldiers jumped to obey and Lucius noted that several looked more than pleased with their assignment.

The next hour was a chaos of screams, wails, bellows, bleats, crashes and the crackle of burning thatch. A few women tried to flee or attacked the soldiers, but they were quickly subdued or killed. The old men accepted their fate with resignation, and despite himself Lucius was impressed by the dignity with which they met death. He wondered if he would have that much courage in similar circumstances. The children were the most difficult, screaming and running everywhere, dodging the slower, armoured soldiers with ease.

Eventually, everyone had been herded together and the last lowing cow slaughtered. The women and children, many still wailing and weeping, were led out of the village. Bodies lay scattered in pitiful heaps around the open spaces, and flames still leaped from a couple of buildings. The old man who had come out to meet them hung dying from a crude crucifix outside the largest building.

The buildings burned fast once the thatch caught, flaring up in a spectacular, noisy inferno, but quickly dying down as the roofs collapsed in on themselves. The smell of roasted meat, from the animals trapped in their burning barns, competed with the acrid smell of burned thatch and the subtler odour of blood. Lucius watched as a chicken, its tail scorched, scratched around in the dust beside a woman's body.

"Signifer, bring the standard," Balbus ordered, "and collect all the evidence. The rest of the centuria will form up across the fields."

Lucius saluted as Balbus rode out behind the captives.

As Balbus led the rest of the centuria out of the devastated village, Lucius and his *contuberium* picked up the rusted Roman weapons.

"That'll teach them a lesson," Herod said. "The other villages will think twice before they attack Roman soldiers. Here, hold this," Herod handed the still filthy, broken standard to Appius, knelt beside a stone water trough and began washing his hands and arms.

Appius stared at the standard, turning it round and round.

"Might as well clean that, too," Drusus suggested.

Appius went to the trough and began cleaning off the dirt. The others stood around, waiting for their two companions to finish.

"I'm not so sure this will discourage the other villages," Lucius said, thoughtfully.

"They had to be punished, though," Drusus said. "If we let them get away with attacking Romans, they'll just become more and more arrogant. Besides, there must have been warriors from a lot more than this village. This sends *them* a message."

"Of course, they had to be punished," Lucius said, "It's just that in the past the more villages we've burned, the more battles we've had to fight."

"Then we'll burn more villages and fight more battles," Herod said, standing and shaking water off his hands. "Eventually they'll get the message not to cross us."

"We may be giving the wrong people the message." Everyone turned to look at Appius, who was standing by the trough examining one of the medallions attached to the broken fragment of standard.

"What do you mean?" Herod asked.

"Look at this," Appius held the medallion forward and the others crowded round to see. "See that," he gestured at a three-pointed trident engraved on the medallion.

"Neptune's trident," Drusus said. "So what?"

"That's the symbol of the Legion this centuria belonged to. It's not a scorpion."

Everyone stared at the medallion as the implication of Appius's words sank in.

"And look here," Appius turned the standard over. The iron clasp holding the medallion onto the shaft was deeply rusted. "This is old. It's been buried in that dung heap for a long time. As far as I know, the only Legion called Neptune that has ever been in Germania was with Caesar, more than sixty years ago. This is not from the Fourth centuria."

"Then these people had nothing to do with yesterday's massacre?" young Servius asked.

"Of course they did," Herod said angrily. "Just because this is from when they killed some other Romans years ago, doesn't mean they weren't involved yesterday. Where are all the warriors from the village?"

Almost as if in reply, Lucius heard shouts from the edge of the field, followed by the clash of weapons. The group rushed into the open and looked around. The captured women and children stood surrounded by the rest of Lucius's centuria. To their right, a band of Germanic warriors was battling desperately to reach them.

The Bructeri warriors had no chance. Lucius guessed there were about fifteen men and they were being systematically cut down by the Roman soldiers who were converging on them from all sides. Balbus sat on his horse shouting orders and the wails of the women and children blended with the helpless battle cries of the doomed warriors.

It was over by the time Lucius and the others crossed the field. The bodies of the warriors were stretched back in a line to the edge of the trees where the cleaned carcasses of a large buck and two does lay discarded. With a sick feeling in the pit of his stomach, Lucius realized what it meant. The men had come out of the trees, seen their women, children and burned village, and gone berserk. Without any thought, they had dropped what they were carrying and charged, hopelessly, to save their families. It was incredibly brave, and utterly futile. But what really tightened the knot in

Lucius's stomach was the sight of the dead deer. The men of the village *had* been away hunting, just as the crucified old chief had said.

But Lucius had no time to dwell on it. The cohort was busy forming up in marching order, dragging the terrified, tearful, women away from the bodies of their husbands and sons, and setting fire to the fields of grain. Balbus was once again shouting orders.

"Hurry! You men are to lead the column back, and I want you to remove the heads of our soldiers from the trees as you go. Replace them with the heads of these barbarians so that the rest of the cohort can look upon a defeated enemy instead of their comrades."

The centuria set about its grim task. Lucius noticed that all of the heads had a complex twisted Bructeri knot tattooed on their left cheek, just as Freya had described when she had told him about the tribal tattoos.

The thought of his friend made Lucius look around. He spotted her red hair immediately. She was standing by the cohort commander, who was giving orders for the march, but she was staring at the soldiers taking the heads. Beside the officer in his polished armour and red-crested helmet, Freya looked wild and primitive with her fiery hair and wolf-skin tunic—and her gaze was intense.

Lucius felt more alone than he had since Titus had died. He and Freya had always been different, but they had managed to be friends despite that. But Lucius had an uncomfortable, growing sense of distance between them. Was it this afternoon and other events like it? Or was it something else, something more? Whatever it was, Lucius was certain he could explain everything if they just had a chance to talk.

The commander said something to Freya, but she was either too distracted or too stubborn to respond. The officer raised his baton and struck her on the shoulder. Freya didn't flinch. She merely turned her gaze toward the man. If a look had the power to kill, the cohort commander would have been lying withered at Freya's feet in an instant. Instead he shook his head and turned away.

Freya looked over at Lucius. For an instant, her face softened, but then the mask of hatred was drawn down again. Lucius couldn't hold her look. He lowered his head and stared at the ground. When he looked up again, Freya was gone.

Lucius felt as if he were standing on the edge of a black void and slowly, as if in a dream, he was falling forward. If he fell, he would be swallowed, lost.

Cursing, Lucius spun around. He almost fell over the headless body of a Bructeri warrior. Anger overwhelmed him. It was all this man's fault—this pitiful ragged corpse was to blame for everything! Lucius drew back his foot and kicked. It felt good. The pain in his foot reminded him that he was alive. He kicked again. It was almost funny, they way the body jerked and flopped as his foot made contact.

Lucius would have kept going until he collapsed from exhaustion if Drusus and Herod had not soothed him and led him over to join the rest of his centuria. He didn't see Freya watching him, her face a confusion of conflicting emotions.

Freya

"I should have your head." Arminius stood facing Arnulf, surrounded by the major chiefs of the local tribes. All were heavily armed with axes, swords and bows, and each wore an animal skin to denote his tribe and status—wolf, bear or stag. Even amidst this savage finery, Arminius, in his mixture of tribal clothing and Roman armour, dominated. His voice was soft, but the threat in it commanded attention. "You have jeopardized everything for the sake of a little greed and glory. All depends upon the Romans suspecting nothing before we are ready to strike, and your Sicambri rabble could not resist slaughtering an isolated centuria and giving warning."

"You call the Sicambri rabble?" Arnulf tensed, his hand moving toward his sword.

"I do," Arminius replied, "an undisciplined rabble."

Arnulf drew his sword and held the point to Arminius's throat. "No one insults the Sicambri."

"Go ahead," Arminius said, lifting his head to expose more of his neck to the blade. A murmur ran through the assembled warriors. Very slowly, Freya unhooked her sling and dug a stone out of her pouch. Arnulf hesitated.

"Kill me," Arminius went on. "I do not wish to live if we cannot win and we cannot win if we are not disciplined. Either I lead and we win or I die here and now."

Freya slipped the loop of her sling over her finger and slid the stone into the leather pouch. She might not be able to save Arminius, but Arnulf would be dead before her uncle's body hit the ground.

Arnulf's eyes flickered uncertainly. His sword point wavered and lowered. A sigh ran through the watchers.

Arminius stepped forward and clasped Arnulf's arm in a gesture of friendship. "No one doubts that the Sicambri are brave, or that they can kill Romans," Arminius explained with a smile, "But what we plan here requires more than bravery. We do not want to kill Romans." Arminius paused for effect. Every eye in the clearing was on him. "We want to kill *all* Romans. We can kill a centuria here, a cohort there, perhaps even an entire Legion, but that is not enough. To win our freedom, we must kill every Roman soldier in Germania. We must show Rome that it is not worth its time or sacrifice to fight us. Then the Romans will leave us alone.

"To do all that, we need to be clever. We need to lull these Legions into thinking that we are subdued, beaten, a spent force that can pose no threat. Only then, when they are relaxed, can we spring. If we continue to go around killing isolated patrols and centuria, it will put them on guard. Then it will be impossible to take them by surprise."

"I know what you say is true," Arnulf said, "but it is difficult to smile while they walk through our lands taking what they want. The young men are impatient, they want blood."

"And when we do attack they will bathe in blood. But for now, you must make them wait."

"I will try."

A large man with a Bructeri knot tattooed on his cheek stepped forward. "I am Sigmund of the Bructeri. You know me and I would speak."

"All will listen," Arminius said.

"The Bructeri have suffered most from the Sicambri actions. Several peaceful villages have been burned, warriors killed, and women and children taken into slavery, simply because the Romans have not the wit to realize that an attack occurring in one place does not mean those closest to it were responsible."

"The Sicambri are sorry for your losses," Arnulf growled, "but it was the Romans who did the deeds. Surely you do not seek restitution."

"I do not. I wish to thank the Sicambri."

"Thank?" Arnulf asked.

"The Bructeri have been at peace for many years. Our crops have flourished and the hunting has been good. Many children have lived and we have grown strong. Because of this, a number of our village elders have spoken against the Cherusci plan. They have said, 'why should we poke a stick into a hornets' nest when the hornets are asleep.' Many have listened to them and agreed.

"The Sicambri have changed this. Because they attacked the Romans on Bructeri lands, the hornets have woken up. They have shown us that we have become soft, and that we too must now awake. Every Bructeri warrior will march with Arminius."

A rumble of approval ran through the crowd. Arminius stepped forward and embraced Sigmund. "We are united then," he said. "Now, let me show you a part of the plan."

Arminius led the way through the trees to an open area on the slope of the hill. "This is Kalkriese Hill," he said when everyone had gathered. "It is the most northerly place where the uplands push into the great swamp. Anyone travelling west by this route must round the hill between this slope we stand upon and the swamp. An army moving this way must stretch out on a narrow path and cannot spread out easily, either up the hill or into the swamp. It is an ideal place for an ambush. This is where the last of the Romans will die."

"But the Romans do not normally travel this way," a Marsi warrior said. "They use the river to the south."

"Then we must make them travel this way," Arminius said.

"There is more than one path," said a Tencteri, pointing to a narrow thread of hard ground that led away from the point of the Kalkriese Hill, over the swamp toward some low, sandy hills to the north. "What if they choose to go that way?"

"We shall take that choice away from them," Arminius replied. "Paths across swamps can easily become swamps again."

The warriors fell silent imagining the battle that would be fought below them.

"It will not work," Sigmund said at length. "The plan is to destroy all three Legions?"

Arminius nodded.

"And they will be marching through here in narrow file, squeezed between the hill and the swamp?"

"Yes," Arminius said.

"In that case," Sigmund went on, "their column will stretch for near two of their miles. When we attack here, we attack only the head, perhaps half a mile. I agree, this is a good place and we can kill those we catch here, but what of the others? Two Legions will be behind. What is to stop them forming a defensive square and holding out? They could even retreat south to the river and be rescued by their boats. This does not sound like the overwhelming victory you promised."

"You were not listening closely, Sigmund," Arminius said with a smile. Freya was amazed at his calm. "I said this is where we will kill the last of the Romans. What happens here will occur on the third day. If we all work together and keep to the plan, there will be less than one Legion left by the time we have herded them to Kalkriese Hill."

Freya felt a thrill of excitement pass through her. Her uncle had thought of everything. She stood listening hard as Arminius outlined the rest of his plan. People were given specific tasks, times were set and ways to pass messages rapidly established. The sun was turning the western sky a fiery orange by the time everyone drifted away, leaving Arminius, Freya, Arnulf and a few Cherusci and Sicambri warriors on the hillside.

"It will work," Arnulf said.

"Because of you," Arminius said with a smile.

"What?" Freya couldn't control herself. "The whole plan almost failed because of the Sicambri attack on the centuria!"

Freya was amazed to see both men burst out laughing. "I don't understand," she said, helplessly.

Arminius wiped his eyes and spoke. "Even you believed our little theatre."

"Theatre! But you fought! Arnulf nearly killed you because you were so angry at the Sicambri attack."

"Just words," Arnulf said. "Although, when I had my sword at your throat, I was tempted. You can be annoyingly arrogant sometimes."

The two men laughed again.

"All right, all right!" Arminius said, taking pity on Freya. "I knew the Bructeri did not wish to fight, but if we are to succeed, they must. The battle will be fought on their lands.

"Arnulf and a few warriors visited the Bructeri village," Arminius became serious, "and one of our scouts took word of this back to the Romans. As soon as I heard the centuria was to leave, I sent word to Arnulf, who was waiting in the forest."

"The attack was easy," Arnulf contributed. "They had no idea we were waiting, and no Sicambri was even badly wounded. We killed most of them and allowed a few to escape to meet the cohort sent to find them."

"You knew the Romans would burn the village," Freya said, staring at Arminius as the enormity of what she was hearing dawned. "You even knew that the men were away hunting. You planned it that way, so that the village would be undefended."

"I did," Arminius said.

"Old men, women and children died, in that village and the others the Romans attacked in the following days," Freya said in horror. "You killed them!"

Arminius nodded acknowledgement. "It's true," he said, his voice serious and sad. "I knew the Romans would retaliate against the nearest village. But I also knew the retaliation against innocent villages would force the Bructeri to take sides. Remember, I told you we had to become as hard as steel if we are to succeed?"

"Yes," Freya said quietly.

"That is what we have become. I sacrificed a few villages and some innocents so the Bructeri would be with us, so we would have a chance of throwing the Romans out of our lands. If we succeed, countless Bructeri, Marsi, Cherusci, Sicambri and others will grow up in freedom, not as slaves of Rome.

"Is it a fair trade?" Arminius shrugged. "I cannot say. I don't think fairness has a place in our lives any more, but it is a trade I made and one I will have to live with. There is no going back now."

The three stood in silence watching the fragile sunset colours slowly fade. Freya knew her uncle's decision must have been immensely difficult to make. She knew he wasn't a cruel man by nature, and that the choice he had made was essential to the plan's success. Still, she couldn't get the image of the burning village and the hopeless charge of the Bructeri hunters to try and save their families out of her head. She realized now what becoming hardened meant. But could *she* do it? If it came down to it, could she kill Lucius to free her people? Obviously it would be a good trade—one Roman life for an entire tribe's freedom, but was that what was most important? What was their freedom worth if it was based on decisions like that?

A disturbance behind the group made them all turn their heads. A Cherusci warrior had emerged from the trees. He was grim-faced and dressed for battle in a belted wolfskin with the head, complete with snarling teeth, thrown over his right shoulder. On his left arm he carried a round shield and in his right hand, a gleaming battle-axe.

Arminius stood and approached the man. Freya held her breath and waited to see what would happen. For what seemed an age, the pair stood a pace apart, staring at each other. Then the stranger stepped forward and embraced Arminius. "I have come to fight for our homeland," he said.

"And you are the most welcome of all my warriors," Arminius said, returning the embrace.

The pair separated and Arminius introduced the stranger to the group. "Now I know we shall win. We are united. This is Freya's uncle—and my brother—Lothar."

Herculaneum

The reign of Titus Caesar: Year 1
24th august, 10:00 p.m.

My story approaches a climax as, I think, does our adventure here. The shaking of the ground has eased, but Pallas has reported that vast glowing clouds occasionally move with stunning rapidity down the flanks of the mountain. None have approached this way but I fear that, should they do so, our end would be swift indeed. I will not regret a swift end, as opposed to the slow decay of age, but I do wish for time to finish my story. I suppose, since I cannot avoid or control what happens here, I must simply accept what will be.

Not so everyone. You know of the flight of my companions in the villa, but loyal Pallas and I have been visited by our neighbours from the northwest. All day they sat, as we have, watching the mountain and hoping. They observed the flight of refugees towards Neapolis, but could not bring themselves to join the flow, trusting the sturdiness of their villa and the benevolence of the Gods.

As darkness fell, they finally decided to join the flight, but the way was packed with terrified people and landslips had made the road almost impassible. They turned back intending to go to Herculaneum itself and try to take passage on a boat across the bay. It was during this endeavour that Pallas saw them passing and hailed them.

Most generously, they offered to carry me with them to the town, but I declined, not wishing to spend what little time I have left in uncomfortable travel. However, I urged noble Pallas to join them, but he refused most firmly, stating that he had lived for so long to take care of my interests that he knew not what he would do if he did not have me. Never has a slave deserved his freedom more.

After our neighbours left, Pallas confided that he did not think their venture would end well. He had been down to the shore and, apart from the undulations of the water, could not determine where the ground ended and the sea began, so thick was the carpet of light grey rock that floated upon its surface. He doubted that any vessels could either arrive or leave Herculaneum's harbour.

Pallas also brought me a report from the roof. Although it is now night, the lightning playing around Vesuvius gives glimpses of the Hades in which we find ourselves. The cloud still belches forth from the summit in a boiling mass that must reach to the realm of the Gods itself. The land beneath is grey and, with the exception of the confused mass of people and terrified animals seeking escape along the road, devoid of life.

To the south and east, on the slopes of the mountain itself, the devastation worsens. Although it is difficult to see more than glimpses through the swirling ash, Pallas assures me that the ash has reached the height of the olive trees in places and that vast boulders rolling down the slopes have created great paths of devastation.

Pallas asked me what I thought we had done to deserve such wrath from the Gods. I could not answer in the general. Certainly, every man carries with him a burden of evil deeds he would rather not have done, but I doubt our companions in Pompeii, many of whom must already have perished, carried any greater load than others, and there must be multitudes in the Senate of Rome and the halls of Kings and Emperors who deserve the Gods' retribution more.

As for the specific, I take what is happening to me as only my due. I did not deserve to survive so many years ago, nor to exist for so long after in such relative comfort. But I am not so vain as to think this vast destruction is simply the Gods answer to me. They have had many opportunities to dispose of me before without the broad cruelty of this great event.

On the contrary, I am becoming convinced that the Gods hold off on my destruction so I may complete my task. This being the case, I had best not strain their patience.

In the days following the destruction of the village, Varus sent out his cohorts to devastate the surrounding Bructeri lands, but we were never again met with violence. On the contrary, we would most often arrive at a village to find that even the chickens had fled. We burned many abandoned farms, but soon lapsed back into our previous complacency.

Varus became ever more frustrated—angry that he was being deprived of his victory and urged us on to even greater acts of destruction—but what could we do? If there was no one to fight, what honour was there in burning empty houses and slaughtering the few chickens that were left behind?

That summer was the warmest and driest I remember in all my years in Germania. On several occasions we had been called out to battle small, carelessly-set fires that threatened to spread to the surrounding forests. The weather remained dry and sunny into September, but the evening chill and the turning trees told us winter was coming and all were eager to head back along the Lupia to the relative comfort of Vetera.

We had begun loading the baggage train when we heard that Varus had one more task for us. News was reaching us that the campaign in Illyria was finally going well and that Germanicus and his Legions would be returning to Germania in the coming months. Arminius brought word that the Bructeri, far to the north of the area we had devastated in August, were rising in revolt.

They were far enough away from our forts or route home that they posed no immediate threat, but Varus saw one last opportunity to wrest some glory from the disappointing summer. When Germanicus returned, he would be reduced once more to a Provincial Governor, overseeing petty squabbles and road building while others led the Legions on campaigns ever farther east.

We all groaned at the news. Instead of a comparatively easy march due west along good roads with river-supplied forts to stay in each night, we would have to march in a broad arc northward. We would have the forested hills to our left and the endless swamps to our right, and the roads or paths would be rough and slow. Every night, we would have to search for a tiny patch of flat dry ground on which to build our night time encampment.

The soldier's gossip held that Varus had originally ordered one Legion to head north, but that Arminius had convinced him the revolt was serious and that the chances for a decisive battle were excellent. At least in the last part Arminius told the truth.

The Trap

The reign of Augustus Caesar: Year 36
14/15 September

W e've been walking for ten days and we're still in the same place," Drusus complained.

"Stop moaning," Lucius said. "We're making progress."

"It doesn't feel like it. I'm certain that tree over there," Drusus indicated a large oak beside the path, "is the same one I used to sleep against when we were back at the Weser River. It looks identical. And that swamp, it's the one I almost sank into back in Junius."

"When we started out, "Lucius said with a resigned air, "I thought that the Legion being spread out along these narrow paths was a good thing. Balbus would be too far away to hear us talk or threaten us with flogging. After ten days of listening to Drusus complain, though, I almost look forward to a good flogging."

"Very funny," Drusus said, "but what is the point of all this?"

"I'm afraid, Lucius, that I'm with Drusus on this one," Herod remarked. "All we're doing is extending a worthless summer into a worthless September."

"Exactly," Drusus agreed, enthusiastically. "Same old deserted villages. Same old chasing after shadows. Varus won't find his Triumph here."

"Who is Varus?" Lucius asked ironically. "I haven't seen him in days. If he's still up front with the 18th, he must be a good four miles ahead of us, the way we're stretched out along this farmer's track."

"Count yourself lucky," Drusus said. "I was talking to one of the 17th yesterday, and he told me it's chaos in the middle of the column. They've got the baggage train and the oxen are impossible. Something spooks them, and one'll go blundering off into the swamp. It takes ten men an hour to get the stupid beast out."

"And," Herod added, "the 18th at the front have to clear the path of fallen trees and widen it at every corner."

"Well," Lucius said, "that explains why we stop and start all the time. I don't think we've covered ten miles on the best day. At this rate, it'll be year's end before we get back to Vetera."

"At least by then it'll be raining," Drusus said. "I never thought I'd say this in this country, but I'd love to see some clouds and a good downpour. Everything's so dry that if the underbrush gets going the whole forest will go up in flames. We'll all be up to our necks in the swamp, praying for the wind to change."

"Might be sooner than you think," Appius contributed. "There's a lot of smoke up front."

Lucius squinted ahead. It was difficult to see far through the trees, but the sky did appear hazy and the sharp smell of wood smoke caught his nose.

"Someone probably forgot to put out their cooking fire this morning," he commented.

The men marched on in silence until they were ordered to halt beside a small lake. Thick clouds of grey smoke drifted across the open patch of blue sky and darkened the noon sun.

"That's more than a cooking fire." Drusus expressed all their thoughts.

"The wind's not blowing toward us," Lucius said, watching the smoke and the tree tops. "But I wouldn't like to be with the 17th. They must be in the middle of it."

For a nervous hour, no orders or news came back and Lucius and the others stood and waited in mounting frustration. There was some discussion about whether the fire was the result of carelessness or a lightning strike, but mostly the men just watched the smoke clouds roll out over the lake. Gradually, the wind swung around and the smell of smoke grew stronger. Fragments of black ash drifted down amongst them. Eventually, the order to move forward was passed down.

"Again we have to go and get the 17th out of trouble," Drusus joked, but no one laughed.

As they marched, the lake beside them gave way to swamp and then the relatively solid ground of an open meadow. Good place to camp, Lucius thought. He was distracted by a loud crash from up ahead. "Tree down!" someone yelled.

Drusus cursed loudly. "Another delay."

Lucius strained to see what was going on ahead. The fire was still some way off, although he could see occasional flames shooting above the treetops.

About twenty paces away, the path curved to the left around the hillside. Lucius couldn't see the downed tree, but the centuria at the corner had put down their shields and were moving up to remove the obstacle. Lucius didn't envy them, it was hard work moving one of these big forest trees. They'd be stuck here for a while.

"Why did the tree fall down?" Appius asked no one in particular.

"Are you beginning a philosophical discussion to pass the time?" Drusus asked. "Why does a tree fall? Why have the Gods placed us here? Why do my feet hurt?"

"No," Appius said, patiently, "but the fire is still a long way off."

"It was probably old, like the rest of us are going to be if we don't get a move on," Drusus said.

A thicker swirl of smoke blew past, making Lucius's eyes sting. He coughed and rubbed the tears away. There was no doubt about it— something was going on ahead. He stared into the distance, trying to make out what was happening. Twenty paces in front of him, someone had fallen down. As Lucius peered, another man fell, this one with an arrow sticking out of his neck.

"Ambush!" Lucius yelled. "Testudo!"

All around, shields went up, but the centuria wasn't in a tight formation and there were gaps. Arrows thudded into upraised shields, and someone screamed in pain.

When the hail of arrows stopped, Lucius lowered his shield and tried to organize the centuria into a tighter defensive formation to face the wild attack he expected at any minute from the trees. But nothing happened. Lucius scanned the underbrush. There was no sign anyone had been there. A group at the edge of the centuria began to edge toward the trees.

"Hold your position," Balbus shouted from the path. He was dismounted, but his red helmet crest stood out above the nervous men. "No one is to break formation. What are the casualties?"

Lucius turned back from the trees and looked around at his contuberium. Sextus Livius sat to his right on the edge of the path, his head tilted awkwardly to one side and a long feathered shaft sticking almost vertically from the join between his neck and shoulder. He was breathing with difficulty and a strange rattle emerged from his open mouth. Sextus Vipsanius was fussing over him, but there was little he could do.

With an obvious effort, Sextus Livius looked up at his friend. "And so it begins," he croaked. He shuddered once and fell forward.

Sextus Vipsanius, tears pouring down his cheeks, stood beside his fallen friend and screamed incoherently. Lucius stepped toward him, intending to offer what comfort he could, but Sextus ignored him. Hefting his shield, Sextus pushed Lucius out of the way and barged past Drusus toward the trees. When he reached what little open ground there was between the column and the forest, he stopped and clashed his spear against his shield. "You want to fight? Here I am. Come and fight," he yelled. The action was taken up by others in the centuria.

"Back in the ranks," Balbus shouted as he advanced toward Sextus.

Lucius caught a movement in the trees out of the corner of his eye. A sling. The rock caught Sextus Vipsanius dead centre in the forehead, below the ridge of his helmet. He collapsed like a half empty sack of grain.

Instinctively, men raised their shields, but no more rocks came. With Balbus shouting orders, the centuria formed a tight rectangle and swept through the trees by the path. They found nothing but a few patches of crushed underbrush where the archers had hidden.

By the time the men returned to the path, word had come back from the Legate that the legion was to establish a camp and dig fortifications out on the meadow. Lucius's centuria was one of those assigned to protect the others while they dug the ditches and piled the walls. They were stretched in a line along the edge of the meadow, facing the trees. Drusus was to Lucius's right and Herod to his left.

"Must have been a small raiding party," Drusus said. "They were attracted by the fire and took the opportunity to lob a few arrows at us. I thought the damned Auxiliaries were supposed to clear the woods on the line of march."

"Can't trust the Auxiliaries," Herod said, "and anyway, we're so spread out along this path that there must be gaps you could march a Legion through."

"Well, there's certainly a gap between us and the 17th now," Drusus commented. "That fire went through between us and them. Thank Mithras the wind's dropped. The fire'll burn itself out soon enough."

Lucius looked to the north. The darkening sky was still heavy with smoke, but the flames had died down to an occasional flare up and a dull glow.

"What if the fire wasn't an accident?" Lucius asked. "What if it was deliberately set, part of an attack?"

"Of course it was an accident," Herod said. "You know how dry these forests are this year, how quickly a fire can get out of control. Besides, if it was an attack, it was a very weak one, a few arrows and a slingshot! Even counting the two Sextus's, we couldn't have suffered more than half a dozen casualties.

"The Bructeri just want to keep out of our way so we can go back across the Rhenus and leave them alone for the winter."

"What if it wasn't the Bructeri?" Lucius asked.

"What do you mean?" Drusus asked. "Who else would it be? This is their land we're in."

"Have the Bructeri ever attacked us with slings?"

"No," Drusus answered, "but that doesn't mean they don't have them. They've hardly attacked us at all."

"What colour are the Bructeri arrows?"

Drusus thought for a minute. "White, I think."

"They are," Lucius confirmed, "but the arrow that killed Sextus Livius was red."

"So," Herod said, "some Bructeri decides that red arrows look better than white. What are you trying to say?"

"I'm not sure," Lucius said, slowly. "But these tribes set much store in things like their tattoos, which animal skin they wear and the colour of their arrows. I cannot see them changing that lightly." He paused. "But what worries me more is this. Herod, you always say a force of three Legions is unbeatable."

Herod nodded.

"The tribes must know that, too. What if the fire was deliberately set to split us up?"

"Then why didn't they attack us," Drusus asked, peering nervously into the gathering darkness between the trees. "There's no way any help could have gotten back to us through the fire."

"True," Lucius agreed, "but we were beside this meadow. We could form up here and hold off any attack they could throw at us."

"So they made a mistake in setting the fire too close to the meadow," Herod said.

"No," Lucius replied. "Maybe they're just not in a hurry."

"What do you mean?" Drusus asked.

"What are we going to do next?" Lucius asked.

"We're not turning back and abandoning the other Legions," Drusus said indignantly. "Tomorrow we'll press forward and link up with the 17th and 18th. Then everything will be fine again."

"Possibly," Lucius acknowledged. "But what if the attack on us was simply meant to harass us and put us on edge."

"It certainly did that," Drusus said.

"What if the major attack was on the 17th north of the fire? We couldn't help them because of the fire and I doubt if the 18th could have turned around on this narrow track and offered any assistance. The 17th would have been on their own —one Legion attacked by the enemy, not three."

"Nonsense," Herod scoffed. "You're giving the barbarians far too much credit. The Bructeri couldn't organize something as big as you propose and, even if they could, there are hardly enough of them to attack even one Legion."

Lucius was quiet for a long moment. Everyone strained nervously to look into the trees. It was dusk and the darkness could hide all manner of horrors.

"What if it's not just the Bructeri," Lucius said quietly.

"Who else could it be?" Drusus asked.

"The Cherusci use slings and red arrows."

"The Auxiliaries?"

Lucius shrugged. "Why hadn't they cleared the woods? Why weren't they here to help us?"

"A hundred reasons," Herod said, but he sounded unsure. "They missed the small band that attacked us. They couldn't get back past the fire."

"Perhaps." Lucius acknowledged.

They lapsed into silence, each wrapped in his own fears.

Lucius wasn't convinced by his own argument, he was simply speculating. But something odd was going on, and what if he *was* right? He hadn't mentioned this to his companions, but when he'd seen the movement in the underbrush as the stone that killed Sextus Vipsanius was fired, he had caught a glimpse of what might have been red hair. He wasn't certain, everything had happened so quickly, but wasn't Freya always saying that surprise was the greatest weapon in war?

"All right, the camp's ready," Balbus's voice broke into Lucius's thoughts. "Withdraw."

As the centuria retreated away from the trees to the secure walls of the fort, Lucius noted a commotion to the north. At first he was nervous, thinking it might another attack, but he soon saw that it was a detachment of Roman cavalry. About fifty troopers surrounded the bobbing helmet crests of several high-ranking officers. Everyone was black with soot from riding over the burned ground. A number of soldiers were doubled up on their mounts. The soldiers of the 19th stood and watched as the filthy, tired men rode into the fort and the officers ducked into the Legate's tent.

"This doesn't look like good news," Drusus grumbled under his breath.

As if in response, lightning flashed off to the east and was followed by the deep rumble of thunder.

"Good or bad news, we'll hear it eventually," Lucius said.

The first large drops of rain were splashing onto Lucius and the others by the time they had unpacked the *contuberium's* tent, and they were completely soaked as they sat for a meal of cold porridge, hard bread, dried meat and sour wine.

The guard was doubled and the first watch was taken by Appius, Servius and Flavius, but Lucius, Herod and Drusus made no attempt to sleep. The storm had been short but violent, thoroughly soaking everyone and everything. As the rain eased, Herod had managed to get a small fire going and the three friends huddled, shivering as close to it as possible, passing a wine jug around.

"At least we won't have to worry about forest fires tomorrow," Drusus said, morosely.

"I wonder what news the cavalry brought," Lucius said, staring at one of the new arrivals who was standing aimlessly beside the tethered horses.

"Not good," Herod said.

"Let's find out," Drusus said, standing. "Friend! Come and share some warmth and wine."

The soldier looked around. "I'm watching the horses," he said.

"You can watch just as well from here. And the wine's good."

The soldier moved closer and crouched by the fire where he could keep an eye on the horses. "Name's Gaius Agrippa, *equites* with the 18th Legion," he said by way of introduction.

Drusus introduced himself and the others and handed Gaius a goblet of wine. "So what brings a bull down among the scorpions?" Drusus asked.

"Not the wine," Gaius said, grimacing at his first taste.

Drusus shrugged. "What's going on up ahead?"

"It's not good," Gaius began. "The 17th's gone."

"Gone?" Lucius asked, confused.

"Dead, most of 'em."

Lucius gasped. It was impossible. An entire Roman Legion dead in an afternoon?

"How?" Herod asked.

"I can tell you what happened to the 18th from what I saw with my own eyes and what happened to the 17th from what survivors said and the ride down here. You saw the fires?"

Everyone nodded.

"They were deliberately set, and cunningly done. The wind was blowing down from the hill and the barbarians set two huge fires that roared down to the swamp edge, cutting off the 17th from us ahead and you behind. They sent the cavalry back, but there was no way through and small bands of barbarians kept appearing from nowhere, firing arrows and disappearing again. We lost several men. The small attacks kept up all day."

"Same thing happened to us," Drusus said. "Nothing big, just enough to keep us tied down."

"Exactly," Gaius agreed. "That was their purpose. Anyway, what was left of the 17th began reaching us after noon. The barbarians had lit many small fires and they burned down the hill onto the Legion and the baggage train. It seems that the fires were accompanied by small bands of warriors with slings who appeared from nowhere and deliberately targeted the officers. What with the officers dead and the chaos created by the panicking oxen, mules and slaves in the baggage train, the Legion fell apart.

"If you ask me, the goats have always been suspect, but it must have been hell in there. At least some cohorts kept their discipline and retreated from the fires into the swamp, but you can't fight in a swamp. The men sank up to their knees in places. Couldn't even turn to fight properly when the attack came. Barbarians were hiding everywhere, behind every tussock of grass and in every fold in the land, and they weren't wearing armour so they were light enough to run over the top of the swamp. It was a long hard fight—I saw the bodies on the way here—but the 17th never really had a chance. They swarmed over our men like ants."

A chill ran down Lucius's spine as he recalled the dead Sextus Livius's dream. The three friends sat as if riveted to the spot while Gaius continued.

"A lot of the Legion found swathes of unburned hillside between the fires and fled away from the swamp, but that was a trap, too. The unburned corridors had been deliberately left and they led only into closed valleys where the barbarians were waiting.

"I tell you, the slaughter was horrific. Been nothing like this since Hannibal taught us a lesson at Cannae. Only part of the Ist cohort managed to fight its way through to us. Hundreds of others also escaped—I expect you'll see some arrive here during the night—but they're good for nothing, shocked, exhausted and mostly burned or wounded."

"It's a total disaster," Herod said.

"And you haven't heard the worst. That bastard Arminius is leading them."

"Arminius betrayed us?" Lucius asked in shock. "Are you certain?"

"As can be. A large force of the Auxiliary cavalry came in as we were building a camp. We'd been wondering where they were, but suspected nothing. The line of guards let them through, but as soon as they were in among us, they started killing the men building the fort. At the same time, another Auxiliary force launched an attack from the trees. A lot of our men were cut down before they could drop their shovels."

Gaius went silent and the others waited patiently for him to go on. Eventually he raised his head, took a long draught of wine and continued.

"We managed to organize and fight them off eventually, but the casualties were bad, about a third of the Legion, I reckon. Our boys and what's left of the 17th are camped about four miles north of here. We were sent across the burned wasteland by Varus himself to tell you to move out at dawn and join us there."

"It's a disgrace," Herod said, angrily. "Varus had us so spread out that only a small number could fight at any one time. We'll never live this down."

"I'm just happy to be alive at the end of this day," Gaius said.

"Tomorrow will be different," Herod said. "They took us by surprise today, and Arminius will pay for that. The 19th is still intact. Once we join up with the 18th and the remnants of the 17th, we'll be a formidable force and these barbarians won't take us by surprise again."

"I hope you're right," Gaius said as he stood to go. "But I'd best get back to the horses. Thanks for the wine."

All three sat silent, deep in their own thoughts. Paramount in Lucius's mind were Sextus Livius's final words: Was this, then, just the beginning?

~~~~

By dawn the next day, the story brought in by the filthy, exhausted cavalry unit was all through the camp. Small groups were discussing what had happened animatedly as they buckled on armour and prepared for the march. Some were loud and angry at the betrayal, others were quietly sad at the thought of all their dead comrades.

Lucius remained silent. He hadn't slept the night before, even when he wasn't on guard duty, and he was no closer to answering his question. But he was resolved. Whatever the day brought, Lucius would fight as well and as long as he had to and if it was his day to die, then so be it. Mithras could take him to sit and drink wine and talk about old times with Titus.

But one thing saddened Lucius the more he thought on it. It was the growing conviction that the flash of red he had seen before the slingshot felled Sextus Vipsanius had been Freya. True, he hadn't seen the attacker's face, and red hair was quite common amongst the barbarians, but he was certain nonetheless. The news that the Auxiliaries had attacked the 18th had merely confirmed his thinking. This uprising must have been planned all summer, which explained why Freya had been avoiding him. Now there truly was an unbridgeable gulf between them. He felt no anger at Freya's betrayal, just a bottomless sadness that they would never again sit and share stories about his life in Rome and hers in Germania.

"Form up," Balbus shouted orders at the centuria. "Today we go and avenge our comrades. Keep tight formation on the march. If anyone breaks ranks today, I'll have them crucified outside my tent before the sun sets tonight."

The day's march was slow and hard work. Wisps of smoke rose from some blackened trees, but the rain of last night had turned the ash that coated the ground into a slippery, filthy mess that made it hard for the soldiers to keep their footing. The Legion's cavalry, along with the men from the 18th, ranged widely through the trees and this, and the vistas afforded by the burned underbrush, provided some safety from a major surprise attack. However there were numerous minor skirmishes. Wherever the brush was unburned or some feature of the ground offered cover, there was the likelihood of a small group attacking and then disappearing with lightning speed. Often, the first warning of an attack was a scream as an arrow or spear found a target. None of Lucius's *contuberium* was injured, but everyone was kept on edge and there were long delays as the Legion took up a defensive posture.

The going was also slowed by the need to manhandle fallen trees out of the way, many of which, Lucius noted, showed signs of having been deliberately felled. As they progressed, the thousands of marching feet sometimes broke into deeper pockets of ash and threw up a thick cloud of choking black dust that coated everything, stung eyes and caught in noses and throats. But the worst part of the march was seeing the results of the battle the day before.

The corpses of horses and oxen marked the route, their legs sticking up like forlorn signposts, and charred, soldiers' bodies lay everywhere. Some were alone, but most were clustered in small groups, indicating the spots where they had fought hopelessly until they were overwhelmed either by the fire or the enemy.

Three hours into the march, the Legion passed the swamp that Gaius had told them about. Hundreds of bodies lay in ranks where they had fallen and many others were scattered as far as the eye could see—no doubt men who had been overtaken on their cumbersome flight over the spongy ground. Most of the bodies had been stripped of their weapons and armour and some had been mutilated.

The Legion marched in a sullen silence and Lucius felt a bitter anger growing. His first reaction to Arminius and Freya's betrayal had been sadness, but the sight of so many dead soldiers made a cold hatred settle in his heart. The hatred grew as the Legion left the heavily burned area and entered an unburned forest where many of the trees were decorated with Roman heads. Perhaps Herod had been right all along. Perhaps the barbarians were just untrustworthy savages who could never aspire to civilization. Perhaps Freya, despite her intelligence and interest in the wider world, was fundamentally a savage who would revert to barbarism at the slightest excuse.

Lucius shook his head. He couldn't believe that of Freya, but it was hard not to when faced with the horrors around him. And if he, someone who knew the Cherusci better than most Romans, was having doubts, Lucius was convinced the others were certain. No one said anything except Drusus, who muttered "Savages!" under his breath at each new atrocity.

The biggest attack of the day came close to noon, after they had been travelling through the trees for almost an hour. The Legion was passing along a narrow pathway between a lake on their right and a particularly steep section of hillside that, higher up, gave way to dark cliffs of rotten-looking rock. Worryingly, smoke was rising from the base of one of the cliff sections. Lucius was glad when the tortured progress along the narrow path beneath the threatening cliffs was behind him. But he barely had time to savour his relief. Almost as soon as the Legion halted, the sounds of fighting came from both the head of the column around the curving hillside and the tail, still struggling along below the cliffs Most of the soldiers, including Lucius's centuria, were stuck and could go neither forward nor back. All they could do was stand helplessly and listen to the sounds of others fighting.

"You two," Balbus pointed to Flavius and Servius. "One of you go forward and the other back and find out what in Mithras's name is going on."

The pair hesitated for an indecisive moment before Servius headed forward and Flavius back.

The skirmish didn't last long, and Servius was soon back with news.

"The path widens at the end of the lake," he said, nervously. "The way was blocked by a tangle of large trees. When the leading cohort moved forward to clear the way, they were attacked from the hillside. They formed a testudo, but one of the soldiers told me that only a few of the barbarians fired on the cohort. Most shot arrows at the cavalry. A lot of horses were killed. Then the attackers just vanished."

"Thank you, soldier," Balbus said. "Rejoin the ranks, we're moving on."

Servius saluted and moved back into position. He looked pale and visibly frightened.

"Are you all right, lad?" Drusus asked.

"It was the horses," Servius said. "The wounded ones screamed like children in pain." He shuddered. "It was horrible."

"Better horses than men," Drusus said.

"Where's Flavius?" Servius asked.

"Not back yet," Drusus said. "He'll catch up."

"They targeted the cavalry?" Lucius asked.

"Yes," Servius answered, "Some were killed or wounded, but most lost their horses."

"And there was cavalry at the rear where the other attack occurred?"

"Of course," Drusus answered brusquely. "The cavalry always goes ahead and behind a marching Legion. You know that."

"They're blinding us," Lucius said.

"What do you mean?" Servius asked.

"He's not as dumb as he seems," Drusus said, thoughtfully. "He means that the cavalry are our eyes. They can roam through the woods and spot an enemy attack before it builds up and gets close. Without the cavalry, we're open to an ambush almost anywhere. That used to be the Auxiliaries' job," he finished, bitterly.

"We certainly taught them well," Appius volunteered.

"It does tell us one thing," Lucius said, thinking once again of Sextus Livius "Yesterday was the beginning, not the end."

"What do you mean?" Servius asked again, fear making his voice quaver.

"Why would they bother to target the cavalry unless they had something else planned?" Lucius explained.

"Why don't we turn around and go back to the forts on the Lupia?" Servius asked, an edge of hysteria entering his voice.

"Calm down, lad," Drusus said. "Would you have us desert the 18th? Our mates are up ahead and we have to go and join them. Perhaps then, Varus'll decide he's had enough of this ridiculous search for glory and take us back to the river."

Drusus was just beginning a reassuring story about honour and loyalty in the Legions when a deep roar from behind interrupted him. Everyone instinctively turned to look back. Huge rocks were bouncing down onto the path. Behind them a large section of cliff was slumping down and sliding toward the lake. A thunderous roar swept over the marching men and a grey cloud of dust rose into the air. Panicked figures at the end of the column fought against the crush of soldiers on the path to get out of the way of the avalanche. Others disappeared beneath the rumbling cascade of rocks and rubble.

Lucius watched in stunned silence as the vast mass of rocks, trees and earth crushed anyone too slow to escape and thundered into the lake. Waves rose and raced over the water to lap against the far shore.

"Flavius!" Servius cried.

"He's probably well on his way back by now," Lucius said, reassuringly. "He'll be here any minute."

"On top of everything else," Drusus said, bitterly "the Gods are now throwing the earth at us."

"Are you sure it's the Gods," Appius asked.

"Of course," Herod said. "No man could cause that."

"Don't be so certain," Appius commented. "You saw the smoke coming from the hillside. It puzzled me because it seemed to be coming from the earth itself, and not the forest."

"The barbarians can't set the earth on fire," Servius said.

"True, but think: how do we break down walls when we lay siege to a city?"

"We dig a cave under the walls, support the roof with timbers and then set the timbers alight," Drusus said. "When the timbers burn through, the cave collapses and brings down the walls above it."

"Those cliffs," Appius went on patiently, "didn't look too stable to begin with. The rock was rotten. If someone dug under an overhang on such an unstable hillside, support it with timbers and then burned out the timbers, it could trigger an avalanche. You'd only need to get it started."

"Cunning devils," Drusus said, wonderingly. "Lucky the entire Legion wasn't underneath it when it came down. Looks as if it only caught a few stragglers at the rear of the column."

"Lucky, yes," Lucius said. "But now we're cut off from the river. There's no going back that way. We have to keep going around the hills, whether we want to or not."

"We'll make these barbarians pay for all this," Herod said, angrily.

"Maybe," Lucius said, quietly, "but think on this. In the last two days, these uncivilized barbarians have reduced our force by more than a third, destroyed all our supplies in the baggage train, blinded us, and forced us to travel the route they want us too. It might not be as easy as you think to make them pay."

They all stood silently watching the dust settle over the place where the path had been.

"Oh God," Servius whimpered, tears rolling down his cheeks. "I just want to go home."

~~~~

"Two days of fighting and a Legion destroyed and I haven't even drawn my sword," Drusus said ruefully

"And three of our *contuberium* dead," Lucius added.

Flavius hadn't reappeared and everyone assumed he had been caught in the landslide. Drusus, Appius and Lucius were squatting miserably around a small fire in the 18th Legion's camp, discussing the day. Lucius was absent-mindedly rubbing his Mithraic medallion.

Herod and Servius were taking the first shift at guard duty. Drusus should have accompanied Herod, but he had sent Servius instead. The boy was terrified and Drusus had sent him to walk the walls with Herod for something to do so that he wouldn't dwell on their situation.

"You'll get your chance to use your sword," Lucius assured Drusus. "I'm certain of that. Everyone else has. It'll be our turn tomorrow."

The 19th had arrived at the 18th's fort in late afternoon. The fort had been attacked on and off all day, but the warriors had withdrawn, taking their dead and wounded with them, as the 19th approached.

Lucius had been shocked at the state of the Legions in the fort. The 18th had not suffered as much in the fighting that day and the day before as Lucius had feared. More than half the Legion was still a coherent, disciplined force, but the men were exhausted and hungry. Most of the supplies had been lost with the baggage train and the soldiers had been reduced to subsisting, and fighting all day, on the meagre rations they carried in their packs. Most worryingly, increasing numbers were deserting, sneaking off singly or in small groups to try and slip away from the barbarians or else surrender to them in the hope of mercy. The arrival of the 19th had stiffened many soldiers' resolve, but the news that the way back was cut off by the landslide was a blow.

With the exception of the Ist cohort and a few other intact centuria, the survivors of the 17th were not much good for anything. Filthy and with eyes that stared into the distance, most of them stumbled around aimlessly.

"The Scorpions are still in pretty good shape," Lucius mused. "We've marched a lot and had some casualties, but as Drusus points out, we haven't fought a battle yet. Add to that the Bulls and what's left of the Goats and we're still a formidable fighting force."

"And we're forewarned," Drusus added. "We're together and we won't be surprised again. It's a disaster, no denying it, but I think the worst is over."

"We must be close to the most northerly projection of these hills into the swamp lands," Appius said. "Once we round that, we're heading south again and, according to the chronicles of Caesar and Germanicus's expeditions, the hills are lower on that side and the ground dryer. There's a big river that flows north and drains much of that land. The going should be much easier."

Lucius knew what they were doing. It was an old soldier's characteristic, sitting around convincing each other that things were not as bad as they appeared. It was comforting and, just maybe, they were right.

As Drusus and Appius talked on, Lucius's mind drifted away. Where was Freya? He remembered the last time he had seen her, at the burned village. Had she known then what was going to happen? And what was she doing now? In barbarian camps all across the hills, Romans, prisoners and deserters were being sacrificed to the Gods. Had Freya reverted to the ways of her people to the extent that she could nail a Roman head to a tree? Had the Goddess Freya taken over the human, delighting in accepting enemy souls as slaves into the afterlife? Lucius hoped not, but he wasn't sure.

And was he being fair? He didn't want Freya to revert to the savage but, if he was honest, he would happily watch as barbarian prisoners were crucified from every available tree trunk by his Legion. Was there really any difference between them?

Lucius glanced down at the medallion in his hand. "Mithras, protect me," he whispered under his breath. "And Freya," he added as he tucked the medallion back under his shirt.

"He's gone." Lucius looked up to see Herod approaching.

"Who?" he asked stupidly.

"Servius." Herod crouched and warmed his hands at the fire. "We were patrolling a section of wall. Every time we passed, he kept asking me if it would be all right. I admit it was wearing on me and I was getting short in my answers, but one time, I turned round and he was gone. Slipped over the wall and off. Must be hoping he can outrun the barbarians in the dark and get back to the river. Fool, but he's not the only one who's gone over the wall tonight."

"I hope he makes it," Lucius said. "I remember how scared I was when I first joined and this is much worse."

"We've all been scared enough at some time to wonder if it would be better to go over the wall," Drusus said.

"Not me," Herod said, indignantly. "What makes us superior to them is our discipline and organization—the fact that we *don't* run away at the first sign of trouble."

"Sometimes, Herod," Drusus said, "you can really get on my nerves. Don't be so pompous. Servius is just a scared boy who wants to go home. If you ask me, these barbarians you disparage so much have given us something to be scared of over the last couple of days.

"Now, I'm going to try and get some sleep. It'll be a long day tomorrow and, if it's to be my last, I want to be awake for it."

Drusus stood and walked over to the tent. There'd be plenty of room for the four of them in it tonight. Appius and Lucius followed him. Lucius doubted he would be able to sleep, but he was unconscious as soon as his head hit the ground.

Lucius knew nothing until the sound of the Legion's bugles roused him. He didn't feel rested, but he rose with the others, donned his armour and collected his weapons. As the sun rose over the far horizon, he was ready to march out of camp with his comrades.

The first thing they all saw as they marched north were dozens of naked, mutilated bodies nailed and tied to the surrounding trees. Some were missing limbs or heads and some, Lucius was horrified to see, had been skinned. One of those was Servius.

Freya

"I've failed." Arminius was pacing back and forth on the edge of the clearing, taking short, hurried steps.

"How can you say that?" Freya asked from her perch on a fallen, partly-rotted, moss-covered log. "Look at what you've achieved!"

"Achieved! I have achieved nothing."

"That's not true! You have crippled the Roman army in Germania. One Legion is destroyed, another mauled and the remnants forced to do your bidding. It is a great achievement and we shall complete it tomorrow."

"After all I have taught you, you still do not understand. I must achieve *everything* or I achieve nothing. Victory alone is not enough. It must be total—so crushing that the Romans will not dare return."

Arminius stopped pacing and stared at his niece. "Yes, we have done all the things you say, but it is not enough. The first day went as planned, when we had surprise, but today was difficult. I knew the landslide catching the 19th on the march was taking a chance, since no one knew how long the timbers would take to burn through. Because the 19th survived, I launched more attacks on the 18th in the fort. If they were weakened, I thought we might overwhelm them. But neither plan worked and the Legions have joined up again."

Freya was secretly pleased that the landslide plan had failed—it meant that Lucius was probably still alive. She knew he had to die, but she couldn't help feeling happy that he had survived another day. Freya had killed her fair share of Romans with her sling in the past two days, including one of Lucius's friends. Her emotions as she had fired her deadly stones had ranged from hatred to cold professionalism, but with Lucius it was different. When she had seen him that first day, standing confused amidst his Roman friends, she could no more have killed him than flown in the air. She simply did not have the hardness in her soul that Arminius demanded.

"But they are weak," Freya said to her uncle. "The soldiers must be tired and hungry and many are wounded. They have no supplies, their cavalry are destroyed and they have nowhere to go except into tomorrow's trap."

"But is the trap big enough? I had counted on there being only a single Legion on the third day. Today's failures mean there are almost two, and that is formidable. And, remember, however tired and hungry they are, they are soldiers fighting for their very survival."

"But if any cohorts survive tomorrow, they still have a long way to go. We can hunt them down."

"Individuals, yes, but if any units survive tomorrow with any discipline, they will be free to go home. It is hard enough to get these tribes to come together for three days—already the Chatti are saying we have done enough and wish to go home—after tomorrow, our army will vanish. They will take their plunder, whatever prisoners they feel they need to sacrifice and they will melt back into the forest as if they had never been. I will not be able to convince them to follow a last remnant of the Roman Legions when they are so eager to celebrate such an extraordinary victory."

"But does it really matter if one cohort struggles back to Vetera? Will the effect of our victory not be as great?"

"Freya, you may have Roman friends, but you do not truly understand them. If a cohort survives, they will tell their story. Other Romans will listen and say, 'This is where we went wrong. If we do this differently next time, we will not fail.' Then they will cross the Rhenus once more in even greater numbers and we won't have a second chance to destroy them.

"But," Arminius began pacing again. He was becoming more animated, describing shapes in the air with his hands to emphasize his point, "if not one returns, it will be as if the entire army has been swallowed by the Gods. It will be mystical. The superstitious will say the Romans are not meant to rule east of the Rhenus, that they are presumptuous and are overreaching themselves and in doing so have angered Mars, their God of War. Then, they may leave us alone."

"It will work tomorrow," Freya said as encouragingly as she could. "You'll see."

"I hope so," Arminius stopped his pacing. "We have only this one chance." He smiled at his niece. "I am proud of what you have done in the past two days. You have proved yourself a true warrior. If all are like you tomorrow, perhaps all will be well.

"But now I must go and organize. The Romans will set out early and we must be ready. Try to get some rest. Whatever happens, tomorrow will be a busy day."

"I will," Freya said, standing, but she doubted she would. There was too much on her mind. The anger at the injustices of Roman rule and the heady idea of throwing them out of the Germanic lands had swept her along, but now she was tired, not just physically from all the hard work, but emotionally from all the killing. She hated the idea of the Romans with their arrogance and thoughtless superiority, but it was hard to translate that into hatred for an individual soldier coughing his life away with a Cherusci arrow through his throat or one of her sling stones embedded in his temple. More and more, she found herself seeing Lucius in every dying man's face.

A group of Sicambri warriors burst into the clearing. They were wild with victory and dragging along three pitiful, nearly naked Roman soldiers. One of the Romans, a short man with terrified eyes, looked up. He stared pleadingly at Freya, but when confronted with her cold gaze, his head sank in resignation.

"Come join us for the sacrifice," one of the Sicambri yelled. "The Gods are happy. The swamps are running red with Roman blood."

Freya shook her head. Their Gods were insatiable, but hers was satiated.

She kicked the rotting tree trunk viciously. A large section of it disintegrated and a puff of fungus spores rose in the air. Why couldn't the Romans just go and leave them alone? Why had they come in the first place? Even after all she had done and been through, a part of Freya regretted that she and Lucius couldn't simply be friends. Beneath her hatred of Romans, she still wished she could travel with Lucius to Rome and see the wonders he had told her about.

It wasn't fair, but there was no way out now. Arminius was right: tomorrow they had to win and win totally. And Freya would do her part. She would kill and kill again until there were no Romans left.

She looked up into the branches above her head. "Please, Woten," she said quietly, "do not let my path and Lucius's cross tomorrow."

Kalkriese Hill

H erod was the first of the four companions to die. A barbarian spear plunged over the top of his shield, punched through his armour and buried itself deep in his chest. Another spear from the first volley tore Appius's arm open and yet another thudded into Lucius's shield so hard it knocked him off his feet.

"Testudo," Balbus yelled, but it was too late. The spear volley had done its damage and dozens of the centuria were already dead, dying or wounded. Lucius saw Balbus's horse go down with a spear through its throat, but the centurion struggled to his feet and continued giving orders. With an unearthly scream, hundreds of barbarians poured over a camouflaged earthen wall in the trees and pounded down the slope onto the shocked Romans.

Lucius hauled himself to his feet, rammed the pointed end of the centuria standard into the soft ground and hurled his *pilum* into the charging mass. Others were doing the same, and it was impossible to miss a target among the packed bodies, but the spears did little to slow the charge.

The front row of Roman legionaries barely had time to draw their swords and set their shields before the weight of the barbarian onslaught crashed into them. Lucius was swept up in a chaos of screaming men and clashing weapons. He fought thoughtlessly, aware only of the man in front, trying to kill him. He caught axes on his shield, parried sword swings and stabbed at any exposed flesh he saw. He felt no fear, working on instinct alone, like an animal. Metal flashed, he raised his shield to catch an axe, thrust forward with his *gladius*, sensed it sink into flesh, felt warm blood flood over his hand, and the pressure in front of him ease. Drusus was beside him, grinning wildly.

Gradually, the pressure slackened. The line moved forward, stepping over bodies or kicking them out of the way. Lucius grabbed the standard and held it behind his shield, leaving his sword hand free. Then the attackers were gone, pouring back up the slope behind the wall.

"Hold!" Balbus screamed as some soldiers began to surge after them.

Lucius glanced around. The roar of his heavy breathing eased, allowing his brain to take in the sounds around him. The ground was covered with men. Some lay still, others tried to stand, groaning with the pain or twisting and writhing in agony. Occasional piercing screams cut the air.

At Lucius's feet, Appius lay dead, a huge axe-gash in the side of his head. Farther off, Herod's body sprawled on the road, impaled by the spear. Lucius felt nothing. The adrenaline the sudden attack had sent coursing through his body was still swamping his normal emotions. He noticed the dead, but his entire being was focused on searching out the next crisis, every muscle in his body was tensed, ready to react.

Drusus stood beside Lucius, covered in blood, though most of it didn't seem to be his. His shield was chipped from axe blows and he was hunched forward, grimly wiping blood off the handle of his sword.

As far as Lucius could tell, the attack had erupted all along the line of march. Here and there, it looked as if the line had been broken and the casualties everywhere were severe, but the surviving centurions were organizing their men.

In the trees, Lucius could see the wall that had concealed the attackers. It was about six feet high and wound through the trees parallel to the path. Remnants of the branches and foliage that had concealed it were lying trampled and broken at the foot. That's why they targeted the cavalry and blinded us, Lucius thought, so we wouldn't find the trap. As he watched, archers appeared above the wall.

"Testudo!" Balbus shouted. Shields went up on tired arms and arrows thudded into wood.

"Retreat out onto the flat ground and form a square," Balbus ordered.

Lucius glanced behind him. The ground was swampy and dotted with countless small hillocks and tufts where enemy soldiers could be hiding.

"No!" Lucius shouted. "It's a trap! Remember what happened to the 17th! Stay with the standard."

"Who said that?" Balbus said. "*Signifer*, obey my orders."

The soldiers hesitated.

"He's right," Drusus said. "It is a trap. Our only chance is to break through the wall."

"How dare you," Balbus managed before a half dozen arrows found chinks in his armour. For strange moment, he stood still, a puzzled look on his face and arrows sticking out of his arms, legs, side and neck, then he toppled forward.

"Come on," Drusus screamed. We have to take the wall." He stepped forward and others followed.

Lucius took a look around. Along the line, some men had followed Balbus's order and retreated into the swamp. Lucius watched as figures rose from hiding all around them.

"We'll die in the swamp!" Lucius shouted at the others. "We must take the wall. With the standard!"

Lucius pushed forward beside his friend and began to trudge up the slope. Even though the incline was not great, it was painfully slow going burdened as they were with heavy equipment. His shield felt twice its normal weight and the muscles of his sword arm ached horribly, but he had to go on. Most of the other soldiers along the line were following Drusus's lead. It was not the coordinated, disciplined advance Lucius would have liked, but enough were going forward together that, if they could break through the wall and drive the barbarians away, they still had a chance.

Lucius took a last look over his shoulder, and his heart sank. The swamp was alive with barbarian warriors. As far as he could see to left and right, thousands had come out of hiding. A few were busy killing isolated groups of Romans who had sought the false security of open ground, but most were surging forward like ants. The Legion was doomed, trapped between the wall and the advancing horde. It was Sextus Livius's dream come true. But there was nothing for it but to fight on. Dying swiftly in battle was preferable to being sacrificed to the Gods.

The closest Roman units had now reached the wall. Many had laid down their cumbersome shields and were struggling to climb the steep front. Others were frantically hauling at the sod and dirt foundations in attempts to bring the fortification down. Both groups were being attacked by warriors along the wide top of the wall who hurled missiles at them and hacked at those who managed to climb.

"Lift me," Drusus ordered. It took Lucius a moment to realize what his friend meant, but he quickly understood. Drusus held his shield over his head while Lucius and another soldier dropped their own protection and lifted him by the legs.

When he was high enough, Drusus began hacking at the unprotected legs of the warriors standing on the top of the wall. Enough fell back to allow Drusus to climb up.

"Now me," Lucius shouted, grabbing his shield and the standard.

The top of the wall was about six paces wide and soon there were small groups of Roman soldiers on top, fighting for their lives. The warriors from the swamp were now battling the soldiers who had remained on the path below. The vice was closing, and the only ways out were the few places where soldiers had gained a foothold on the top of the wall.

As Lucius and Drusus fought their way forward, the press of bodies behind them increased. Suddenly, they were over the wall. The drop on the upside was much shorter and the trees and underbrush thicker. About twenty soldiers slithered down the slope into the warriors waiting below. Lucius was exhausted. Sweat and blood were running into his eyes, stinging them painfully. His heavy wooden shield felt as if it were made of solid lead. The muscles in his arms and legs screamed in agony and were going into spasms, but still he kept going.

"Come on, you lazy sods," Drusus encouraged. He seemed tireless, stabbing everywhere with his sword and battering ahead with his shield. "No one said a soldier's life was easy."

Somehow Lucius kept up with his friend, blindly killing anything that got in his way. He had a vague sense of the slope steepening, the trees growing closer together and there being fewer and fewer men behind him. Gradually, he found himself fighting against the underbrush more than the enemy. The sounds of battle faded beneath the pounding of his heart and the rasping of his breath. Nearly blind and staggering like a drunk, one thought dominated Lucius's mind: he had to keep going. Strange lights flashed behind his eyes and the world swam in and out of focus.

An instant before he collapsed, Drusus grabbed Lucius by the arm and dragged him behind a large rock that had rolled to a stop on the hillside decades before. The upslope side of the rock formed a slight overhang and the underbrush concealed the two soldiers from all but the closest examination. But Lucius was oblivious. He didn't care if he was found and killed. His chest hurt unbearably and he struggled to drag air through his raw throat in convulsive gulps. Lucius closed his eyes and wished he were dead.

His wish wasn't granted. Gradually, his breathing eased, his pain lessened and he began to notice the world around him. He opened his eyes to find Drusus was sitting beside him, hunched over his knees and breathing deeply.

"Wh—where're we?" Lucius gasped.

Drusus shook his head.

"Wher're others?"

"Dead," Drusus shrugged.

Lucius rested his head against the rough stone. In the distance he could just make out the sounds of battle.

"They're still fighting," he said.

Drusus shrugged once more.

"We should help." Lucius made a half-hearted effort to stand.

Drusus put his hand on his friend's arm. "No point."

"But—"

"You saw how many there were," Drusus said, staring hard at Lucius. "You saw our lines break. They're doomed."

"Are we all that's left?" Lucius asked.

"There are probably others. Small groups, individuals, hiding, like us. Soon as the barbarians have finished back there, they'll come looking."

"What'll we do?" Lucius couldn't think clearly.

"Run," Drusus said. "What else?"

Lucius concentrated on slowing his breathing. Gradually, his mind began to work again. The ambush had happened as the Legion rounded the most northerly hill. When he and Drusus had fought their way up from the wall, they must have been heading south. If they kept going, they would get onto the uplands and, eventually, reach the Lupia.

"We can wait here until dark—"

"Too close. We must leave now."

Lucius thought for a minute. Drusus was right. "All right, then we have to ditch our armour and shields. They're too heavy to carry and speed is what's important. If we bump into a group of barbarians, our shields are not going to help."

"You're right," Drusus agreed, pushing his shield aside and beginning to unstrap his armour.

Lucius followed suit. It was only now he noticed that the centuria's standard was gone. At least the top part had been severed by an axe in the wild melee at the wall. He felt a sudden surge of regret. He had failed. The standard was the heart of a centuria and it was the signifer's job to protect it with his life. His father had never lost a standard.

"I've lost the standard," Lucius said, stupidly.

Drusus laughed bitterly. "Doesn't matter now. There's no centuria left. Now hurry."

Drusus was right. What use was a standard without a centuria? As quickly as possible, Lucius took off his armour and helmet. The pair stood in their filthy, sweat-soaked woollen tunics. Lucius noticed that Drusus was covered in cuts and gashes, but none seemed too serious. He had a deep cut in his left leg himself, and there was blood coming down from his scalp, but neither hindered him nor hurt too much.

"You look good," Lucius said.

"A good pair of soldiers of Rome," Drusus said with a smile. He looked down at his sword. The blade was broken off half way along. "Piece of rubbish," he said, throwing it aside and grabbing his dagger. Lucius, too, threw away his sword, taking only his dagger, the sling Freya had given him and a bag of stones. "Let's go, before they come looking."

Moving as quickly as aching legs would allow and keeping to the thick underbrush as much as possible, the pair worked their way up the hill. They stopped often to listen and twice had to hurriedly take cover as warriors passed nearby.

Eventually, the hill flattened out and the trees became more widely spaced. They slowed and moved with more caution, skirting open boggy areas. Lucius had an uneasy feeling that they were being followed, but every time he glanced back, there was nothing to be seen.

At length—about mid-afternoon, Lucius judged—they came to a small clearing with a boggy pond in the middle. The water was brackish, but Lucius was so thirsty he simply lay down, pushed his face into the bitter water and drank. He could hear Drusus beside him, doing the same.

When his thirst was slaked, he stood up. At the edge of the clearing, two Sicambri warriors were watching. Both carried blood-stained axes. Grinning broadly, the two men trotted forward.

Without a word, Drusus stood and moved a few paces to the side. The Sicambri split, each silently selecting his victim. With a shock, Lucius noticed that the one heading for him had a broken nose and a curved scar on his forehead.

"I failed to kill you once, Roman," the man said with a sneer. "This time there will be no mistake."

Lucius tugged the sling out of his belt and fumbled for a stone. He could drop one of them, he was sure, but two?

The man coming at Lucius was moving slowly, savouring the moment. The other was much closer to Drusus.

Lucius swung the sling and fired. The Sicambri in front of Drusus grunted and collapsed. Lucius's attacker snarled and broke into a run. Lucius scrabbled with his pouch of stones. One fell to the ground. He cursed. It felt as though he was moving through molasses.

The Sicambri's body crashed into Lucius, knocking him flat. As he struggled to free himself and reach his dagger, he slowly realized the barbarian on top of him was still—dead. Pushing him off, he stood up and looked at the man. It was the one who had attacked him years before, Lucius was certain. He remembered how this warrior had been the only one who had not been stripped after the ambush. He had simply been dragged into the trees. He must have survived. But he would not survive this. The man's pale eyes were open and glazed over. A round pebble was deeply imbedded in his right temple.

Lucius looked up. Freya stood on the far side of the clearing, her sling hanging from her right hand.

"Freya!" Lucius exclaimed.

For what seemed like an age, Freya stood in silence. Then she moved. In a blur she loaded her sling and fired. Lucius just had time to register the sickening crack as the first stone caught Drusus on the forehead before he felt a searing pain on the side of his skull and everything went black.

~~~~

"Wake up, we need to go." Freya's voice forced its way into Lucius's consciousness. "It's late."

With an immense effort, Lucius opened his eyes. He was propped up against a tree on the edge of the clearing where they had stopped for a drink. Drusus's body, and those of the two Sicambri, lay near the water. It was dusk. "Where am I?" he asked, struggling to remember.

"You're in the clearing where I caught up with you," Freya said, "but you'll be in the afterlife if you don't wake up."

"Drusus?"

"He's dead."

"You killed him?"

"Yes," Freya said, matter-of-factly. "And you will join him. There are other Sicambri close by, looking for their friends. Do you want your head nailed to a tree?"

Lucius hauled himself to his feet and shook his head in an attempt to clear it. It was a mistake. Pain radiated from his left temple and made the world swim out of focus. He slumped to his knees.

"Come on," Freya grabbed his arm and hauled him back up. Half pulling and half threatening, she led Lucius into the trees. He stumbled along as best he could, tripping over roots and banging into tree trunks. Night fell, but the sky was clear and a three-quarter-moon gave them some light to travel by. Freya seemed to know the way and moved easily along paths, deer trails and around the edges of clearings and swamps. Despite their movement, Lucius shivered with the cold and his wounded leg grew more painful with every step.

"I have to rest," he said, eventually.

Freya looked around at him and nodded. At the next clearing, the pair sat side-by-side against an old oak. Freya took off her skin cloak and wrapped it around Lucius's shoulders. She produced a piece of dried deer meat and handed it to him. As Lucius chewed, his mind worked over the events of the day.

"You saved me from the Sicambri?" Lucius asked.

Freya nodded.

"Then why did you kill Drusus?"

"For the same reason I should have killed you," Freya said. "He was a Roman."

"Why didn't you kill me?"

"How do you know I didn't try?"

"If you had tried, I would be dead now."

Freya nodded acknowledgement. "I couldn't do it. Arminius says we must harden our hearts if we are to rid ourselves of you Romans. We can afford no softness. Everyone must die, but I cannot be like that."

"You killed Drusus easily enough.'

"You are a Roman and my friend. He was just a Roman."

"Why do you hate us so much?" Even now—after all he had seen and done, Lucius still struggled to understand.

"Because you are arrogant. You think you know how the world should be and you have the power to force that view on anyone you choose."

"But you were interested in my stories of Rome! You wanted to be a Roman!"

"I did," Freya said, thoughtfully, "but the cost was too high. I would have had to watch my people be enslaved, give up their heritage and become Roman taxpayers. And I would have been forced to give up my past, forget everything I knew and deny all that I grew up with. And even then, I could never be true Roman like you. To people like your friend Herod, I would always be a barbarian."

"So you've chosen to live in the forest."

"Yes. It's my home."

Lucius nodded. He understood. If things were reversed, he would fight not to live in the forest.

"I'm sorry," he said.

"You're a Roman," Freya said. "You did not choose to be. Don't be sorry for what your people do."

"That's not what I mean," Lucius said. "I'm sorry I can't take you to Rome and show you all the wonders we talked about."

Freya was silent for a long moment. "I'm sorry, too," she said eventually.

Lucius thought he heard a catch in Freya's voice. He looked at her face in profile in the moonlight. *I could live in the forest with Freya.* The thought leapt unbidden into Lucius's mind. But as soon as the thought formed, Lucius knew it was impossible. Freya was right. He was a Roman and, however much he would enjoy being with Freya, he would always miss that. Too much had happened between the Cherusci and Rome for anyone to cross the divide.

"Come," Freya stood up. "We must go. We have far to travel."

"Where are we going?" Lucius asked.

"I am taking you to the fort at Alterium. There are two cohorts there that will retreat to Vetera when they hear what has happened."

"We'll come back, you know."

"Arminius thinks not. He believes that the scale of the disaster will discourage another expedition."

"He's wrong. Rome does not forget wrongs. The Legions will return and devastate the land."

"Will you come back with them?"

"No." Lucius shook his head. "I will serve out my time somewhere peaceful—I've heard that Africa is pleasant—and then I will return to my father's farm. I think I will study history instead of trying to make it. Perhaps I will write an account of what happened here."

264

"You must!" Freya said, suddenly animated. "My people will tell tales around the fires for generations of this time, but they will not last forever, especially if the Legions return. Stories die with the storytellers. But a story that is written down will last forever. Promise me you will write this story."

Lucius reached out and touched Freya's face, brushing a lock of red hair from her eyes. "I promise."

"Now we must go. We have a long journey ahead."

"Wait," Lucius said. He reached under the neck of his tunic and removed the Mithraic medallion that Titus had given him after his initiation.

"I know it's not your God," he said, handing the medal to Freya, "but he is a God of soldiers. Perhaps he will protect you. I don't need him any more."

"Thank you," Freya said, accepting the gift. She stepped forward and embraced Lucius. "I will return it to you when we meet in the next world."

"I will look forward to that," Lucius said.

Without another word, Freya turned and led the way into the trees.

Herculaneum

The reign of Titus Caesar: Year 1
24th August, midnight

I am alone, a stupid old man scratching an ancient story amidst a world that is ending. I have outlived my span by another lifetime, journeyed to the ends of the earth and been a part of the history about which I write. Yet thoughts of a single person in a clearing in Germania seven decades ago can reduce me to tears. For all our arrogance, we are pitiful, foolish beings.

But I must bring this to an end. Pallas waits to seal my parchment in an old Egyptian jar for protection against what Vesuvius might throw at us.

Freya did take me to Alterium, where my story created a most extraordinary panic. The cohorts there were never attacked, yet they buried all their treasure and fled to Vetera. News of the disaster arrived in Rome at the same time as news of the great, final victory over the rebels in Illyria.

It is said that the Emperor Augustus never recovered from the tragedy in Germania and in his waning years would wander his palace exclaiming, "Publius Varus, give me back my Legions."

Whether that is true or not, when Augustus died five years after the Varus disaster, the Senate appointed Germanicus Commander in Germania. Over two campaigning seasons, Germanicus led eight Legions across the Rhenus, caught and slaughtered the Marsi and devastated the Cherusci lands. He had a burial mound constructed over the bones he found below Kalkriese Hill and recovered the eagle of the 19th Legion. But the country east of the River Rhenus never did become a settled province and the 17th, 18th and 19th Legions were never rebuilt. I hope Freya lived long enough to see the Cherusci finally live the way they wished in lands without Romans.

Arminius did not. The discipline that he admired in the Legions and that he imposed on the Germanic tribes did not survive the battle. The tribes fell to squabbling and the tale is that he was assassinated by Chatti chieftains who were afraid he was becoming too powerful.

I did leave the Legions and return to the farm outside Pisanus. Both my father and older brother died in the same year and I spent most of life content on the farm. I travelled with my trading ships and saw much of the world. I never married.

But enough. I must seal this and await the time when I see Freya again. I will have Pallas carry me up to the roof. I wish to witness what is yet to come.

Vesuvius

The reign of Titus Caesar: Year 1
25th August, midnight and 1 a.m.

L ucius was tired. The journey up to the roof, even with Pallas supporting him, was always a struggle and today had been long. Lucius sat in a wicker chair with the sealed jar on his lap, recovering what little strength he had. Pallas placed a small table and a flickering oil lamp beside him, and went back down to fetch some olives and wine.

Lucius turned his head and looked over toward Herculaneum. In the violent flashes of lightning, he could see the buildings as clear as day. Here and there, tiny figures indicated that others were also on their roofs watching the display. A crowd of several hundred people—all those who had not already fled, Lucius assumed—were congregated on the beach by the boat house. Some were trying to launch small boats and others, he was amused to notice, had brought their horses down with them.

A change in the cloud above the mountain made Lucius look up. The column that for more than twelve hours had been roaring upward out of Vesuvius's summit, was collapsing. With astonishing speed, a bulge was spreading out and shooting downward, making the column look a little like an inverted mushroom. The bulge hit the upper slopes of the mountain and shot outward, creating a roiling, living curtain that raced toward the sea with unimaginable speed.

It's beautiful, Lucius thought in the two minutes the cloud took to reach him. The face of the cloud sparkled with tiny busts of lightning, but the whole thing seemed to glow, lit by an ethereal internal fire. Olive trees exploded as the raging torrent touched them and a panicked donkey careened down the hillside before it disappeared.

Lucius, relaxed, wrapped his arms around the jar and settled into his chair. He knew he was going to die, but he also knew that the end would be swift. That was a comfort, and so was his document, the now complete story that Freya had made him promise to preserve.

Fascinated, Lucius waited, a small smile creasing the corners of his mouth. In the instant before the cloud hit, he murmured one last word: "Freya."

Historical Note

The glowing cloud that killed Lucius on the roof of the villa outside Herculaneum in 79 CE, was travelling at something more than 200 kilometres an hour. It was composed of a mix of superheated gas, ash and fragments of rock torn from the throat of the volcano. The temperature within the cloud was over 1,000 degrees centigrade. That is hotter than it was 300 metres away from Ground Zero at Hiroshima—where the world's first atomic bomb exploded over a city.

Within Lucius's villa, the cloud was fickle. In some places the force crashed through walls and exploded bronze statues. In others it was gentle enough to preserve wax tablets, cloth and the olives Lucius enjoyed.

Lucius and Pallas died instantly, their blood boiling, teeth exploding and flesh vapourizing. They felt no pain since their brains disintegrated before any nerves had a chance to send messages to it. All that was left were charred bones.

Throughout the rest of the night and the next morning, other glowing surges, six in all, swept down the mountain, burying Herculaneum under 18 metres of hard rock and volcanic glass.

Lucius's villa hasn't been discovered yet, but one containing a library of preserved papyrus documents has. If there is a Lucius buried somewhere on the edge of Herculaneum, it might be possible to read the words he wrote that night.

As usual, that far back in time, only the lives of the important people are preserved in any way. Varus is real, as are Arminius, Germanicus, Caesar Augustus and the historical figures they talk about. The rest of the characters—including Lucius and Freya—are fictitious, but that doesn't make them less real. The 20,000 Romans who died in Arminius's ambush and the populations of Pompeii and Herculaneum, saw themselves as just as important and interesting as we see ourselves.

Acknowledgements

There is no shortage of books on Rome and the Romans, but the two I delved into most were *Ghosts of Vesuius* by Charles Pellegrino and *The Battle That Stopped Rome* by Peter S. Wells. There are also many websites on the Romans and their enemies and Wikipedia is a good place to start a search for whatever your interest is, from weapons to food.

If you want to look at the face of a soldier who died at Kalkriese Hill, visit: www.armatura.connectfree.co.uk/jrmes/j0601a.htm.

For a look at the archaeological excavations at Kalkriese there is:

http://varusbattle.com/index.html.

Linda Preussen enlivened the original text and polished where my sloppiness got the better of me.

If you enjoyed *Germania*, you might enjoy others in the Caught in Conflict Collection. For example, **Where Soldiers Lie India 1857.**

"This is an absolutely terrific book...Never lagging with a credible hero and an exotic setting...The pacing is flawless."
    Geoffrey Bilson Award for Historical Fiction Jury Citation

Prologue

Queen Victoria's Jubilee
Sunday, June 27, 1897

The man absent-mindedly scratched the hard knot of scar tissue beneath his left arm where the crocodile had opened his side to the bone forty years before. Was the beast still alive, he wondered? It had been young and inexperienced when it had attacked him and it was said that they could live to be over a hundred years old. He chuckled—it would probably outlive him.

Jack O'Hara was sitting on the stone steps below a small temple, gazing over the Ganges River as it wound across the northern plains of India. When the rains arrived in a week or two, bringing floodwaters from the distant Himalayas, the river would be a two-mile-wide, churning, muddy torrent; but now the water was low, exposing whale backs of sand and mud separated by a weave of sluggish channels.

The river was just as he remembered it: pelicans beat their wings over the water, herding small fish into schools they could scoop into their brightly-coloured beak pouches; cranes stood hunched forward like old men in formal waistcoats; metallic kingfishers flashed down on unsuspecting prey; and half-wild village dogs scavenged in the shallows.

Humans, too, went about their business in the river. Laundresses beat clothes on rocks with large swinging motions that sent fine, glistening sprays of water curving upward in the sunlight. Old men brushed their teeth with crushed twigs or ritually bathed, cupping their hands and pouring the holy water over their heads. A mounted British officer—a scarlet wound on the dun-coloured scene—trotted diagonally across a sandbar in the foreground.

The river hadn't changed since that tragic summer when Jack was barely sixteen. Only the city of Cawnpore behind him was different. Now the railway ran alongside the Grand Trunk Road, connecting all the British stations from Calcutta in the east to Peshawar, nestled against India's western border with Afghanistan. Burned-out bungalows, shops and offices had been rebuilt and new army parade grounds laid out with military precision. General Wheeler's pitiful entrenchment had long vanished, replaced by the red brick walls of All Souls Memorial Church. The entrenchment well, where so many brave men had risked their lives for a cool drink of water, and the sepulchral well were both filled in. Quiet gardens and an elaborate monument—overdone and ostentatious, Jack thought—marked the site of the Bibighar and its own well of horrors. In fact, the only well still serving its original purpose was the one in Aunt Katherine's garden. There, a bullock mindlessly plodded the same circular path that its ancestor had generations before.

Jack often thought of his memory as a kind of well. Like a well it provided something good, and Jack treasured his memories of Alice, Tommy and Hari, and of his long-ago childhood in the Canadian forests. But just as the bottom of a well is dark and dangerous, there were places in Jack's memory that were frightening; places where he tried not to fall.

Nevertheless, despite his best efforts, his mind often refused to cooperate. On these occasions, his memories would drag him back to the dreadful events of 1857. Thoughts of the crocodile were carrying him back now, not just to that moment of terror in the frothy, bloodstained water when the beast had ripped his flesh, but to the weeks that had led up to it—weeks of confusion, fear and tragedy. But also weeks of incredible courage and strength. Weeks that had determined the man whom Jack would become.

Tuesday, May 12, 1857—Dawn

Cawnpore was a mess of a city, spread haphazardly along the southwest bank of the Ganges. In reality it was several distinct towns.

Jack lived with his Aunt Katherine and Uncle James in one of the collection of spacious, immaculately kept bungalows in the cantonment. This was where army officers, East India Company employees and European traders lived their sheltered lives. The only dark-skinned faces seen on the cantonment's wide, tree-lined streets were servants or favoured Eurasian employees—or Jack.

The cantonment occupied the best position in town, a long swath perched on the high bank of the river where any cooling breeze off the water could be felt. Behind this oasis of transplanted British civilization loomed the packed and filthy native city. Narrow alleys—clogged with stalls, rickshaws and aimlessly wandering cattle—teemed with life. Shopkeepers bawled the benefits of their produce, scribes scribbled official letters on tiny folding desks, beggars whined at any passing wealth and skinny, near-naked holy men flitted through the mass of humanity like underfed ghosts. The air was filled with noise, dust and the smells of every form of human activity. On his rare visits to these streets, Jack imagined that medieval London might have smelled the same way before toilets and sewers were introduced.

Surrounding the native city were the infantry and artillery lines. For the native infantry and cavalry—*sepoys* and *sowars*—these gave the impression of bustling villages with hordes of half-naked children running between the rows of rough huts where the soldier's families lived. The European lines consisted of low, verandahed barracks set in open expanses of swept parade ground.

On the northwestern edge of town sat the squat, brick treasury and magazine. The city was connected to the northeast bank of the river and the Lucknow road by a bridge of boats.

No physical barriers prevented people moving from one area of town to another, but most were content—for religious, racial and cultural reasons—to stay within their own prescribed world.

Jack and Australian had explored it all, and many of the scattered villages up and down the Grand Trunk Road as well, but their favourite spot was in the open spaces by the river. The air was slightly cooler and cleaner here and there was always activity to watch. The Ganges was both a place to wash bodies and clothes, and the most sacred site in India. The mere touch of its water could cleanse a person's soul of the most terrible crime.

Jack rode down the narrow ravine that cut through the river's high bank near his aunt's bungalow. He emerged at Sati Chowra Ghat, a series of stone steps that allowed access to the river. When the water was high and lapping at the bottom steps, Sati Chowra was often crowded with people washing and praying. But now, in the dry heat of May, the water was far from the bank and the steps were deserted.

Jack turned Australian past the foot of the small Hardeo Temple to the Hindu god Shiva and splashed his way west through the shallows. At the bridge of boats, he regained the bank. He had intended to skirt the native city and explore the countryside to the west, but the sight of a solitary figure, sitting on a low wall, made him rein in. It was a girl about his age, dressed in immaculately pressed riding clothes. Her long dark hair was held in a tight bun and her left hand lazily held the reins of a piebald pony.

It was unusual enough to see a woman out on her own in this culture that worshipped the idea of womanhood and cherished, pampered and protected any individual considered to be close to the ideal, but two additional things made Jack stop so fast he almost fell out of his saddle. This girl, even seen only in profile, was beautiful, and her skin was nearly as dark as his own.

As Jack recovered his balance, the girl looked at him with two of the deepest, darkest eyes he had ever seen.

"What are you doing here?" Jack blurted out the first thing that crossed his mind.

A gleam of anger flashed into the eyes. "I wasn't aware that this was private property. And what business is it of yours anyway?"

"N...none," Jack stammered. "It's just...I mean... you shouldn't be out alone."

"Should I not?" The glare turned to smile. "And why would that be?"

"It's not..." Jack searched for the right word, "seemly." Mentally he kicked himself. Stupid! He sounded just like his aunt.

The girl laughed. "And it is your duty, I suppose, to protect lonely damsels from harm and ensure that they do nothing that is not seemly?"

Jack felt his cheeks redden. He didn't like being mocked, and besides, why didn't this girl act the demure way all women were expected to act here?

She should be politely thanking him for his concern and waiting for him to offer to escort her back to the cantonment. Instead she was staring challengingly at him with those impenetrable eyes. Jack's brain was turning to mush.

"It's not safe," he said lamely, "or proper." Damn, there was his aunt again.

The smile faded from the girl's eyes. "Let me tell you a story about proper. Do you know what this place is?" she asked, waving her arm to take in the building on the other side of the low wall.

Jack walked Australian forward and examined the scene. The rundown building consisted of two long structures facing a small courtyard that was visible through a pair of wide, wooden doors. The courtyard was empty except for a twisted old tree —a mulsoori tree, Jack guessed. The garden was surrounded by the low wall, but looked untended, the grass long and dry. About forty feet to one side a large banyan tree partially hid the stonework of a well.

"It's the Bibighar," the girl said.

"It's deserted," Jack observed.

"Now it is, but it wasn't always. Long ago it was built by a British officer for his *bibi*—do you know what a *bibi* is?"

"Of course I do. My mother was one."

The girl nodded in acknowledgment. "My grandmother also. So, you know how important *bibis* were in the early days here?"

Jack's confused look encouraged her to continue. "The first British soldiers and traders left their wives and sweethearts at home. They took local wives—*bibis*."

"Like the *voyageurs* did in Canada," Jack interrupted.

"I suppose so. Anyway, the *bibis* taught the newcomers how to do things—how to stay cool in the heat, how to negotiate with local princes—it was a good arrangement but it was doomed. As the empire grew, more and more men began to bring their wives and families out here to live. As you can imagine, the wives did not take kindly to the *bibis*. These local wives were often abandoned with nothing."

"My father took my mother to Canada West."

"That was a brave solution, but it was not possible for everyone. One young officer built this place for his *bibi*. By all accounts she was very beautiful and he loved her dearly. He built her this house close to the river, with a courtyard and verandahs to catch the breeze. He even built it around her favourite mulsoori tree.

The arrangement suited the pair and, for many years, the officer and his *bibi* were happy. But, eventually, the officer was posted back to England. She begged to go with him, but the young man said no."

"He can't have loved her then," Jack interrupted.

"Oh, but he did. That was why he decided to leave her behind. England is not Canada West. The officer knew that she would not survive either the harsh English climate or the even harsher drawing rooms of proper society. He believed he was doing the best thing.

"On the day the officer was due to leave, he came here to say farewell to his love. He found her hanging from the mulsoori tree. The officer was devastated and, so local legend has it, died of a broken heart on the voyage home."

"That's a terrible story."

"It is." The girl stood up on the low wall and mounted her pony. "Now you see the consequences of doing things the proper way." She pulled her pony's head around and walked back toward the cantonment.

"Wait," Jack shouted. "I don't know your name."

"That's because we haven't been properly introduced," the girl said with a laugh. She flicked her riding crop and her pony broke into a trot.

Jack stared after her until she disappeared behind the Old Cawnpore Hotel. He felt stunned. He had never met anyone like her before. She was nothing like the simpering daughters of the sahibs and memsahibs who giggled inanely and pretended to be utterly helpless whenever a male was near. She had opinions and spoke her mind—and she was beautiful. As beautiful as the *bibi* in her story, Jack wondered? His gaze wandered back to the Bibighar and the mulsoori tree. There was a thicker branch on its left side. That must be where she hanged herself. In Jack's imagination she was still there, her body twisting mournfully in the breeze.

A Selection of Books by John Wilson

Norman Bethune: A Brief Biography

As a young man, Norman Bethune served as a stretcher-bearer in the First World War. The experience left him with the dedication and passion to lead crusades to find a cure for tuberculosis, to introduce universal health care in Canada, and to introduce mobile blood transfusion units to save wounded soldier's lives on the battlefield. He served with the Republican armies during the Spanish Civil War and in China where he died of blood poisoning in 1939. Because of his left wing politics, Bethune was ignored for decades in his home country. His childhood home in Gravenhurst, Ontario sees large numbers of visitors each year, although a majority are tourists from China where he is revered as a hero for his work with Mao's army in its fight against the Japanese. Regardless of politics, Bethune deserves to be more highly regarded everywhere for his lifelong struggle against injustice and suffering wherever he encountered it.

"I couldn't put the Bethune story down...It is an inspirational tale as well as a historically important one."

-Times-Colonist

"...John Wilson makes the private man come alive...[a] gripping story of a larger-than-life Canadian hero."

-Quill & Quire

John Franklin: A Brief Biography

Sir John Franklin was many things in his life: an officer in the great naval battles of Copenhagen and Trafalgar; governor of Van Diemen's Land; an explorer from Australia to the Arctic, but it is for his mysterious death and the deaths of all 128 of his crew that he is remembered today. The mystery of the disappearance of the Franklin Expedition to the Northwest

Passage has captivated thousands in the 174 years since his men buried Franklin in an unknown grave in the frozen land that kept calling him back. For most of that time only a handful of graves, scattered bones, fragments of debris and Inuit stories have fuelled the speculation as to what killed them all. Now, the wrecks of both of Franklin's ships have been found, preserved in the frigid waters off King William Island, and may contain answers that have been sought for generations. This is the story of the man whose name will forever be associated with the greatest tragedy in Arctic exploration history.

"This book, admirable in its succinctness...is the best life of Franklin yet produced...there could be no better introduction to the life and journeys of Franklin than Wilson's...wonderfully engaging book."

-Russell Potter, Arctic Book Review

An *"...excellent overview, the reader is left with an appreciation of the enormous task early exploration of the Arctic represented...a first rate story and a very useful addition to our understanding and appreciation of an important and unique segment of Canadian history. Highly Recommended."*

-CM Magazine

Heretic: The Heretic's Secret book 1

In the style of Bernard Cornwell, The Heretic's Secret Trilogy is a rollicking historical adventure set during the bloody 13th century wars against the Cathar Heretics of Languedoc. When the armoured knights of Pope Innocent III swept south in 1209, most thought they would be gone by summer's end but, led by the fanatical Arnaud Aumery and the ambitious Simon de Montfort, they stayed for three fiery decades. In that time they slaughtered thousands of Cathars, burned countless towns and castles, destroyed a thriving country that rivalled France in power and culture, and created the foundations for the shape of western Europe we recognize today. John and Peter enjoy arguing about their differing views of the world. Peter sees the Church and an unquestioning acceptance of

God's word as the way to salvation. John sees developing an understanding of the wonder of the world around him as a way of becoming closer to God. As the brutal holy war expands and the flames of the Inquisition spread, Peter and John find themselves on opposite sides of a dangerous search for a secret that may have the power to change the world. **Quest** and **Rebirth** follow John and Peter's thrilling adventures to their heart-rending conclusion."...*a brave book, an unsettling book, and one that is very much needed at this time.*"

-The Globe and Mail

"...*an astonishingly nuanced and masterfully told story...*"
-Quill & Quire

The Alchemist's Dream

In the fall of 1669, the Nonsuch returns to London with a load of fur from Hudson Bay. It brings something else, too—the lost journal from Henry Hudson's tragic search for a passage to Cathay in 1611. In the hands of a greedy sailor, the journal is merely an object to sell. But for Robert Bylot—a once-great maritime explorer—the book is a painful reminder of a past he'd rather forget. As Bylot relives his memories of a plague-ridden city, of the mysterious alchemist John Dee, and of mutiny in the frozen wastes of Hudson Bay, an age-old mystery is both revealed and solved. Set against the thrilling backdrop of the quest for the Northwest Passage, The Alchemist's Dream is a riveting tale of exploration, ambition, and betrayal. Also available in an expanded edition that includes extracts from Hudson's journal, **The Final Alchemy**.

"*In this engrossing historical adventure, John Wilson paints a vivid picture of a bygone era involving Henry Hudson's fateful search for the elusive Northwest Passage, an alchemist, mysterious passengers, and enigmatic maps. The Alchemist's Dream fascinates from start to finish.*"
-Governor General's Award jury citation

The Third Act *(soon to be a major live-action movie)*

The Third Act deals with the intercultural struggles faced by Chinese students studying in North America in the present day and by an American playwright, Neil Peterson, caught up in the Nanjing Massacre of 1937. The contemporary story focuses on three Chinese friends (Tone, Pike and Theresa) who grapple in their own ways with the pressure to succeed in an unfamiliar culture. The historical tale concerns Peterson's effort to find his literary voice and save the woman he loves amidst the chaos and horror of the fall of Nanjing in the Second Sino-Japanese War. The two stories are tied together by a play that Peterson attempted to write after his return to America. The students in the present day get caught up in putting on a performance of the missing third act of Peterson's play, and in doing so they are forced to confront their cultural and personal pasts and futures.

"I recommend The Third Act to students who enjoy both historical fiction and mystery novels. The novel has a strong, well-developed female character in Theresa...Highly Recommended."

-CM Magazine

The Ruined City: book 1 of The Golden Mask *(The inspiration for the upcoming animated feature, Heroes of the Golden Mask)*

Howard is a lonely, geeky tenth-grader dealing with a father who's had some kind of breakdown, a flaky, overprotective mother and frightening waking dreams. Then he meets Cate, a strange girl who convinces him that he is an Adept, which means he can communicate through dreams with other dimensions and, under certain circumstances, travel between them. Howard discovers that our world is only one of several dimensions swirling in time and space, and that one of the others, peopled by unimaginably powerful monsters, is approaching Earth for the first time in millennia. The last time the dimensions coincided, our world was saved by the breaking of a powerful golden mask in the Bronze Age Chinese city of Sanxingdui. Together, Howard and Cate travel through time and space, meeting other Adepts and avoiding lurking monsters, in a quest to find the three fragments of the golden mask and prevent it from falling into the wrong hands.

"A tale of adventure and monsters, The Ruined City, with more than a nod to H.P. Lovecraft, should appeal to readers who enjoy a mystery and slimy monsters from another dimension. Highly Recommended."

-CM Magazine

"An ambitious story...Fascinating."

-Kirkus Reviews

A Soldier's Sketchbook: The Illustrated First World War Diary of R. H. Rabjohn

A unique First World War diary, illustrated with more than a hundred stunning pencil and ink sketches, for children learning history and also for adults interested in a new perspective on the war and authentic wartime artefacts.

"The extracts from the diary describe intimate wartime experiences of death and destruction in gruesomely dispassionate terms...it's a story of unmitigated horror, highlighting more than any textbook the futility of war...This unique compilation of firsthand impressions of the Great War will be a valuable resource for adults and teens with an interest in this turning point in world history."

-Kirkus Starred Review

"The excellent and succinct text . . . provides context for Rabjohn's short diary entries, many of which merely scratch the surface of the suffering he experienced during his time at war."

-Starred Review, Quill & Quire

Ghost Mountains and Vanished Oceans: North America from Birth to Middle Age *(new edition complete with the original maps and appendices included)*

This book is more than the story of how a continent formed over 4 billion years. Told in readable, entertaining prose and filled with personal and geological anecdotes, Ghost Mountains and Vanished Oceans tells the story of our world and, in doing so, it tells our story. As the author puts it, "We are not just passengers on a dead piece of cosmic debris whirling through space; we are an integral part of an exceptional, dynamic system that produced both our earth and us."

"...a fascinating read for anyone interested in the planet on which we live and how it came to be as it is..."

-Geoscience Canada

...this book is a true, well-crafted page-turner...if you've ever wondered how the continents and the particular slab of rock you live on came about, you will love this book...Highly Recommended."

-Amazon Reviewer

Shot at Dawn

Allan McBride has fought in some of the First World War's bloodiest battles. He has seen his comrades, and his best friend, killed. But tonight he waits in a shed outside Amiens, accused of desertion, to discover if dawn will bring a last-minute reprieve—or execution by firing squad.

"...the powerful writing and strong characters will grip readers from beginning to end."

Quill & Quire

Graves of Ice

Thrilled at being a part of such a great adventure, George Chambers volunteers to join Sir John Franklin's expedition in search of the elusive Northwest Passage. But as the ice traps both *Erebus* and *Terror* in a desolate, frozen landscape, the explorers' search for the fabled passage deteriorates to a grim struggle to avoid death by starvation, freezing or scurvy. Eventually, only George remains alive searching vainly for a rescuing sail on the horizon.

"...a compelling story...a haunting story that keeps the reader riveted."

CM Magazine

Lost Cause *(The SEVEN Series)*

Steve travels to Spain and uncovers his late grandfather's involvement in the Spanish Civil War. Followed by a sequel, **Broken Arrow** and a prequel, **The Missing Skull.**

"I had to force myself to take a break for food and sleep. I just wanted to keep reading."

ALSA's Top Ten review program

The **Caught in Conflict Collection** is an imprint of fast-paced, historically accurate, morally-complex quick reads for Adults and Teens. They can be read in any order.

Germania: Roman Empire 9 CE

"This riveting, haunting tale will leave readers clamouring for more."

-Best Books

Where Soldiers Lie: India 1857

"This is an absolutely terrific book...Never lagging with a credible hero and an exotic setting...The pacing is flawless."

-Geoffrey Bilson Award for Historical Fiction Jury Citation

Flags of War: Shiloh 1862

"...action-filled, tightly written prose. Realistic battle scenes illustrate the senselessness of war...the story offers a fresh take on the conflict - the idea of Canada as refuge for fugitive slaves and the irony of how it was nearly drawn into the war on the side of the South."

- Albany Public Library, NY Flames of the Tiger: Berlin 1945

"Equal parts philosophical debate and historical fiction, this book... presents a compelling and thoughtful story of war that should appeal to a wide range of readers."

-Quill & Quire

Battle Scars: Libby Prison 1863

"Readable and exciting."

-Booklist

Death on the River: Andersonville 1865

www.ingramcontent.com/pod-product-compliance
Lightning Source LLC
Chambersburg PA
CBHW020302200626
46814CB00006BA/2045